BROTHER OF DEMONS

Fictive Kin book four

BROTHER of DEMONS

Nico Silver

WHITE RAVEN PRESS

Copyright © 2023 by Nicole Silver.
All rights reserved. This book or any portion thereof may not be reproduced or used in any manner whatsoever without the express written permission of the publisher except for the use of brief quotations in a book review.

Second Edition, 2024.
ISBN: 978-1-998212-23-1
This book was previously published as by Nicole Silver.

White Raven Press
North Cowichan, British Columbia, Canada

Cover design and digital alterations by Nik Sylvan
Model stock © Neo-Stock via www.neostock.com
Animal stock (background) © Ondřej Prosický via Dreamstime.com
Animal stock (foreground) © Marcin Perkowski via Shutterstock
Background stock (road and moon) © Dary423 via Dreamstime.com
Background stock (city) © Songquan Deng via Dreamstime.com
Fog brushes © Krist A via brusheezy.com
Title typefaces: Eva Antiqua Heavy by Spiece Graphics, and Snell Roundhand by Linotype

Content warning: This book contains material that is not suitable for all audiences. It is recommended for readers 18+. Some content that may be triggering for readers includes explicit sex, violence, and sexual violence.

For anyone who has ever felt helpless,
but carried on anyway.

Chapter One

IT STARTS WHEN I kiss her goodbye. I could say it started before that, with the mood swings and irrational anger I keep telling myself are stress. Work stress. But my job is not stressful.

I could say it started with the nightmares, each ghost in my head replaying its memory of fear and brutality and death. They are not simple unpleasant dreams you awake from and they fade away leaving only a lingering bad feeling. They are *memories*; not mine, but they might as well be. Each beating, each violation, each torture I live through in a dream, and can't wake up until the ghost dies in my dream and when I do it takes time to remember those things did *not* happen to me, and each time it takes longer to remember.

When Su is with me, I do not have those dreams. Instead I dream of the forest, a lake, the stars. Wild dreams. I dream of slow lovemaking, her skin against mine. I dream of fucking, of burying my face between her thighs, of her voice crying out in pleasure. And then I wake up and I can kiss her for real, hold her, smell her, taste her.

But something makes me retreat from her from time to time, as if I need to see those terrible ghost dreams. Like I can only be rid of them once I see them all over and over until they *are* my memories. Or until they drive me mad.

But I don't hear the voice until I'm kissing her goodbye.

She's leaving, my Su, on a trip to Germany with her friends Alex and Li. It's a long story, and complicated, but there's magic involved – Alex is a witch, a *hexen*, and Su... To save my life, Su combined her own magic with Alex's, and ended up bound to her friend as a familiar and they can't undo it. And Su needs to be free.

Su is... I don't know what Su is. She is a thing that shouldn't be possible, just as I am. But she was born a *hexenfuchs*, inherited from her German father. And later she was made something else. A fox woman. Three old fox ladies were trying to save her life, and ended up *changing* her. What she is now is simply glorious.

And she needs to be free, so she's leaving me to find a way.

"I'll text you," she says, and I smile, remembering my attempts to teach her how to use her new smartphone.

"I know," I say. "I'll miss you."

"I know," she says. "Me too."

"My heart," I say.

She smiles, her eyes taking on an amber glow. If she lets them, they can become fox eyes, slit pupils and all. A strand of black hair escapes its pins and elastics, and I twine it around my finger.

She grins, takes hold of the strand, and severs it with a quick snap of her fox-sharp teeth. "To remember me," she says, as I stare at the lock of hair she twists around my wrist as a bracelet.

"As if I could forget you," I say. Then I kiss her, soft, tender. She parts her lips, deepens the kiss, and I wish we had more time, even though we spent most of last night making love.

Throw her against the wall and fuck her, says a voice in my head, and I know that voice. I almost choke on our kiss.

"Are you all right?" she says. "Ev?"

I nod. "Yes," I say. "I just tried to breathe at the wrong moment." I don't like to lie, and I abhor lying to Su. But she needs to go to Germany, to get free of the magic that binds her to Alex, and if I told her the demon had re-formed itself again, enough to make words in my head, she would insist on staying to help me.

She puts her hand on my cheek, warm and vital. I can feel her pulse on my skin. My own pulse is slow, so slow compared to hers, even after a sexy kiss to speed it up.

"I love you, crazy Russian vampire witch boy," she says.

"I am your very own abomination."

She frowns. She doesn't like to hear me called abomination, even when I try to make it a joke. I forgot that. How could I forget that?

"I love you, my glorious foxy German-Chinese woman," I say.

"You forgot Korean," she says. "One of my grandmothers was Korean."

"German Chinese Korean," I say. "North American woman."

Outside, the taxi driver leans on the horn.

"Gotta go," Su says.

I nod.

On the floor, says the voice. *I bet you've never fucked her up the ass.* I pretend not to hear it.

I have to step back away from the spear of sunlight as Su opens the door. If not for the sun, I would see her to the airport, drive her there myself; Magne would lend me his truck.

She turns and waves one more time as she gets into the taxi, and then it pulls away and she is gone.

And I am alone, except for the demon in my head.

My name is Evgeny, and as Su said, I am a crazy Russian vampire witch boy. I was born in Russia, and lived there long enough before my parents brought me to the New World to always sound like I'm not from around here.

I don't have a Russian accent anymore, not unless I want to, but I've never quite shaken the slightly-too-formal English my parents taught me before we left the motherland.

I didn't know I was a witch until after I had been made a vampire. Being "reborn" as the other vampires like to say – they prefer to be called that, as well. Not vampires but Reborn. I don't associate much with my kind. They haven't treated me well.

But there are two kinds of non-human sentient creatures lurking in the shadows. Some, like witches and *hexenfuchs*, are born what they are. Some, like vampires and werewolves, are made what they are. No *other*, it is said, can be both born and made. Either one dies in the process, or one's inborn nature defeats the invader, or the invader defeats the genetics.

Mostly, it means death.

But it can happen. Su was born *hexenfuchs*, and made a fox woman. She lived, and now she's both. Or something greater than either. She thinks it's because *hexenfuchs* – that means "witch-fox" – and fox woman are both foxes, so they didn't fight, so to speak.

But that doesn't explain me. Though I didn't know it, I was born a witch. Witches, for reasons unknown, are all female, except in a few rare families. The royal family of Imperial Russia was one such family. They all died, but young Prince Alexei lived longer than anyone supposed. Long enough to have a son, and to be used by a mad sorcerer trying to create a powerful puppet.

The sorcerer was defeated and my great-grandfather had to be burned alive and his ashes imprisoned in a jar to defeat the demon he was becoming.

History repeats. I was a vampire before I knew I was a witch. I should have died, but instead my witch powers grew. And the other witches saw me as an abomination. Not for being a male witch, but for being both witch and vampire. An impossible thing.

They tried to use Great Grandpapa's ashes as a focus to combine their power and take over my mind, to force me into the sun and kill me. It almost worked, but instead they unleashed the demon, a consciousness born of the senseless death of a whole village of innocent people in pain and fear.

And Su defeated the demon and the witches, but it bound her to Alex, and that's why she's gone, and I am here alone with the demon we thought was dissolved into memories.

You should have tied her up, the voice in my head says, as I retreat to my dark bedroom. It is rich with the smell of Su, of our sex. I ignore the voice and burrow into the blankets and breathe in what's left behind of my lover.

"Su," I whisper, as if her name alone can keep away the voice. *It's only a voice*, I tell myself.

Only a voice.

In my dream, she's there, behind me somewhere. I can't see her in the shadows when I turn to look. Contrary to popular superstition, vampires don't have good night vision. We use other senses to hunt. Not that we're stupid enough to hunt much these days. It is too risky, and bagged blood is no different from fresh once you heat it up. As long as it's not *too* old.

I can see vague tree shapes, but once I've looked back the way I'm headed, I can't turn to look for her again. I can only stare ahead as a tall, lean form steps out of the dark.

My stomach clenches. *Demon*, I think. But the demon never took such form.

Instead, it's a man with Asian features. Japanese, I think, as he steps near enough I can almost see him clearly. His eyes look flat black and I think I have seen him before.

"Evgeny," he says. His voice is cold. Not devoid of emotion, only filled with something I can't name. The faint moonlight finds a gap in the tree cover and glints for a moment off his teeth and I can see the slight gaps where his canines would fit if he extended them, unfolded like the fangs of a venomous snake. Vampire.

I shiver, and from behind me, I can smell Su's fear. I didn't think Su was so afraid of anything. Something nags at my memory, like I should remember more about this man, this vampire who feels older than time, but who has nothing of the shriveled look very old vampires usually get.

I don't answer him. I'm not sure I can make my vocal apparatus work.

He looks at me closely, shakes his head. "How disappointing," he says. "I thought you would become something interesting. Perhaps you are not as strong as I believed." He steps away again, disappearing back into the trees and darkness.

"You're just like all my other degenerate offspring. No better than your father."

The "father" he refers to is not my human father, but my vampire sire. Su calls him "Papa Vamp." He was cruel and clever and it may be because he fed me on witch blood – which is supposed to be toxic to vampires –

that I didn't die in the process of being reborn.

"Su killed him," I say. I don't know why I say it, though it is true.

The other vampire pauses, a blacker shadow under the trees. "I believe she did," he says. "A pity you didn't do it yourself."

"He was evil," I say.

His shape moves and I think he may have glanced back. "Some would say we are all evil."

"I refuse to be," I say, and I think I can feel Su draw closer behind me, feel the heat of her skin.

The old vampire laughs. "That may be your undoing," he says. Then he's gone, between one eyeblink and the next, but as I wake, groggy and disoriented, I think I also hear him say, "Or it may be your salvation."

I suppose for some, being made a vampire would be an exciting change, an adventure full of new possibilities. For me, it is mostly an inconvenience.

My existence is no more exciting now than it was before. In many ways, it is more mundane, save only that I would never have met Su if I hadn't been reborn.

I still need a job so I can pay rent and buy food, only now I have to work after dark and my groceries are in liquid form. Mostly. I refuse to give up all human things. As a vampire, I need not eat solid food, but I still *can*. Not a lot, mind. It doesn't digest well in large quantities. But I can still taste flavors, even if some are stronger than they once were. And I have always loved to cook.

So I go to work each night, walk my night security rounds at the local mall, evict drunk teenagers from the roof. I collect my pay, pay my rent, buy groceries.

I am trying to return to the creative pursuits I once had. Before I was made what I am now. Right now, the only thing that makes my life mean anything is Su, and Magne keeps telling me I shouldn't invest everything I am in another person. It's not healthy, he says. Like he should talk. He's so besotted with his witchy new girlfriend. Nosy werewolf.

Except he's probably right.

So it's Magne's fault, I suppose, that on my first night off after Su leaves, I gather up my camera and a portable flash unit and go looking for something to photograph.

Before I was made a vampire, I liked to shoot street scenes: people doing strange things, juxtapositions of signs and objects, little oddities and quirks people don't notice until they're pointed out.

At night, there is nearly as much going on in some parts of the city as during the day. In some places, there is even more happening. The light is more difficult to work with, more contrasty with bright hot spots and shadows devoid of detail, but the challenge should be fun. Exciting.

Instead, I see nothing at all I want to capture in my lens. The camera hangs from my shoulder like a stone, banging against my ribs, and I'm really regretting bringing the extra burden of the flash. I wander the streets, wishing Su was next to me. She always noticed the little details, pointed out things to make me laugh. She was always so happy to simply exist, even with all the terrible things she's seen, the terrible things she's had to do, and to endure. I used to be like that. I remember how the shape of a leaf or a smile from a stranger could make me feel good to be alive.

When did that change? When I died and was brought back as something different from what I used to be?

Magne would tease me if he knew I was pining for Su like a lovesick boy. *Su* would tease me. Though she would be nicer about it. Here I am, trying to find a way to exist without her, and she is all I can think about.

I find my steps have turned away from populated areas, have carried me to the park. Here, Su and I had to defend ourselves from a whole pack of vampires who had been sent to capture me. It wasn't the first time I discovered how easy it was for me to kill, but it was the most obvious example. Su managed to disable two of them, and in that time, I took out the rest. I don't know how many there were, and I try not to think too hard about it. I don't want to know.

Instead, I steer my thoughts to happier memories. Last time we were here, we sat on a bench and shared a dairy-free milkshake. Chocolate tofulati with a hint of peanut butter. Su drank most of it, but she made sure I had plenty of sips.

This bench, here, is where we sat, drawing glances for drinking a cold summer treat after dark, when the air was rapidly cooling to night chill.

And we just grinned back at those people and they smiled and shook their heads at two people stupid in love.

I sit on the bench and lean back, watching the moths flit in the light of an electric lamp nearby. A pale blur, too large for a moth, I think, captures my eye and I have to get up, walk over to it, fluttering at the lamp's base.

It *is* a moth, pale green with reddish edging on its upper wings, and transparent spots. It is the size of my hand, almost, and so fuzzy I want to stroke it like a kitten. I reach out a finger tentatively, and touch it lightly in the center of its back. It flips its wings fully open, but it doesn't seem bothered.

Its hind wings taper into long, gently twisted tails and I think I have seen a picture of one of its kind before. A lunar moth? No a *luna* moth. No "r". I stroke it again and it is a soft as the delicate fur behind a cat's ears. It fans its wings.

Then I reach for my camera, check the aperture and shutter speed against its built-in light meter. I still shoot film, not because I'm a Luddite, but because I like the hand-work involved in developing my own film and printing my own images.

I wish I had brought a tripod instead of the flash, but I brace the camera on my knee and am for once thankful for my vampire nature, that lets me go more still than is natural for any other creature. I hope that and the lamplight will be enough for a sharp image.

The click of the shutter cheers me. Magne was right, I do better with something outside of Su to focus on. Though of course the whole time I'm thinking how I can show her the image when she gets back, or scan it and email it to her, maybe bring her here to see if another luna moth will come so she can see it for herself.

I bracket my shots, one f-stop on each side of what I think is the correct setting. Then I bracket the shutter speeds, too, just because. One the five should be useable, I hope. I almost I wish had loaded color film, to capture the delicate green of the animal's wings, but black and white will exaggerate its ghostliness, and it suits my mood.

As I put my eye to the viewfinder for one final shot, I notice a detail I didn't see before, something Su would have noticed right away. Something

I would have noticed if I'd been paying attention to my sense of smell instead of concentrating only on what I could see.

Where the pale moth rests on the grey concrete, there are splatters of dried liquid. It looks black in the contrasty lamplight, but I know in daylight it would be dark red.

There is blood on the ground here and, unless my vampire olfactory acuteness has suddenly failed me, it's not entirely human blood.

Chapter Two

I LICK MY FINGERTIP and press it to the largest of the dark spatters, then hold it up to my face. Not red at all, as I thought it would be, as it should be, but dark green. Red and green, contrary to popular belief, are easy to confuse. Red-green color blindness is, I have read, normal in all mammals save primates, and even we humans – or almost-humans – can suffer from it. Especially males, especially at night.

Dark green, but very definitely blood. I bring my finger closer to my nose and inhale. It smells something like stagnant water, but the sort that teems with life. It smells delicious. I can't stop myself from touching my fingertip to my tongue and suddenly my mouth is watering. It tastes divine, like avocados or perfectly steamed asparagus, but there is also an animal flavor, gamey but savory. Roasted venison crusted with herbs and garlic. But of course it is also nothing like any of those things.

My teeth unfold from the roof of my mouth with a wet sound and my mouth is full of saliva. Then a sudden pale green ghost flutters in my face and the moth flies off, as if I startled it, though only my hand has moved from blood to mouth.

For a long moment I stare at the retreating, fluttering creature, clinging to my view of it because what I desperately want to do is lick the dried blood from the concrete.

Finally, when the moth has disappeared into the darkness, I stand, in control again. I shoulder my camera, heft the flash unit in my left hand, and begin walking.

I intend to head for home, but instead I turn deeper into the park and it's several minutes before I realize I'm breathing more rapidly than usual, taking deep, quick breaths to test the air for scents. I'm *tracking*.

The realization stops me dead and I hold my breath until it hurts. For a vampire, that takes a very long time. How could I be following a scent and not know? It is a thought more frightening, somehow, that the sinister voice in my head. *That*, at least, is silent. For now.

I don't know what else to do besides try to pay more attention, to be deliberate and aware. To not let my mind wander while my body does something else.

But the green blood does have me intrigued, so I breathe deep again, turning my head one way then the other to find whatever thin thread of scent I was following unknowingly.

There. I feel it tickle my nose, and almost immediately spot a dark splash on a leaf to one side of the path. It would have been invisible except for a bright patch of moonlight lighting it up like a spotlight. I resist the urge to pluck the leaf and taste it. Instead, I step off the path and follow the next splash and the next, until I find myself on the rocky bank of the pond that forms the park's center. All paths lead here eventually, though my shortcut through the bushes has delivered me much more directly.

There isn't much natural left of the pond. The rocks lining its banks were added by the city to keep its shores from eroding under the constant tramp of feet. But there are ducks here, and frogs, turtles, salamanders, even fish of the kind that can survive in the lower oxygen environment of a small body of water mostly unconnected by stream and river. And there is bright green pondweed, leaves floating and covering at least half of the water's surface.

And there is something else living here, it seems. Something *other*. Its blood splashed and dripped across the rocks, drying in inklike splodges. I crouch at the edge of the pond, where a larger smear shows where the *other* paused, propped itself with a blood-smeared hand – the one it had perhaps kept pressed to a wound – before entering the water.

I slip my fingers into the water, bring them to my nose, and sniff. The water here has some of the qualities that the blood did, but much less concentrated. Stagnant scented, but full of life.

I gaze across the pool, watch as the waning moon creeps above the trees to reflect in the water, almost a perfect half-circle. I can feel the moonlight on my exposed skin like heat, nothing like the full fury of the sun, but a reminder of it.

And then I see her watching me, and smell her fear.

Her head is a bump on the flat plane of the water, and if it weren't bright green-blonde, it would look like a smooth rock breaking the surface. If she had hidden among the pond weed, I might not have noticed her at all.

She is still, staring from almost exactly the middle of the pond, her eyes reflecting the moon, then vanishing for a moment as she blinks.

My stomach rumbles, and I ignore it.

"Hello," I say. Fear wafts off her so strong I can taste it in the back of my throat. *Mmm*, the demon-voice says, but I remember Su's fear in my dream and the voice is silent again.

"I won't hurt you," I tell her, this strange pond-dwelling *other*. I try to remember the folklore books Su and I read, when she still did not know what she was and we were searching out possibilities.

The bright head, glinting eyes, drift a little closer, trailing bits of pond weed, but barely stirring the water otherwise. She looks familiar, what little of her I can see, but I can't think where I might have seen her before. I can see so little of her, but maybe she can pass as human, and I walked by her on the street once?

She lifts her head from the water enough to speak. "You're no like the others," she says. Her voice has a lilt. Irish, maybe.

"Which others?" I say.

In answer, she drifts closer still, raises herself up in the water so I can see her neck and the tops of her shoulders. A t-shirt, white and nearly transparent with water, clings to her where her body meets the air, and drifts ghost-like beneath the surface. She tilts her head to one side and gestures at her neck, the hollow where it meets her shoulder.

Two neat puncture wounds, dark but not bleeding.

She tilts her head the other way. Two more, beneath her ear. Then she holds out both arms so the pale inner skin just breaks the surface of the pond. Two sets of bite marks on one side, inner elbow and wrist. One set, jaggedly torn, mid-forearm, on the other.

"Bloodsuckers," she says, and sinks back down into the water so only her eyes are visible, her pale forehead, her long, bright hair drifting and weed-entangled.

"Vampires attacked you?"

She nods.

"Why? Who?" My kind don't usually attack *others*. It's too risky. Even more risky than feeding from humans. And many types of *others* are toxic to us, or just taste terrible. Like my Su. She smells more delicious than any living creature I've ever encountered, but tastes foul beyond words. Her blood, I mean. Every other part of her tastes sweet and the mere thought makes me grow warm.

"How would I know, anyway?" the pond woman says. Then, "What d'you want? Why follow me?"

"I found your blood," I say. "I thought you might be hurt."

She stares at me.

"I'm not going to hurt you," I tell her again.

She stares.

I decide to change the subject. "You said I'm different. Different how?"

She shrugs, and the water ripples away from her, "You feel different, is all."

"I don't feed from the living," I say.

"Why not?" Strangely, she actually sounds interested.

"One," I say, "It's too dangerous."

"Aye," she says. "We monsters need to stay hidden. But that didn't stop your lot trying to make a meal of me."

"Not my lot," I say. "I don't have any vampire friends."

"No mates," she says. "You must be lonely. That why you came after me?"

I smile. I *am* lonely, but only because Su is gone, and Magne too busy with his new love to socialize. "My best friends are a *hexenfuchs* and a werewolf," I say. "And a witch." I don't know if Alex counts as a friend, but I include her anyway.

"I don't know what this *hexen* beast is," she says. "But witches never did me no favors. Weres neither."

"German fox shifter," I say. "Sort of."

She shrugs. "That's only a practical reason for not feeding on *others*," she says. "Not very comforting." She's drifted even closer now, and perches half out of the water. Her hair hangs heavy around her, like a curtain, and her t-shirt shows every detail of her thin, almost emaciated, body. What I can see of her face through the locks of hair is delicate, elfin, and probably very beautiful if I could see it whole.

Tasty, says the voice, and I must make some reaction because the pond woman looks at me sharply.

"What?" she says.

I shake my head. "I also don't feed on people for moral reasons."

She raises an eyebrow.

"I don't believe in killing sentient, thinking beings," I say.

"You *are* different," she says. "And I think I remember you."

"Do you?" I say.

She shrugs, and her shirt slides over her skin. She's nearly as white as the fabric, and her nipples show through as dark circles, surprisingly large for the slightness of her breasts.

Wouldn't you like to suck on those? the voice says, and I can't help shift away from her, as if the voice could make me do the very thing it mentions.

She senses my unease, perhaps, because she slides back into the water a ways.

"Do you know who attacked you?" I say. "Could you recognize them again?" I don't know what I think I can do, but I feel as if I ought to do something. The local vamps used to be ruled by a sort of council of elders, but Su and I kind of destroyed it some time back, and it doesn't seem to have re-formed yet. If vamps are stupid enough to hunt, especially to hunt *others*, then someone has to do something to control them, and I feel responsible, even if I really have no desire to associate with my own kind.

"Big tall one," she says. "White. Brown hair. Skinny little girlfriend, darker skin. Latina, maybe. 'Nother white boy. Red hair, short. Lots of freckles, though I can't say how a bloodsucker could get enough sun to freckle. Two Asian twins, middle height and muscular. They all smelled like curry."

"Curry?" I say. It's an odd detail, and I can't imagine how it happened. If they were human, I'd assume they had just come from a restaurant, but most vampires don't bother with real food once they start on blood.

She shrugs, the pond woman, and drifts a little closer again.

This one would make a nice substitute for your usual fuckbuddy, the voice says. *I bet her cunt tastes like watercress.*

I hold myself very still and push the voice away. I swear I can feel the demon chuckle. The demon that should no longer exist, except as fragments of memory, of fear and pain and cruelty.

"They said they knew me," the pond *other* says. She's half out of the water now, staring at me. "From that place."

The way she says "that place" makes me shiver and I have a sudden flash of memory, of darkness and then glaring fluorescent lights, cold metal against my back, the prick of an IV needle in my arm, both arms, and the slow drip of my blood into a plastic bag that shouldn't be audible but it's louder than my own heartbeat pounding slowly in my ears.

I blink and find I've shrunk back from the edge of the pond, but the *other* has followed me and her eyes, an improbably bright green, stare into mine.

"You remember," she says. "They drugged us and bled us, and they fed us to you."

Another flash of memory, a tube forced down my throat, blood in the tube, different flavors piped directly to my stomach so I only taste them when my body tries to vomit them back up. No, my brain wants to vomit, my vampire body won't let me. Only a trickle of taste seeps back up to my mouth.

I blink, and the pond woman is almost in my lap. She's wearing nothing but the t-shirt and she's painfully thin, almost albino pale. But there's something alluring about her, a fragility that beckons.

"I remember," I say, and gently push her away with a hand on her collarbone. Her skin is cool like the pond's water, colder even than my vamp-cold temperature.

"Good," she says. "We must never forget what it is they did to us. Those bloodsuckers who tried to snack on me – they forgot who turned them into real monsters."

That facility underground – the Reborn council had set up a lab to create new and improved blood formulas for vampires. Their true goal, though, was to create something that would make us invincible, some combination of *other* blood that would let us live in the sun. Vampire blood makes us stronger, so maybe the blood of different *others* would too. And I was their prize, a vampire who could drink witch blood and not die. They tried to use me as a living filter. Feed me witch blood, then drink of me.

But Su rescued me and we set all the captives free.

"No," I say. "They didn't make new vampires." But I suppose they could have. I spent most of my time there in a cell, strapped to a table.

The pond woman smiles, and her teeth are almost as green as her eyes. "No," she says. "But they made regular-as-dirt bloodsuckers into something far worse. They made them monsters without conscience. Without a mind." She tilts her head, then leans close, presses herself to me, and whispers, "Chosen," in my ear.

I pull away. "What?"

"You," she says. "Chosen to make bloodsuckers rule us all. But you showed them." She waves both arms in the air, pulling the wet shirt close against her breasts, and I can't look away. The demon won't let me. "You and the fox girl spoiled all their monster plans."

She notices me looking and smiles. She puts a finger under my chin and tilts my head up so I have to look at her face.

"Come swim with me, pretty Chosen," she says.

I shake my head, but the demon is already pulling my eyes back to her chest. I try to fill my head with Su, thoughts of her become thoughts of sex, and the demon chuckles in my head.

Leave me alone, I think desperately at it.

You'll never be alone again, it whispers.

"Come swim," says the pond woman, and she stands up. The t-shirt barely covers her crotch, and it clings everywhere to her thin frame. "Come swim with Jinny."

She cups her own breasts in her hands, rubs until her dark nipples stand against the fabric, and then reaches out one hand to me. "I can see where you're looking," she says. "I can tell you want to."

The demon laughs and twists suddenly in my head and then I am only a passenger, helpless and able only to watch as my hand lifts and takes the cold fingers of the pond woman and my body follows her into the frigid water, camera forgotten on the bank.

My feet sink into the mud as I wade into the water after the *other*, weeds tangle my legs. The water is chill, but it doesn't bother me, and the woman's skin is colder still as she presses close to me, runs her hands up under my shirt, bites my ear hard to enough to leave it throbbing.

"You are a pretty one, Chosen," she says. "It's almost a shame to eat you."

For a moment I'm afraid, but then she ducks under the water, and I feel her hands on my fly, tugging the cloth away. When her cold mouth closes over my manhood, I want to shrivel away, to scream, to flee. I want Su, who is warm and kind, and loves me.

But the sound that comes out of my throat is not a scream, but a laugh, and the voice belongs to the demon. *Just relax and enjoy it*, he says, and he tangles my fingers in the woman's hair as she sucks and when he – I – we – are done he moans, loud and triumphant.

"Fuck, but I missed that," he says. "You need some variety in your diet, Evgeny the prude."

Inside my own head, I feel like I'm thrashing to get out. I've been taken over by the demon before. A few times, when the witches first released it on me, before Su saved me. But now it seems her sacrifice to get me free was in vain.

The pond woman surfaces, my hands still tangled in her hair, and grins at me. "Such a salty boy," she says. "Such spunk." And she giggles.

Then she untangles my hands and pulls me deeper into the pond until my feet can't touch bottom and my clothes are heavy and I have to fight to stay afloat.

I have to fight. The demon is gone, I realize, and my body is my own again.

"You don't swim so well, do you, Chosen?" the pond woman says.

"What's your name?" I say, testing my control of my voice, trying to distract her from my attempts to move closer to shore.

She laughs. "Now you want my name, pretty bloodsucker? Now, after I drained your cock for you?"

"I'm sorry," I say. "I wasn't myself."

"I already told you anyway," she says. "I'm Jinny." She takes my hand and pulls me again toward the center of the pond. "You should study more, so you won't be caught off guard."

The name tugs at my memory. Something I read in one of Su's books, maybe? But I'm too distracted by the demon, by what just happened, to think straight.

"Now I think you owe me," she says.

"What?" I say. The water pulls me down, her hands dragging at my shoulders, the weight of my sodden clothes.

"Did you forget already? You moaned so load I could hear you under the water. I suck you off, you lick my cunny, yes?"

I shake my head and try to pull away, the horror of what's happening setting in and threatening to drown me as surely as the water.

"I'm sorry, I can't," I say, trying again to swim for the bank. "I shouldn't even be here."

She laughs. "You can't get away from Jinny so easily," she says. "And I saw your face, pretty bloodsucker. You want me as much as I want you." She grabs my hair and dunks me under. I struggle but she's strong, improbably strong, and we're in her element – possibly literally – and I quickly lose all sense of up and down. Her thighs wrap around my head and her pubic hair tickles my nose and I'm barely conscious of anything save the need to get away, to flee. It seems like forever that I thrash and struggle and her legs remain clamped around my head like the tentacles of an octopus, until finally I hear a muffled screech and she lets go and I flail my way to the surface.

She floats, only her head above water, her hair drifting around her. When I gasp in air she turns her eyes to me and smiles.

"Still alive?" she says. "Were you human you'd be drowned and I'd soon be feasting on your flesh in a completely different way."

I can't find words, only suck in clean air. My vampire-slow metabolism is the only reason I didn't drown, but it's not so slow I don't need to breathe at all. When my lungs stop hurting finally, I realize I can smell her sex, all over my face, and I scrub frantically at my skin, but the pond water only seems to intensify it.

She laughs again. "Smell me, do you? My whole pond is full of it, from all the pretty boys who lick me off while they die."

Kill the bitch, the demon says in my head, but whatever let him take me over before seems not to be in effect, because I can shove the voice away easily.

"They made you a monster, too," I say, finally, my voice sounding weak. Then I flail my way to the bank and haul myself up on the rocks. I stand unsteadily, notice my fly is open and I'm hanging out limp and pathetic-looking, I tuck in and zip up, but my hands fumble and it seems to take forever.

"I was already a monster," says the pond woman. "But I like you. Too bad you know so little of the world beyond your own *other* kind."

I turn to flee, not thinking about where I'll go, and her laughter follows me.

"Come swim with me again, Chosen," she says. "Next time maybe I'll let you fuck me."

Oh yes, says the demon, and I shove the voice down again and run faster.

Chapter Three

WHEN I WAKE UP, I'm surrounded by darkness and warmth, and the soft bed I'm lying on smells like Su. Somehow, in my mad flight last night, I ended up at Su's loft and not my own apartment.

There is no sense of the voice in my head, and I wonder if it is driven off by whatever of Su's presence is left behind in her home. I hope so. I need to feel safe.

I'm so comfortable it takes me longer than it should to realize I am not alone. Beyond the heavy black drapes that surround the bed – installed even before Su met me because her fox nature likes small, enclosed spaces to curl up in – there is the sound of someone breathing.

It's so quiet only a person with extra-sharp hearing could even detect it. Then his scent reaches me, faint through the curtains. Werewolf.

"Magne," I say.

"You're a heavy sleeper these days," he says. What he isn't saying, but I can hear it anyway, is that something must be wrong. Vampires, unlike the movies would have one believe, are light sleepers. Our existence depends on being able to wake and defend ourselves, as it does for any other predator,

"I had a stressful night," I say. But I can't tell him what happened, not yet. He may be one of my closest friends, but he was Su's friend first. If I can't explain well, if it sounds like I cheated on Su, he won't be my friend at all anymore. There might even be violence. Werewolves can be very... physical in their expression of emotion. And they don't take betrayal very well.

He grunts and I hear him get up from the couch. "Coffee?" he asks.

"What time is it?"

He pauses. I can almost hear his hesitation and I know it's because I shouldn't need to ask the time. Another thing a vampire's survival depends on is being able to sense the passing of night and day, because we always need to know exactly how long we have to get out of the way of the rising sun. Translating that sense into human timekeeping is simple after so long.

"Nearly five," he says. "You work tonight?"

"Yeah." I part the curtain cautiously and peer out. The sun isn't shining directly in the windows this time of day, but there's enough ambient light to make me uncomfortable.

"You want to talk?" He's started making coffee even though I didn't answer whether or not I wanted any.

"Not really," I say. "Not yet." I'm about to ask why he's here, but then I see my camera and flash unit on the coffee table and I don't need to. My wet clothes are strewn across the floor between the door and the bed and there are muddy footprints, too. Mine.

"Must have been quite a night," he says. "One of my packmates found your gear." His voice is carefully neutral and I can tell he wants to question me, that he's worried about me, but also worried that I might have done something unforgivable. He knows my history, or at least as much as happened since I met Su. He was there for a lot of it, and saw some of the worst.

"Thanks." I pull the quilt around me and inhale its scent. It smells like clean laundry, but also like Su. Me and Su together. But I have also tainted it with the odor of stagnant water and pond woman.

I want to cry, but I can't. Not with Magne here. He might be kind and understanding and an excellent friend, but he's also a werewolf. Macho is big with wolves, and macho men don't cry, not even alone.

"Have you heard from Su?" he says, handing me a cup of coffee and pointedly changing the subject. Except maybe he isn't changing the subject at all.

I shake my head. "Just a short text to let me know they got there safe."

He sits on the couch and lets out a long sigh. "I sure hope they find what they're looking for."

"Yeah."

For a few minutes we just sit and sip our coffee, and I try to figure out how I'm going to get home for clean clothes after the sun goes down and still have time to get to work. I haven't eaten yet today either, and I can't remember if Su cleaned out her fridge before she left, if I might find a few bags of blood in there or not.

I stare at the damp heaps of denim and cotton, wondering if I can just use the building's dryer, brush off the mud, and wear yesterday's clothes to work. Except I'll get hell for not being in my mall cop uniform.

Then I hear a sharp inhale from Magne and he thumps his mug down on the table, missing the coaster. He's up and across the room before I can do more than stare at him with my mouth hanging open. Werewolves are fast, but he shouldn't really be able to get the jump on me.

He grabs my face and twists my head to the side, and I don't even have the presence of mind to flinch away.

"What the hell happened to you?" he says.

"What?" I say. I must sound genuinely confused, because his grip softens and he steps back.

"Come here," he says, and he takes my arm, pulls me off the bed and into the bathroom.

I cringe, but the light isn't strong enough to be painful, just uncomfortable. I manage to put my coffee down – miraculously unspilled – as he pulls me across the room.

In the bathroom, he stands me in front of the mirror and I can only stare. My olive complexion looks almost green under the compact fluorescent lights, and there are dark bruises just beginning to show around my neck and shoulders.

"What the hell happened to you?" he says, but his voice is gentle, like he doesn't want to scare me.

Then he inhales, bends closer to smell my hair, my cheek, and his grip on my arm tightens. I would not be surprised to acquire even more bruises.

"What the *hell* happened?" he says again, but his voice is as hard as his grip and I can't tell if he's angry at me or at what might have happened to me.

I stare at my pathetic self in the mirror. I look sad, hurt, and weak. But I'm not weak. I pull sharply away from Magne, easily break his grip, though he's much larger than I am, bulky and bulgy-muscled where I am lean. I want to remind him that for all his big muscles, I could kill him with hardly a thought.

It's a mistake, I realize as soon as I move. It makes me look guilty. And I would never, could never, harm Magne. He's big and sometimes violent – though never to anyone who doesn't have it coming – but he's the best kind of person, kind and giving.

He stares at me, his teeth slightly bared. Even fully human, werewolves have very big canines. "What did you do?" he says.

I slump down, sit on the toilet, and put my head in my hands. Leaving the back of my neck vulnerable isn't quite as submissive as baring my throat, but Magne relaxes a little.

"Ev?"

"I can't," I say. "Not yet."

He shifts to sit on the edge of the bathtub and his hand on my back is warm, and more comforting than I'd ever admit to him.

"Are you all right?" There is still suspicion in his voice. Like I said, he was Su's friend first, and I smell like another woman, but he's willing to hear me out, if I want to talk.

I sit up. "I think so," I say, knowing it's a lie even as the words come out. I hate lying, but I can't stop it. "But it wasn't a good night."

He nods. "And that's why you came here?"

"Yeah." I look out the bathroom door at the bookcase on the other side of the loft. Su and I built it together to hold all the books we took from Papa Vamp's lair. I'm hoping there might be some answers there.

Magne follows my gaze. "You need some help?" Suspicious that I might somehow have betrayed Su, but still offering me help – that's the kind of true friend Magne is. I want suddenly to crawl into his arms and find comfort there, but I know he would definitely *not* welcome that. He isn't that sort of friend, and I'm fairly certain he's as straight as they come.

If I didn't have Su, I would be very disappointed about that.

"No," I say softly, but it's only half in answer to Magne's question. It's also a denial of the thoughts in my head, thoughts that might not be entirely mine. Sure, I like men. I've had male lovers. But since I met Su, she has been all I wanted, all I have thought about. We're so perfectly matched – in bed and out – that I can't imagine any other lover coming close.

Since I met Su... until the demon invaded my head. But is it the demon who lusted after the pond woman, who wants to feel Magne's bare skin on mine, or is the demon just showing me what my love for Su kept hidden?

Except my feelings for Su have not changed since she left for Germany. If anything, they've grown stronger.

"Ev," says Magne, laying his arm across my shoulders for a brotherly squeeze. I try not to lean into it, and try not to flinch away.

"You know if you need anything, I'm here," he says. "Don't be stupid and try to face shit alone."

I nod.

"Su would kill me if anything happened to you." He mock growls and bites my ear like a dog play-nips another. "And besides, you're my friend, too."

I can't say anything because I'm too busy trying to ignore the erotic flush that fills me at the touch of his teeth, exactly where the pond woman bit me last night. It stings and throbs fiercely, but the pain brings pleasure – though I've never been aroused by pain before – and I have to bunch the quilt in my lap to hide the fact that I'm getting hard. Suddenly and painfully.

The demon is still silent; I can't even feel its presence. But I can imagine its voice taunting me.

You know you want to fuck him, it would say. *You know you can take him even if he fights. You know you would* like *it if he fights.*

No, I want to scream. *Nonono.* I *don't* like that. I *don't* want that. Not now, not ever.

I curl over into myself, feel the cold of the bathroom tiles and Magne's surprise and concern.

"I'm okay," I whisper, to keep him from lifting me off the floor in his arms. "I'll be okay." The lie is bitter in my mouth.

I'm not okay, and I'm not sure I will be. Because what if the demon – or my imaginings of what the demon might say – is right?

What if I *am* that kind of monster?

I think it's only because he's a werewolf – and therefore into dealing with emotions in the manly way of either suppressing them or punching something – that Magne finally leaves me alone to clean up for work.

I find some of my own clothes in Su's dresser drawers, washed and neatly folded, and as soon as the sun is down far enough to make long shadows I can travel in, I pull up the hood on my sweatshirt and run home.

My vampire speed comes in handy, though I've never used it to travel such a long distance before, and I get home with just enough time to change and race to the bus stop. I consider simply running to work – it would be faster – but I'm so tired when I reach the bus that I realize I may have overtaxed myself. So much speed for so long leaves me exhausted and it takes far too much effort to get up from my seat and climb down the steps off the bus.

"Jesus, man, you look like hell," says Luke, the other night guard.

"Bad day," I say. I'm not known for being friendly, so he leaves me alone after that.

Luckily, it's a quiet night, because I'm so weary even an ordinary human might be able to sneak past me. In fact, they might even be able to outrun me by the time my shift is over.

I feel weak and helpless, but at least now I know my faster-than-a-normal-vampire speed is finite. I won't be so frivolous with it again, because next time I might really need it and I don't want to waste my energy.

My weakness, too, not to mention my hunger, makes me worry all night that the demon might take over my body again. I can't imagine finding the energy to fight it off, in the state I'm in. Every time I find my attention drifting, I think he's back. Every less than virtuous thought has me wondering if it's my own, and the worry alone would have worn me out if I weren't already a wreck.

Half an hour before sunrise at the end of my shift I run into Luke again as we're both clocking out.

"Get some sleep, man," he says. "The boss sees you looking like that, he might wonder if he should still keep you on." When I don't say anything, he shrugs. "But whatever, dude. You wanna keep your job or lose it, that's your business."

I realize I've been rude, and as annoying as Luke can be, he did seem to be trying to help.

"Thanks," I say finally, when he's almost out the door. "I just had a really fucking bad day." I don't usually swear much, but I throw in the curse to sound more natural, more human.

Luke nods. "See ya tomorrow," he says, and the door closes behind him. I think it's the longest conversation we've had since I started working there.

Even though my place is much closer, so close I normally walk to and from work when I'm not too tired to think, I head back to Su's when I leave the mall. I know I'm cutting it close – in summer I'd barely make it back to my place even with my hours carefully scheduled to have me working only when the sun is gone, and I definitely wouldn't have time to make it to Su's. But I get inside before the sky grows too bright and pull the drapes over the huge window that makes up most of one side of the loft. It makes the space dim and cave-like. Perfect, at least until the sun comes over the top of the building across the street.

Once that's done, I check my phone. No more texts from Su, but I send her a quick message to let her know I'm thinking of her. Then I make a pot of her favorite green tea. I know I should sleep, but something's niggling in the back of my mind. Not the demon, thankfully, but a vague memory of something I read or saw in one of Papa Vamp's folklore books.

While I wait for the kettle to boil, I scan the spine titles and try to think which one might hold answers. And I try to pin down what it was the pond woman said that sparked the little flutter of familiarity in my mind.

"Jinny," I say softly. She said her name was Jinny, but she also spoke about herself in third person when she used her own name.

Jinny doesn't sound Asian, so I skip the shelves of Japanese and Chinese stories and the volumes of Thai and Korean lore. It might be a version of *Jenny*. An Irish variant, maybe? Scottish? That would fit the lilt in her voice. But I'm no good at distinguishing accents that aren't related to Russian. It could be English or Welsh, for all I know.

By the time the tea is ready, I have a small pile of Celtic and English folklore books and fairy tales on one end of the bed, and the bedcurtains drawn around leaving just enough of a gap for a bit of light to read by. Because, of course, vampires actually need a good bit of light to see. And when I sit I can still smell Magne from when he dragged me out of bed last night. It's comforting, and knowing he's just downstairs in the second floor loft if I need him is also heartening. Mercifully, today I feel no erotic stirrings when I think of my hairy friend. I only feel bolstered by his strength.

I sip tea and flip pages, but it's not until halfway through the last book that my eye is caught by something that almost makes me choke on my tea.

On the right-hand page is a black and white line drawing, faintly Art Nouveau in style, of a fairy woman. The image shows a pond choked with water weed and the woman's head barely above the surface, her hair floating around her and tangled in the weeds.

Her eyes are shadowed, but bright with malevolent interest. I think, in an oddly detached way, that I must remember to look up the artist, because they've captured the very essence of this woman perfectly, though obviously it's not the same woman I met so recently. Only one of her kind.

Jinny Greenteeth, the caption says. For several long moments I can only stare at the picture, as caught by the eyes of the drawing as I now realize I was caught by the eyes of the woman I met at the pond in the park.

I realize, too, that my breathing has sped up. Not with erotic thoughts, such as the demon might use to taunt me – though he has been silent, *absent* even, since I fled the park. Mercifully.

No, instead my pulse races unnaturally fast in fear.

I don't recall being afraid when I was actually there with her. Jinny. Not even when she was taking pleasure from what would have been my dying struggles if I had been human. Or even if I had been merely a witch and not also a vampire.

But I am afraid now. So terrified I wonder if the stench of my fear might drift through the vents and reach Magne's keen werewolf nose in the loft below. It makes no sense for me to be afraid now, when I'm safe in my lover's home, when I was only confused the other night. I *should* have been afraid then.

She must have some kind of mental powers, not so different from those that witches have. She must have used them to lull me, to entice me, and to make me unafraid when I should have been terrified.

Except I have lately been so sure of my own superior strength I might not have been afraid even if I should have been. And, too, no witch has been able to take over my mind since the *hexen* sent the demon after me. Surviving that made me stronger, when I was already stronger than vampires – and witches – much older and more experienced than I.

I wrench my gaze away from the drawing and turn to the text. Maybe I'll find answers here, or at least an indication of where to look next.

Jinny Greenteeth. A pond fairy, always female, and given – as most water fey are – to enticing humans into the water where she drowns them. Some stories claim she devours her prey immediately, while others says she drains them of vitality very slowly, vampire-like, keeping them alive but captive until they are of no more use to her. Still other sources say her predation is accidental, and she is merely lonely and wanting company. Jinny Greenteeth, also called Jenny, Ginny, or Jeannie, is said to haunt only stagnant ponds with an abundance of green duckweed, though whether she causes the state of the pond or chooses locations already to her liking is unknown. This fairy woman is native to the British Isles, especially where Anglo-Saxon, rather than Celtic, cultural influence is strong. Her lore may even have been imported to the New World, to places heavily settled by migrants from rural England.

I set the book aside and sit back. I can still feel terror lurking in my guts, but at least I'm not hyperventilating anymore.

I glance at my phone where it sits on the bed next to the books and my empty tea cup. I know that if I emailed this news to Su as I desperately want to, she would be on the next flight home to help me. To put the demon to rest again, and even to deal with the pond woman. Jinny Greenteeth. Together, we could do anything. We make an excellent team, though somehow it always seems to be me who needs rescuing, and Su who is the hero.

I look back to the book, still open to that chilling image. No. I can't ask Su to come home, or even tell her what has happened, or she would come without my asking. I might need her help, but right now she needs more to help herself. Not for the first time, I wish I could have gone to help *her*. But vampires and long-distance air travel don't work well together.

I stare at the image and finally let the realization of what actually happened sink in. Until now, I had been thinking of my encounter with the pond woman as unintentionally cheating on Su. But that's not it. I was forced into that encounter against my will. Maybe from Jinny's point of view it was wholly consensual, but from mine it was not. With her luring me, and then using her strength to keep me there, and the demon in my head making it impossible for me to resist, to fight back, I was...

I was...

But I can't even form that last word in my private thoughts to myself.

Chapter Four

WHEN I FINALLY crawl under the covers, I still can't sleep for a long time. Now that I have admitted to myself that what happened to me was not because I was weak-minded and gave into my baser nature, I can't keep thoughts of it out of my imagination.

I wasn't weak of mind, of resolve, but I *was* weak of body. I don't know if it was the demon controlling me that made me less able to fight back, or if the Jinny Greenteeth was actually that much stronger than me. The latter seems impossible – I have met no *other*, except maybe Su, who could come close to me – but the former is not a comforting thought, either. If the demon, only recently re-consolidated enough to make words in my head, could control me so easily, I don't know that there is any hope of me ever being free of it.

I might end up like Great Grandpapa, burned alive and my remains stuffed in a magic bottle to keep the evil contained.

When I close my eyes, Jinny's eyes are there, too green to be human, compelling, alluring in a way that makes me feel sick. Eyes open and staring into the dimness within Su's bedcurtains, I remember the demon's delight as she led me into the water unresisting.

Close my eyes again and I am submerged, flailing weakly, her legs clamped around my head, her sex in my face. I start awake violently, gagging.

Few men, I think, would admit to being overpowered by a woman. And fewer still would claim they were forced into a sexual situation. We're supposed to *want* sex, and even being with someone we're not attracted to is a conquest, not a violation.

But it *is* a violation. I would like to think I'm not constrained by what our society says a man *should* be, and yet it is difficult to admit, even to myself, even in my despair, that I *was* violated. I was assaulted. I was... But even in admitting my powerlessness, I can't use that word yet.

And if I can't admit it to myself, then how can I face my most manly friend Magne and tell him the truth of what happened? And I have to tell someone or go mad. My first choice would be Su, but obviously that can't happen until she's back. And since I left behind my old life a few years ago to move here, I don't have any of my old friends – not that I was so close to any of my old friends.

So it has to be Magne, but the thought of how he might look at me, how he might think of me, if I tell him... if I tell him I was raped.

And even though my mind fills up with all sorts of reasons why what happened with the pond woman wasn't *really* rape – no penetration, to start with; from her point of view I was willing because she couldn't know about the demon, to go on with – just forcing myself to think that word does something to settle me.

It's not that I feel any less awful, or fearful, or sick. But it eases something I must have been struggling against in my own mind, and it lets me sleep, finally.

There are dreams, and then there are *true* dreams. In regular dreams, your mind makes up scenarios for you, and while they might reflect your state of mind, or even present a solution to a dilemma, they don't really impact your waking life. They aren't *real*. Those dreams are all most people – human or *other* – ever experience.

But since I met Su, I've learned there is another kind of dream, what we eventually started to call a "true dream." Sometimes, true dreams let one person experience in slumber what another is experiencing in real life, like when Su could see what was happening to me in the vampire council research facility, as if she was looking through my eyes. Sometimes, true dreams show the dreamer events of the past, either experienced through the eyes of someone who was there, or as if you are a ghost, observing events from outside of them.

But the dream I have that night is the third kind of true dream – or if it is a regular dream it sure *feels* true – the kind where two dreamers meet somewhere outside of either of them (or maybe *inside* of one of them).

I gradually become aware, in this dream, that I am standing in a featureless grey place. It is so much of nothing that I can't visually distinguish between the surface I'm standing on and the space around me, though I am not floating. I can feel ground beneath my feet, at least.

It is the sort of place that would invite madness if one had to endure it for too long. Fortunately for my sanity, I soon spy a figure in the distance, though I could not have said it *was* a distance save the humanoid shape is tiny as it would be if very far away.

The figure casts no shadow, so watching it approach is simply observing it grow larger as its legs make walking motions. The person is of medium height and powerfully built, though not bulky. Male, Asian, dressed in a dark suit of a style so plain it could probably blend into any number of years past. His hair is long and gathered into a clip at the nape of his neck, and his face is unnaturally smooth.

He seems familiar, but it isn't until he is standing right in front of me that I realize it's the ancient vampire from a previous dream. As if recognition was a cue, I abruptly feel threat washing off of him in waves, leaving me terrified. More fearful than when I found the illustration of the Jinny Greenteeth, by several orders of magnitude.

It makes me want to curl up into the smallest ball I can make of myself, but I stand very still instead. It's not that he feels evil, or even that the sense of threat is directed at me, only that I feel I am faced with a being so powerful he is dangerous simply by being present.

Perhaps he notices my discomfort, because the feeling diminishes, though my brain keeps sending me weak alarm signals, urging me to flee.

It is then that I remember where else I have seen this man. Not in a dream, but in real life. That day Su bound herself to Alex to save me from the demon, we met this vampire in the forest. He was there and gone so quickly that afterward I thought he might have been an hallucination, something the demon inside me had brought on. Except Su remembered him too, and he terrified her.

Karasu. He had told us to call him Karasu. We looked it up later – it's the Japanese word for crow or raven, but can also refer to a type of demon or fairy spirit called a *tengu. Karasu tengu* was supposed to be the most powerful tribe of vampire-like crow spirits.

He stops in front of me and just looks at me, then steps around as if to examine me like a prize horse. Or a specimen. I turn as he circles me and he frowns, so I stop and keep very still as he inspects me.

When he's facing me again, he reaches out a hand and I almost don't flinch. He acts as if he doesn't notice the small movement, and strokes his fingers down the side of my face.

His touch is cool, not ice-cold as I had expected, and the callouses on his fingers rasp a little against the stubble I didn't realize I had neglected to shave away.

I don't know if it's possible for fear to give a man an erection, but I'm certainly not aroused in a sexual way, yet grow hard anyway. I find myself praying to a God I haven't believed in since Papa Vamp fed me my own family before I had been reborn long enough to remember who I was, that Karasu won't notice the bulge.

"So," he says. I couldn't have formed words even if I knew what to say. "Such a pretty, delicate boy to carry such power."

Does he mean the demon in my head? Or the vampire and witch powers that have combined in me in ways that should not be possible?

He drops his hand, waves it, and suddenly I am naked, my erection obvious. But he looks at it just as he looks at the rest of me, dispassionately, as he circles me again.

I feel the brush of his fingers across my back, my shoulders, and then he traces part of the large tattoo that wraps its wings across my back and chest.

"Interesting," he says. The tattoo is a black shape, a bird up the left side of my torso, its tail on my hip and its beak almost in my armpit. A raven.

Then he looks into my eyes and my penis droops and I wonder very sincerely how I manage not to piss myself. I can hardly move enough in my terror to even draw breath.

"Perhaps you are not so delicate after all." He touches my right pectoral muscle. "Merely thin." Then he grasps my chin as Magne had done, only not as hard. But where I could easily break Magne's grip, I have no doubt I could not even move this old vampire's fingers.

He twists my head to one side, to inspect my bruises.

"Someone has not treated you well," he says, releasing my face and looking back into my eyes. I'm certain I can feel him sifting my memories, rummaging in my thoughts.

Then he takes a step back. "I would tell you to kill her for what she did, but there are... parties who would not take kindly to vigilantes, especially not with what you are becoming."

He strokes his chin as if in thought. "But if you survive what is to come, you will be stronger than any number of Jinnys Greenteeth."

"What is to come?" I gasp out, my voice sounding small and young in my own ears.

His face doesn't change, but I think maybe something in his eyes shows he is impressed. "Alas," he says. "I cannot say. No one has survived it in a very long time, and it is different for everyone regardless." He strokes his chin again.

"No one has survived what?" I say.

He ignores me as if I have not spoken. "I wonder if your little witch enemies would have chosen to do what they did if they knew they might not only fail to destroy you, but might actually unleash a *koldun* upon the world."

The word – *koldun* – resonates in my thoughts, but I'm still too concerned with not collapsing in terror to think about why it seems familiar.

Karasu turns away and his figure begins to recede.

"Wait," I say.

He turns.

"What is happening to me?"

His smile is cold, and he doesn't answer.

"Is it the demon? The thing in my head made of fear and pain?"

His smile grows, just a fraction, and I feel my thoughts shifting, arranging, making connections. *Koldun.* It *is* something to do with the demon, with what the *hexen* did to me. With Great Grandpapa.

"Am I evil?" I say, but my voice is only a whisper.

In a flash, a movement so quick I don't even see it, he's next to me, not touching me, but so close I would feel the heat of his skin if he weren't vampire-cold.

In my ear, he says, "You are what you are, and you will be what you choose to be."

Then his shape is tiny in the distance.

"Remember, my son," his voice says, sounding still as if he were right next to me. "You choose, but choices are never simple, nor easy. And the results are often unexpected."

Then he is gone and I am in the grey nothing alone again, where I stay, naked and cold and afraid, unable to return to normal dreams until finally Su's alarm clock sounds and jolts me into waking.

Work is back to its normal tedium, though Luke seems determined now to make friendly gestures, telling me I look much better, and buying me coffee unasked when he takes his lunch.

I feel strange, suddenly having to be courteous to a co-worker I've previously only exchanged a few words at a time with, but I'm not so rich with friends, nor yet so jaded, that I'll outright reject the tentative gestures towards friendship.

After work, I debate going home – it's been days since I was at my own place for more than a few minutes to grab food or change clothes. But all the books are at Su's, and it's time I explained to Magne what happened the other night. Or at least enough to ease his suspicions.

When he opens his door, his brown hair is tousled and he's wearing only boxers that he must have put on in haste, because they're backwards. I can smell his girlfriend Cara and the air is thick with sex.

It makes me linger too long on the shape of Magne's muscles and the pale tracery of scars that crisscross his torso, and I think maybe I should retreat back to Su's and spend some time thinking about her naked, expend a little erotic energy by myself, before having a talk with my wolf friend.

But he just steps back into the apartment, leaving the door open, and waves in the general direction of his living area. There is a couch, but it's so buried under cushions – as is the floor – that it is nearly hidden. I push a few aside and perch on the edge of the seat.

"I was just making coffee," Magne says.

"With Scotch," says another voice, and Cara appears out of the bathroom. She's wrapped herself in a bright green silk robe that makes her dark skin vibrant. Magne certainly is a lucky man.

She turns to look at him and says, "You're on backwards, wolf boy." He glances down, shrugs, and drops his boxers right there, turns them around, and puts them back on.

He has his back to me, but the sight of his muscular buttocks is almost enough to send me scurrying to the door. *You want to shove your cock in there,* I imagine the demon voice would say, and though it remains silent, I'm fairly confident I sense it chuckle from wherever it's buried in my brain. He doesn't even have to say anything now – I imagine his commentary for him.

I shift to ease the tightness in my trousers, and hope Magne can't smell my arousal. It's a problem with associating with *others* – many of us have animal-keen senses and certain things are difficult to hide. It doesn't help when Cara's robe slides off her shoulder as she bends to sit on a huge cushion against the wall, and I catch a glimpse of the curve of her breasts.

I'm not usually such a mindlessly randy creature. I have good self-control. But whether the demon is making me weak, or Su's absence has made me lustful, I've started to turn into the sort of man I detest: one who can't separate anything else from sex.

"So what's up?" says Magne. "Or is this a social call?"

I glance at Cara. I don't think I can talk about Jinny and her assault in front of Magne's lover. Not that I think Cara will judge me – in fact, she's probably less likely to look down on me than Magne. It's just that I don't know her well.

Since they got together, she and Magne have been nearly inseparable, but I still haven't spent much time around her. I guess I haven't seen that much of Magne lately, either.

But I can't ask her to leave, so instead I opt to broach the other subject I came to speak to Magne about.

"What do you know about *koldun*?" I say.

He frowns, and pours the coffee. "Only what you and Su found out in your research."

That stops whatever words I might have said next, and I stare at him as I take the mug he offers. All I can manage to say is, "What?"

He looks at me oddly, glances at Cara, and looks back at me. "Are you having memory issues?" he asks, carefully.

"I don't think so," I say. "Or at least I *didn't* think so." I sip the coffee absently. It tastes slightly scorched and is stronger than I like, but not everyone is a food snob like I am.

"Su and I researched it?" I say.

Magne sprawls on some cushions next to Cara and manages to look completely relaxed, though I can sense tension in him. He puts a hand on Cara's foot and she wiggles her toes. Her nails are painted the same iridescent green as her robe.

"How much do you remember about the *hexen* and what they tried to do to you?"

I shrug. "I would have said everything, but now I wonder." I sip my coffee again to compose my thoughts. "They had Grandpapa – or Great Grandpapa, or whatever – they had a jar of his ashes, and used it as a…" I feel around for the word, conscious now that this is a story I should have clearly burned into my memory.

"A focus," says Cara, her voice soft with guilt. "We used it as a focus to combine our powers, to force you to do our will."

"You were one of them," I say. "I forgot." My voice is as small as it was in the dream of Karasu. How could I have forgotten one of my best friends is fucking one of the witches who tried to kill me?

My hands tighten around the coffee mug until the heat of the beverage inside feels like it's scorching my flesh. *Not fucking*, I tell myself. *They're in love.* And the younger witches were only acting on the direction of the leader of their coven, a woman with reason to fear what I might become. They had no way to know that what she was having them do might unleash the demon that drove Great Grandpapa mad, no way to know they might turn me into something worse than the abomination they already thought I was.

Of course, they *did* know, or they should have, that they were trying drive a thinking, sentient being to his death.

Cara's voice shows no trace that she's trying to avoid responsibility or ignore her guilt. "I was," she said. "And I'm sorry."

"She's the only one save that hag Mathilde who lived," Magne growls.

"You tried to control me," I say, but I carefully keep accusation out of my voice. I don't blame Cara – I don't even really blame Mathilde for being anything other than rash and ignorant. And arrogant. "But you ended up letting the demon free."

"It isn't really a demon," says Cara. "But yes. And you and Su and Alex defeated it." She looks at me expectantly, as if waiting for me to affirm that the demon is still safely locked away in my mind, disintegrated into memories, and harmless. I say nothing.

"While we were trying to figure out what the demon – or whatever – was," says Magne, "Su came across mention of something called a *koldun*."

"That's a Russian word," I say, the language of my childhood returning to me. "It's a kind of sorcerer in fairy tales. Evil."

"Yes," says Cara. "And it turns out someone tried to make your great grandfather into one."

New memories, or old ones I had forgotten, return slowly to me, of how the demon took over my body, first turning me into a raving monster, and then trying to manipulate those around me. It's how I know, now, exactly what Magne's naked chest would feel like under my hands, and how his tongue would taste in my mouth.

I look down at my coffee in confusion, and see that my trembling hands are sending waves across the surface that dance in a mesmerizing pattern.

"How," I say, struggling to remember the details of what we had already learned of my ancestors, and of Russian sorcerers.

"Take one rare male witch," says a new voice from the door, one that sends waves of fear down my spine and makes my legs feel so weak I'm thankful to be sitting down.

Magne half-stands and crouches, teeth bared, between Cara and the door. His face has started its transformer-robot-like shift to wolf, so his canine teeth are extended and huge, his face projecting in a snout. Cara, on the other hand, looks calm and composed, though I can smell her fear, sharp and thick.

"Make that witch a vampire," says the voice, and I force myself to turn so I can see its owner.

"Then add a spirit born of the fear and pain of countless slaughtered innocents."

I find myself standing and then the demon's voice speaks in my head. No, it speaks through my mouth. "And if it survives, you have the most powerful *other* in existence."

"Indeed," says Karasu, stepping the rest of the way through the door – no invitations needed for vampires in the real world. "You have a *koldun*." He places his palm on my forehead and I am hit with an intense headache that leaves me writhing on the floor, but the demon is gone again.

He looks down at me. "It is a good thing that mere *others*," and he waves his hand at Magne and Cara, "are not the only things that go bump in the night. As you would know, boy, if you paid more attention to the enchanting fox who shares your bed."

Chapter Five

"ARASU," I MANAGE to gasp out, as I lift myself from the floor.

"So you remember," he says.

I can't make myself look up at him, but I'm certain I can feel him staring down at me.

"You *other*-folk," he says. "So weak, sometimes. It is disappointing my progeny turned out to be so susceptible to base animal fear."

Then that fear is gone, or not gone but lessened to something sensed in the background rather than an overwhelming force, and I am able to climb the rest of the way to my feet, to face him.

Magne and Cara rise, too, and Magne's face shifts back to human, though his teeth stay partly extended.

"Your progeny?" says Cara.

He looks at her, and something that might be a smile – or maybe just a grimace – passes across his face.

"Not you, of course," he says. "These two."

Magne and I must both look comical, but my astonishment is not for Karasu's words, but for his expressions.

He has them.

Most vampires, when they are reborn, lose the involuntary shifts of expression that all humans have. They are, corpse-like, still and blank unless they choose to put on an expression. Young vampires often sport comical, exaggerated facial movements – when they remember to use any at all – because they are merely mimicking human expression. Older vampires do better, look more natural, but it's fairly easy to spot when you know what to look for.

Su says that I am unlike most of my kind in that I still have a full range of automatic reactions and involuntary twitches, though I can go vampire-still when I choose to.

Karasu's expressions are subtle, but I don't think they are faked. Though perhaps he is simply so old and so practiced that even another vampire can't tell.

"You're a vampire," says Magne. "How does that make me your offspring?"

"Do you not know your own genetic history?" Karasu says.

"Vampires and werewolves are created by a symbiont," I say, and that faint smile flicks across the old vampire's face.

"The same symbiont," he says.

"But not exactly the same," says Magne.

"No," says Karasu. "Your kind," and he nods to Magne, "chose to reproduce in what they deemed a more 'natural' way." He waves his hand as if to indicate Magne's scars. "Though as you surely know, the path to becoming a werewolf is considerably more brutal."

"Vampires used science," I say.

"Yes. We mutated and refined the symbiont, removed the more... inconvenient effects the organism had on our bodies."

"They can't become wolves," says Magne, his chin jerking up defiantly.

"Neither, technically speaking, can you," says Karasu. And he's right. The change to full werewolf actually takes many years, and results in a creature that can shift the way its joints fit together, can bend and twist and rearrange into something that only *resembles* a wolf.

Magne's nostrils flare and the very corner of Karasu's mouth twitches.

"So we're two different animals born of the same disease," says Magne, a growl in his voice. "I still don't see how that makes you my sire."

"I'm not directly, and yet you two are my descendants. I was one of the scientists who worked on transforming the symbiont, but I had other offspring before I found a more... *humane* way to reproduce."

"But that would make you..." says Cara, trailing off in thought.

"Very old, yes," says Karasu. "And now children" – and this time I'm certain the fleeting smile is genuine – "this boy and I have matters to discuss."

"We're his friends," Magne says and Cara nods, taking his hand. "You can tell us anything you tell him."

"Perhaps. He will have to choose whether or not to reveal our discussion to you later, but there are things no *other* needs to know, just as there are things all *others* agree no human should learn, save those few who can be trusted completely."

With those enigmatic words, Karasu steps from the room, moving more quickly than is natural, but so smoothly it doesn't seem wrong until he's already gone.

I look at Magne and he just shrugs. I follow Karasu and as I pull the door closed, Magne says, "We'll grill you later."

Karasu waits by the stairs and I follow, not bothering to explain that those who live here and their friends always use the elevator, even to go one floor up or down, so anyone in the building can hear when we come and go. It's a courtesy and we all follow it, except now.

I'm hesitant to let Karasu into Su's loft – after all, it's her home, not mine, but he obviously knew where it was and it isn't like I could stop him if he really wants in. Inside, I make tea and he sits on the couch and watches. I'm awkward under his scrutiny, but I manage not to burn myself or spill anything. I feel like a child who has just been allowed to use the stove alone for the first time.

He waits until I'm sitting and we each sip before speaking. "Very good," he says, and I hear surprise in his voice – another unusual thing, because vampire expression deficiency extends to vocal intonation, too. "Your lover has excellent taste in teas." Then he just looks at me as if I'm supposed to say something.

"She does," I finally manage. Then, "Why are you here?"

Not for sweet, sweet lovemaking, says the demon – or I hope it's the demon and not just my own imagination – and I almost bite my tongue. I had been starting to think I was safe from it here. What triggered it? If I could figure that out, maybe I could defeat it, or at least avoid setting it off.

I realize Karasu is still watching me, his tea half-raised to his lips. When he sees I've noticed, he takes a sip, then sets down the cup.

"Do you want me to remove it from you?"

I've opened my mouth to answer, "Yes," but he raises his hand before I get the word out.

"Before you answer, listen," he says. "It is not as simple a choice as you might think."

I want to tell him that of course it's simple, of course I want it gone, but if I've learned anything over the past year, it's that the world isn't ever simple.

I nod, and he seems to relax, though he doesn't stir at all.

"Do you remember our conversation the other night?"

I nod. "You said I would become what I choose."

"If it doesn't defeat you," he says.

I think about that. "And if it does defeat me?"

"You follow your great-grandsire into madness." He spreads his hands. "Or you die. Or that which you call 'demon' takes your body and lives your life."

"Could that happen?" I would sooner let it drive me mad than let it have my body if it would keep Su and my friends safe from it.

"It is the least likely outcome."

Then I remember what he said when he appeared at Magne's. "What did you mean about more things that go bump in the night than *others*? About things *others* are unaware of the same way humans are unaware of us?"

"Ah, that," he says, leaning back on the couch. "I suppose everything you have learned from your werewolf and witch friends tells you magic is not real, that werewolves undergo a physical alteration, that vampire abilities are merely those of a human, enhanced by the symbiont."

"That witches manipulate probability and use mental tricks," I add. "Yes."

"But you have also been told that you should not exist as both *hexen* and Reborn."

"Nor should Su exist," I say.

"Ah, but where does a *hexenfuchs* even fit in *other* lore?" he says, waving a hand in the air.

"We always thought she was a sort of were," I say. "A werefox." But Su and I have spent hours talking over all her abilities that are nothing like she should be able to do as any *other* we've ever heard of.

"Does she change shape the way a werewolf does, or a were-seal?"

"No," I say.

"No. She becomes physically smaller. She becomes a real fox in a way no werewolf ever becomes a real wolf. Even her thoughts become fox thoughts, with only the strength of her self keeping any remnant of human in her. Is it not so?"

"So?" I say. "Are you saying magic is real?"

He smiles a bigger smile than I've seen on him yet, but it has teeth in it.

"How do the three fox women who saved your lover's life fit into were lore? *Other* lore?"

They answer is simple, but something none of us has said aloud: they don't.

"How do I?" Karasu spreads his hands and his form seems to waver like a mirage over asphalt on a hot day. I blink, thinking the demon is meddling with my vision somehow, but the distortion remains. And then the old vampire dissolves all at once into nothing, into pale mist that seeps out from his suddenly empty clothes to swirl once around my head and then puddle on the floor to spread thin and seem to vanish altogether.

I feel dizzy and I clutch my tea cup like it is the only thing keeping me rooted in reality. "You're a *koldun*?" I say.

Like a shadow, but vague white instead of grey, the mist reforms on the floor, then gathers and swirls and seeps back into the clothing laid out on the couch, lifts and fills it and reforms into a solid body until Karasu sits before me again, regarding me from his flat black eyes. It could be a trick. It could be the sort of mental manipulation that *hexen* specialize in. But I don't think it is. I think it's real. I think *magic* is real.

"I am not a sorcerer," he says. "Not a *koldun*. But you and I are something alike."

"Magic is real," I say. Despite hints of it before now, despite knowing Su couldn't be *other* if being *other* was what we were taught it was, I still can't help but be astonished.

"It isn't the word I would choose," he says. "But yes." He regards me seriously. "Do you see why I did not wish to discuss these matters in front of your friends?"

"Not really," I say. "They know Su, they know me."

"And they are almost certainly trying always to fit you both into the world they understand, just as humans only see things as if they fit the human world, or else they are thought crazy."

"If I tell my friends magic is real, they'll think I'm crazy?" But I can see what he means. They will try to fit everything into what they know simply because magic is impossible.

"So what are you, if not *other*?" I say.

"I am *other*, or at least I was. I was a vampire before werewolves split off from us to live wild in the forest and those who followed the way of science took to calling themselves Reborn. But I have been alive a very long time, and in that time, I have learned that *others*, as they are now, are much less than we once were. That once we ranked among the minor deities, the demons, the fey-folk, and might even mix with gods from time to time."

"Could vampires now become like you? Turn to mist?"

He smiles. "I can also take the form of a wolf, a true wolf and not such semblance as your friend Magne can adopt. A bat, even." He sips his tea and carefully sets the cup down again. "But no, the symbiont is too weak now, too disconnected from the elemental magic that created it, to allow such powers. Even re-combining the Reborn and werewolf strains could not create such a one as I. And even in my youth, the abilities I have were not common."

"What about me? Am I not *other*? How am I like you?"

"You are *other*, but you can be more. How much more I cannot say. I do not think it possible to know what you could become until you become it."

"But a *koldun* is a powerful *other*, that's what Magne said, and you agreed."

"I did, and I do. A *koldun* is much like a strong witch, but with the potential to grow beyond what any *other* is capable of, to use real magic. Or so the stories say."

"And this demon in my head?"

"As you learned, it is a consciousness created at a moment of fear and pain and terror so great it took the torture and death of many innocents to create it."

"Why is it back? We defeated it, turned it into the memories of those who died in its creation."

"It was a most impressive feat, and if you were not who you are, it might have worked and left you with nothing but ill dreams. But that being was created specifically for your bloodline. It is in your genes to respond to it, to awaken it."

"But you can remove it? Destroy it?" I think about his hand on my forehead and the headache it produced, the feeling that my brain was being seared from inside my skull by the heat in his palm. If that was only to subdue it temporarily, what will it take to destroy it completely? Would I survive?

"I believe I can, if you choose. The process would almost certainly be very unpleasant, however."

"Could someone have done the same for Great-Grandpapa?"

"I could have. I *would* have. He chose not to."

I had not considered that my ancestor might have chosen his fate. I thought I remembered learning that the demon was inflicted on him by a mad human who fancied himself a magician, a prophet. "You knew him?"

"There are few beings of my age. Some of us hide, and some of us meddle. I chose to keep an eye on your family. *Hexen*, as you may perhaps have realized –" He looks at me closely and decides my look means I don't know where he's going. "– Or may not have realized, can sometimes have powers not easily explained by their *otherness*."

"Like the ones in fairytales."

"Perhaps. The pretty dark-skinned *hexen* your downstairs friend is so taken with has the potential to do much more than pluck the strings of probability and trick people into believing they see things that aren't there."

"What about Magne?"

"Just an ordinary werewolf, I'm afraid, though impressively developed in his wolf-form for his age."

I absently sip my tea just to be doing something. It has gone cold, but it helps me ignore the feeling of Karasu watching me. The sense of threat he exudes is still there, on the edge of my awareness, but perhaps I'm getting used to it because it doesn't bother me as much now. I wonder why he doesn't keep it dampened all the time. Maybe it's more effort than he lets on. Or maybe he likes to make people afraid. Or perhaps he simply doesn't spend very much time around people who are affected by him.

"Take it out," I say. I don't care how strong it might make me, if it means I might become evil and harm Su. I don't need real magic if I have her.

"You have not heard all I have to say."

"Take it out," I say again. "Nothing else you can say matters. I won't take the chance that I might become evil."

He regards me, all expression gone from his face so he is unnaturally still. Maybe the emotions I thought I saw were artificial after all, because there is nothing of them now.

"The only way to remove the demon from you without killing you is to sever its genetic connection."

"Okay," I say. "Do that."

"To do that," he says, "I will have to reshape your DNA to eliminate the aspects of your being that the demon-ghost exists to bond with."

"Fine. Whatever it takes."

"Do you know what doing that will make of you?"

A thought niggles in the back of my head, but I can't quite catch onto it. "It doesn't matter," I say.

"You will consent to being genetically altered?"

"This sounds more like science than magic."

"It is both," he says. "I am a scientist, after all. Or I was, long ago, even if science then was still half magic." He tilts his head to one side, but still shows no expression. "I will do nothing until you understand how the process will affect you."

"I'll be free of a nasty voice in my head that sometimes takes over my body. I don't see how there is any negative to that."

"The demon-ghost will not be destroyed. I do not have that power. I can merely imprison it again."

"Does anyone have the power to destroy it?"

He blinks. His eyes are blacker than ever in the shadow of the loft, though I can feel the sun climbing higher in the sky outside. I wonder suddenly if he is trapped here until the sun goes down, or if he has some magic to ward off sunburn. Soon I'm going to have to retreat behind the bedcurtains.

"You do," he says finally.

"There," I say, holding out my hands like I've made some argument-winning point. "You pull it out of me, and I destroy it."

"You misunderstand. *Either* I can remove it *or* you can destroy it, if it does not destroy you. Whichever you choose, it will leave you changed."

It finally sinks in that I really need to shut up and stop insisting he get rid of my demon. I need to listen to what he has to say. So I say nothing, and he nods, even relaxes a little.

"If you choose not to have the creature removed, you will have to suffer through whatever trials lie ahead. You will have to survive its manipulations, its voice, its attempts to steal your body."

"And then I can defeat it?"

"To defeat it, you must absorb it, integrate it. But I can not tell you how to accomplish that. It has never been done during my lifetime."

"Then what?"

"Then you will be a *koldun*. A sorcerer, and one of the most powerful beings in *other* lore. One with the potential to be more than *other*, to be powerful in any lore, known or hidden, that I have studied."

"More powerful than you?"

He smiles. "Perhaps. Perhaps not."

"So possible madness, or death, or maybe untold power. Will I still be me?"

"That is up to you, but you will be changed."

"And if I ask you to remove the demon? You don't seem keen to do so."

"I am not." He rubs an eyebrow with one finger, the most human gesture I have seen him make yet.

"Why?"

"As I said, it would mean removing or altering the parts of your genetic makeup that attract the demon, the parts it was created to bond with. Perhaps I am merely unwise in my age, preferring a path that could easily lead to disaster, but I am hesitant to take that from you."

"What does that mean, to remove or alter those parts of me?"

"It means, that in order to get it out of you, I have to take away what makes you a vampire, and what makes you a witch."

I feel cold in the pit of my stomach, a sort of fear, but unlike that terror Karasu inspired when we first met.

He sighs. "I would have to make you human."

Chapter Six

I TELL KARASU I need to think, and he leaves and when he's gone I pace until the sun becomes too uncomfortable, and then I toss and turn on the bed until the sun goes down. Then I climb out the window and down the fire escape.

I don't want Magne to corner me, to "grill" me, as he put it. I really do need to think, but I can't do it here.

Of course, Magne could very well follow me, and he almost certainly will hear me, but by leaving though the window I've – I hope – given him the clear message that I need to be left alone. He of all people, will understand.

I let myself wander the streets without thinking about where I'm going, but when I realize I've turned towards the park, I stop myself and head for downtown instead.

If I choose to have Karasu remove the demon-voice from me, I would be left human. It was not so long ago that I would have – well, not jumped at the chance, exactly, but… Or would I have chosen that? To be human again sounds wonderful. Normal hours, normal food, the sun on my skin. *Others* would no longer want me for what they think I can do for them, though some of them might instead want me for a snack.

But having seen the wonders of the world that humans are unaware of, that we *others* keep secret from them, do I want to go back? Do I want to give up the intensity of awareness I have grown accustomed to, the ability to defend myself – from attacks physical and mental – without even thinking about it?

Passing the window of a café, I spy a familiar face. He waves, and I wave back. He beckons, and I wave again, as if to indicate that I'm in a hurry. I wonder if he can sense the lie, somehow, because he follows me out, jogs to catch up.

"If you have to be somewhere," he says, "I'll just tag along for a bit." He grins, and I don't have the heart to say no. I've never really noticed how good looking Luke is before. Perhaps it's the new context. Now, instead of the guy I usually end up working security at the mall with – though we don't really work together, more like separately in the same general area – he's an attractive young man of about my age with a grin that shows engagingly crooked teeth, and hair that's on the blond side of ginger.

He has freckles and I find them adorable. I wait for the demon to make a lewd comment, but it stays silent.

"I don't really have to be anywhere," I say. "I just need to think."

"Girlfriend got you down?" he says.

"No," I answer, but I can't help the smile that curls my lips. As if Su could ever be the cause of my troubles. So far, she has been entirely the solution. "More like choices I'm going to have to make. Or one big choice."

"Ah," he says. "So no girlfriend, then?" He almost sounds hopeful.

"She's overseas," I say.

"Too bad." And I can't tell if he means too bad she's away, or too bad she exists. I never considered the possibility that Luke was being friendly because he was interested in me. But maybe I'm imagining it; maybe he *is* just being friendly.

"Let me buy you a drink," he says suddenly, pulling me towards the door of a pub. It's an Irish-style place, frequented mostly by traditional musicians and traditional music fans who also happen to be gay. I went there once, before I met Su, and found it laid back, comfortable, and not the sort of meat-market my ex always used to want to go to.

I hesitate. "I don't know," I say.

He flashes his teeth. "Afraid people will think you're queer?" he says. "Don't worry. No one here will care if you're in love with a woman."

"It's not that," I say. "I've been here before. I just... I need to think."

"Ooh. Playing both sides, are you?" Luke says.

"If you mean, am I bi, then yes," I say.

"Or you're indecisive," he says.

I feel my shoulders tense up. I have no desire to get into an argument about how bisexual people are just greedy or can't make up their mind or we don't exist or whatever other nonsense gets tossed around by the gay community just as much as by the straight community. Things like this are why I choose to build my own community, instead of joining an existing one. The easiest way to avoid an argument seems to be to just give in and let him buy me a drink, so that's what I do. It was either that or quite literally run away, and how would I explain my astonishing speed next time we met at work?

He waves at the bartender, who looks enough like him they might be relatives, then leads me to a corner table, far enough from the music session up front that the sound is not too overwhelming.

The bartender appears with two pints of dark beer as we're settling into our chairs.

"So you want to talk over this life-changing decision of yours?" Luke asks. "My mother always says talking something through with a disinterested party can help make everything clearer."

"And are you disinterested?" I say. I take a long gulp of my beer to hide my dismay. Am I flirting? Why am I flirting? I'm not sure I can blame that stupid comment on the demon. I'd like to, because I have no business flirting with Luke.

He just laughs. "Are you coming on to me, Alexeyevich?" he says, calling me by my surname.

"I'm sorry," I say. "I shouldn't have said that."

"I don't mind," he says. "And for the record, I *am* interested. But I thought you mentioned a girlfriend overseas."

"She's why I shouldn't have said anything."

"I don't mind sharing," he says, but he sees I'm not laughing along and becomes more serious. "Is your big decision to do with her? Not marriage is it?"

"No," I say. "It's not about her." But as I say it, I realize that my answer to Karasu *is* going to be partly about her.

"What, then?" He rests his face on his hands and looks at me. He looks younger that way, which makes it easier not to think about him as anything other than a co-worker who might become a friend.

I don't want to talk about this, but I also kind of do. It's really Magne I should be talking to, and Su, and I wonder if I should just get up, walk out, and go back to Su's loft. But Luke watches me without judgement, waiting patiently for me to say something.

Sometimes, at work, his comments rub me the wrong way, grate on my nerves, but right now he seems so sincere and kind I think maybe I *can* talk to him. Not in specifics, of course. I can't tell him I'm a vampire and have a demon imprisoned in my head. But maybe I can be hypothetical.

"What if," I say, and he shifts so he can use one hand to lift his beer and sip, never letting his eyes leave my face. "What if you were given... a talent, something few other people have, but then you discover that talent might carry a terrible price?"

"Wow," Luke says. "I thought you were agonizing over buying a house or going back to school." He sips his beer again. "Is this, like, an artistic talent?"

"Maybe," I say. "Or maybe more like an athletic talent. Or both." I trace lines in the condensation on the sides of my beer glass. "What if you could avoid the terrible price, but it would mean losing the talent?"

"That's a hard one," he says. "I guess it would depend on how terrible the price was, and whether or not you would want to live talentless. Like, how much having that talent defines who you are."

"And what if," I go on, "You could avoid the terrible price in a different way, to keep the talent, but it would make you a very different person, and there was a chance it might kill you, or make you go insane, or get you locked up."

"I hope you're going to tell me what this is all about some day," he says.

"Maybe someday," I say. *But almost certainly not*, I think.

"And where does the mysterious overseas girlfriend fit it? Or does she?" He taps the back of my hand with one finger, but quickly moves his hand back to his beer glass.

"I don't know yet," I say. "I don't know if I should distract her from her important work to tell her. She might want to come home and help me."

"So she should. Or else she doesn't deserve you."

I snort at that and he grins.

"But she needs to live for herself, too," I say.

"I don't know if I can be much help without specifics," he says. "But it seems to me you need to figure out what the talent means to you, what being without it would mean, and if you can live with yourself if you can't pay whatever the mysterious terrible price is."

"The thing is," I say, examining the palms of my hands. "I don't know if she'll still want me without the... talent. Because then I'll just be an ordinary human being."

He slides his hand into mine, squeezes his fingers, cool from the beer glass, around mine, and says, "I'm pretty sure it's impossible for you to ever be an ordinary human being." He leans closer over our beer, so I can feel his warm breath on my face. "And if all she loves you for is your talent, however marvelous it may be, then she doesn't deserve you."

One would think I would be intelligent enough not to get drunk when I have an evil demon inside my head, one that has already shown it's capable of taking over my body at times. But it's been so long since I've been able to just hang out with another guy, and talk about guy things. And the beer is very good.

To be honest, I wasn't even sure I *could* get drunk. The vampire metabolism deals with alcohol differently from a human. I'm pretty sure I won't be able to stay drunk for very long.

It lasts long enough to make me silly, and to let me flirt with Luke while walking him home – his place is on the way to mine, so it seems to make perfect sense to take him right to his door.

That doesn't mean I have to kiss him when we get there. But I do. I'm drunk, and happy in spite of the demon and my impending decision and the fact that the love of my life is far away and I can't help her with whatever she's going through.

When I lean in and brush my lips against his, Luke starts to pull away. And that's when the demon strikes. He – the demon – doesn't speak in my head or even force me to do anything terrible, it merely takes over when I'm about to apologize, to pull away.

And he – I – it – puts a hand on the back of Luke's neck and pulls him closer, kisses him harder. And Luke responds, pulls me close so I can feel the shape of his body against mine, can feel him getting hard against me as I know he can feel me.

I don't know how long we spend at the front door of his building, making out like teenagers. If I were myself, and single, I would have enjoyed it, but instead my body enjoys it, while my mind flails helplessly against the demon.

Any moment, I'm expecting things to turn violent as the demon acts on the sorts of things it likes to say to me, but they don't. The demon doesn't even fill my head with vile language. In fact, it doesn't even reach my hands below Luke's waist or under his clothing. Instead, the demon makes me touch Luke gently, tentatively, as if exploring the possibilities of a new relationship. It makes me act in exactly the way I would act if it wasn't controlling me, and I were not already with Su.

Then, just when Luke whispers an invitation to his apartment, the demon vanishes back into the depths of my mind.

I step back, too suddenly.

"What?" says Luke. "Too soon?"

I don't want to hurt his feelings. I'm the one who started this, after all. Even before the demon took over, I'm the one who kissed Luke, not the other way around.

"I'm sorry," I say. "I need to think. I don't know what I'm doing."

"Okay," he says, and he brushes his fingers down the side of my face. It's comforting even as it reminds me what I've just done. "I understand," he says, but I see hurt in his eyes, and confusion. "Let me know if you want to talk," he says.

"See you at work," I say and he nods, as if he was hoping for more than that. "I just need to think," I say.

The demon waits until I'm back in my apartment on the top floor of a big old Victorian in a nice, quiet neighborhood where the neighbors don't even dream there's a vampire in the green house with the white gingerbread trim.

All it says is, *You really needed that. And you wanted it, too.* Then it is silent again.

I take a long shower and can't help but stroke my own cheek the way Luke did. When I close my eyes, the too-hot water can't muffle the memory of the pressure of his body against mine. He's almost exactly my height, and heavier built than me, though not as muscley as Magne.

He tasted like dark beer and peppermint candy and his tongue was strong and slippery against mine. I want to wash away the memory of him, and I want to savor it, and by the time I emerge from the shower, my heart rate is up and I feel flushed, and not only from the hot water.

I lie on the couch – I can't quite bring myself to go to the bedroom where I know Su's scent still lingers – naked and erect. For a while I just lie still, unable to stop re-imagining that kiss with Luke, the feel of his mouth, the sound of his breathing, the way he nibbled my earlobe so close to where Magne nipped it, where Jinny bit it so hard her teeth left marks.

I feel my blood throbbing and my erection bobs with it. It would be comical if I didn't feel the need for release more badly than ever before.

Finally, I touch myself. I can't bear to linger any longer. I know I shouldn't even be thinking of Luke. But maybe this relief will get him out of my head so I can go back to thinking of Su again.

I jerk at myself with short, abrupt strokes, like it's a punishment. I've never been into orgasm simply for relief – I figure if I'm going to have one, I should really enjoy it. But it feels like enjoying it now would be a betrayal of Su, and I won't let the demon do that to me.

So I tug and jerk and now, instead of lingering over thoughts of Luke, I turn my mind away from them, away from everything except the pressure in my groin, the need for release, the purely physical, mechanical operation of jerking off.

It's entirely unpleasant, and I wonder what sort of psychological damage I might do to myself, by forcing myself to orgasm and not liking it.

When my own touch becomes uncomfortable, bordering on painful, I stop. But my erection remains, stubborn and needing release. I think of Su, but I can't hold a solid image of her in my head, though it has only been a few days since she was here. Or is it a week? Longer? I have lost track.

Instead, Luke's face appears in my mind, then Jinny's, then Luke's again. His lips. I remember his mouth on mine, then imagine it on my erection. I banish the thought as soon as if surfaces, but I'm too late, and I touch myself again, more gently, caressing, squeezing, pulling, imagining Luke's kiss, his hand on my cheek.

I'm sorry Su, my heart, I think. *But I need this.* And I do need the release, the pleasure, and I can't even bring to mind the last time Su and I made love, even though we spent our whole last night together practicing it.

"I'm sorry," I say, feeling guilty. Tears trickle down the sides of my face, but I imagine my hand is Luke's hand, touching me, teasing and stroking, bringing me towards orgasm.

And just as I'm about to climax, the demon makes me stop, and says, *Beg me,* in my mind, and I can't help it. I think I even say it aloud.

"Oh God, please don't stop."

Don't stop what?

"Don't stop touching me. Please."

Please what?

"Make me come," I say, and I'm crying for real now, weeping stupidly like a weakling even as my back arches and I moan and spurt hot fluid – hotter than any vampire's semen has any call to be.

Now you are my slave, it tells me.

"No," I whisper, and I'm not sure if that is aloud or just inside my own head. But the demon is gone again and I can walk, shaking, to the bathroom to clean myself up, then finally I dare the bedroom where I am buried in Su's lingering memory. And I sleep, and dream again.

Chapter Seven

ICANNOT TELL if this dream is a true dream or an ordinary dream. That should bother me because I should be able to tell. Surely, if I can't tell, then it must be only a normal dream. Mustn't it?

In this dream I am in the grey place, only this time there are shadows. There is a ground, and something like a sky, and there are vague shapes around me, and a darker shadow ahead, person-shaped.

I look down at my hands, and they are grey, too, as if I am in an old black and white movie. I look back up at the person-shape and it looks as though its deep grey might hold traces of color. Ahead of it, even farther off, is a flash of orangey-red, fox color.

I walk towards the shape, and as I move, the vague shadows around me take on more solid form until I am walking through a forest. The trees tower over me, ancient oaks and beeches, and other kinds I don't know. This is a primal forest, old growth, and so little light reaches the ground that there is almost no undergrowth. Old leaves, layers and layers deep, muffle the sound of my footsteps and rattle quietly against my toes.

I am barefoot, I realize, though otherwise dressed normally for an early spring day, in black jeans and a sweater. And it is chilly – a cold wind winds between the trees, gusting against my face from time to time.

I walk, and stare at my feet as they flicker through the leaves. My skin is on the dark side for someone of European descent – I have a Romany great grandmother – but my toes look pale as fungus against the shadow of the forest floor.

When I look back up, the person-shape is still there, but farther away, as if it is walking just a little faster than I am. As if it knows I am following. The flicker of red appears and vanishes beyond, as if the figure is following the bright color as I am following the figure.

"Hello?" I say, but the sound is quiet, the ancient presence of the trees refusing to allow my puny voice to disturb their peace. I think maybe the figure looks back.

I walk faster, and though I don't catch up, the person doesn't get any smaller in the distance. I walk faster yet and I think I might be gaining on them.

Then that cold wind shifts and reaches the figure, tugging at it. It gusts and the person's hair flies free of whatever was holding it. It is a long, magnificent cascade, inky-dark like a curtain of deep black silk. I know that hair. I know how it gleams in different kinds of light, though I do not know how it looks in full sun, save only from far away, glimpsed from a crack in the window shade. I know how that hair feels in my hands. I know the scent of her shampoo, and how she smells when she hasn't bathed as often as she likes.

I know the feel of that hair on my bare chest and how it shifts back and forth with her movements when we make love.

"Su," I say. Only a whisper, but it carries better than my earlier words spoken at normal volume.

"Wait for me," I call, and it comes out muffled.

She pauses, then the flicker of red appears ahead of her again, and she continues.

"Wait!" I yell, and the sound is almost inaudible.

"Su." A whisper, again, and she hesitates, stops, turns.

"Wait," I whisper. But the red flash – not merely a color now, but an animal, a fox – appears again to draw her away.

If this is a true dream, that fox might represent Su's goal. I should not distract her from it. She needs to concentrate. If she turns away, even in this dream, she might lose the trail, and then it will be my fault if she fails.

I will not be the cause of her failure.

I hold my tongue, and she turns away, follows the fox.

But, too, I need her. I need to remember her, to remember *us*. To keep me strong against the demon, to keep me from making a big mistake with Luke.

He said I was far from ordinary, but I am nothing – will be nothing – if I can't overcome the voice in my own head. And to do that, I just need to see Su again, to hold her, to touch her, to know if I am making the right choice, even if I don't yet know what that choice is.

So I use my vampire speed to catch up to her. I run. I put everything I am into it and when I feel entirely drained and stumble to a halt, I have almost caught up. She is right there, just ahead of me.

The red creature, the fox, is there too, and it looks at me, shakes its head as if I have done something wrong. And Su begins to turn, to see who has come up behind her.

And I am filled with doubt. I need her, but she needs to not be distracted by me. She doesn't need me. She is stronger than I am, and she is more than I will ever be.

Unless...

I can't let her see me. Not only because I will distract her from her purpose, but also because *I* need to *not* need her.

It's not that I am ashamed to have to rely on a woman – I am not that kind of misogynist asshole. It's that I need to figure out how to rescue myself this time. If I always wait for Su to save me, I am no better than a mere human to her. Not that she would look down at someone for being human; that's not who she is.

And then I have my answer to Karasu, I think. If I want to be the man Su deserves – a full and equal partner who can stand by her side – then I can't be human, and I can't let the demon overwhelm me. I am going to have to defeat it, to become whatever a *koldun* is.

I just can't let it change me.

So as Su turns to see what the dream fox is looking at so disapprovingly, I wrench my consciousness away from the dream and force myself to wake up.

It's disorienting, waking up so suddenly from a true dream – assuming that really was a true dream – and for a long time I have to just lie in bed, fighting the bedspins as if I am still drunk.

Maybe I am still drunk, because when the disorientation fades, it's replaced by a headache the likes of which I don't think I've ever had before, not even when Karasu subdued the demon.

It stabs between my eyes like sunlight and it seems to bore right to the back of my skull. Mercifully, it doesn't last long, but it leaves my head feeling like someone has scooped out my brains with a dull spoon, like a badly-hollowed Halloween pumpkin.

I'm glad the heavy drapes keep my room as dark as a cave. Even a little light might bring the stabbing pain back.

Finally, I feel well enough to stumble to the bathroom, but the movement nauseates me, and I spend far too much time staring at the inside of my toilet bowl while my stomach heaves up all the beer I drank, along with some half-digested fries I don't even remember eating.

I can't remember if I was supposed to be at work last night.

Eventually, I am able to get to my feet and sip a little water. Not too long later, I can drink some blood, heated in the microwave to a touch hotter than normal human body temperature. Finally, I almost feel myself again.

Then I go to my bedroom, and stare at myself in the big mirror on the dresser. I look terrible, eyes bruised, and skin green-tinged. The bruises around my neck are faded and nearly gone, at least. I do heal fast.

I almost imagine I can see the demon lurking in my eyes, like it makes them darker than they should be. Almost midnight blue instead of pale. I have to lean close to the mirror to see the line where iris meets pupil.

"Pussy." It takes me a moment to realize it's not the demon talking in my head, taunting me. It's my own voice. I'm reminded of the Betty White joke about how it's inappropriate to use words for female genitalia to refer to weaklings, because, "those things can take a pounding." I almost smile, until I realize it's a word I never use. I would never call myself that, and I would never use it for anyone else, either. It's a lazy, vulgar word, a word that should refer to a most delightful part of the female body. A word that should be beautiful, not ugly.

And that brings fear to my gut. Just a little. Is the demon taking hold of me? Is it taking over me, or is this part of how I must assimilate it in order to defeat it?

If this is one of the ways the demon-ghost will change me, I don't want it. And if I dislike one new word in my vocabulary, however uncharacteristic, what am I going to think of the other ways it might affect me?

In the dream, when I forced myself awake, I was sure of my decision to keep the demon and triumph over it. Now I'm not so sure. Will it turn me into something I hate? Will I even know it has made me hateful, or will I be like one of those assholes who always think someone else is the *real* asshole?

I turn away from my reflection, and glance down at my left wrist, where the bracelet of Su's hair stands out dark and black, like a tattoo on my skin. I run my fingers over it, and smile, and then I go to the kitchen, get a pair of scissors, and cut the circlet free with a snip. I return to the bedroom and tuck the hair into a little box on my dresser, a place where I keep mementos from my past. A silver ring marked with my name in Cyrillic that my first love gave me in high school. An unopened condom from the first box I ever bought. It had been in my pocket while its twin did its protective work when I lost my virginity to the girl next door. The next one in the box, I had used with her brother.

There is an old love note, a scrap of poetry, a deep red rock found on a beach during a romantic walk. All my mementos, I realize, are about love or sex. And until now, there has been nothing of Su in the box, because she is not a memory. She is now.

The hair curls on top of the other items like a question mark. Like an accusation. Like guilt.

"I'm sorry, my heart," I say softly. "I need to do this on my own." Then I close the lid, walk out of the bedroom, and go to warm up some more blood in the kitchen.

I would very much like to stop going to work, to curl up in the dark in my apartment, and let whatever change is going to happen to me happen. Not needing to deal with the day-to-day would surely make it easier to deal with the demon.

But my apartment won't stay mine if I can't pay the rent, and I haven't managed to save much since I moved to town, so I can't pay the rent if I don't go to work.

The real problem is, Luke is at work, and I'm not at all ready to face him yet. I can't stop thinking about him, but I can't talk to him, either. So my week becomes a farce of near misses and slapstick escapes as I put as much effort into not running into Luke as I put into my job. More, probably, since my job isn't exactly difficult.

Though I avoid him, I can't quite abandon him, either. He can be annoying, and if he hadn't flirted with me, I'd never have kissed him – *Oh, you would have*, the demon says – but he was also genuinely kind to me. He listened to my cryptic attempt at explaining my dilemma, and tried to offer useful advice. And it was useful. So after work, I risk being out too long to follow him and make sure he gets home safe. There are a lot of dangerous things out in the dark, both *other* and merely human. And some of the *others* aren't as averse to hunting – and risking getting caught – as they should be. My run-in with Jinny Greenteeth at least taught me that.

She was a tasty morsel, says the demon in my head. *So much better than a pansy ginger boy*. And that's another thing that happens during the week. The demon's voice becomes more common. He's not as lewd all the time, encouraging me to fuck everyone in sight, but he comments on all kinds of things.

At first, it's so subtle I hardly notice. He sounds just like my own thoughts, and the things he thinks, notices, snickers about, are often exactly the things I would notice anyway. But now I feel like I'm hyper-aware all the time, as if having another consciousness in my head has given me a whole extra set of perceptions. I seem to notice everything that's going on around me, and with my super-human vampire senses, I was already more aware than most.

But gradually, day after day of observing people and the voice starts to sound more like the demon, and less like me. At the same time, though, it bothers me less and less, even while I know it should bother me more.

Look at that fat chick, it might say. *You might suffocate trying to fuck her*. I am horrified, feel my face burn as I walk through the mall. I cannot meet her eyes for fear that she'll know what I'm thinking. She isn't even as large as the demon seems to think, she's strikingly beautiful, and she looks confident and happy. The young man she's walking with looks like he's quite in love with her.

But I guess you wouldn't even have to get it in, says the hateful voice, and it laughs as I leave via the nearest staff exit so I don't have to deal with his commentary around other people. *Just pick a fold and fuck it.*

Then the voice is gone again, dissolved back into my own thoughts. And over time the things it says bother me less, while for every less-than-charitable idea I have, I wonder if the demon planted it there, or if I am become as monstrous as he is.

Self-doubt is not something I need right now. I set that bracelet of Su's hair aside because I need to believe I can get through this on my own, that I can absorb this demon and make it a part of me without succumbing to its nastiness.

It was born from rape and torture and fear, I remind myself, of course it sees the world that way. And I bury my own fear and my own violation as deep in my head as I can so the demon can't use those thoughts against me, at least.

I hope.

Now that I'm back in my own apartment – avoiding Su's place as much as I'm avoiding Luke – the nightmares return, the dreams of the ghostly memories of events that caused the demon to take life. Every night I re-live the horrors, and though I should be haggard from lack of sleep, I feel surprisingly good.

Maybe, I dare hope, the dreams are bothering me less, just as the demon's taunting bothers me less. I certainly wake in terror less often, and surely that's a good thing.

It nags at me that I am becoming used to such images of horror, that reliving the pain every night bothers me less and less. Some small part of my mind thinks it's a bad thing that the dreams, the memories, don't horrify me anymore. Some part of me does not want to become someone who can have such dreams and wake up feeling good.

Once or twice, too, I get the feeling of being watched, of being followed. I catch the scent of werewolf and think maybe Magne has given up on giving me space and is checking up on me. I see fleeting shapes in the corners of my eyes and wonder if a new vampire council is forming and trying to figure out how to use me.

And I feel deep terror at the fringes of my mind and wonder if Karasu is lurking around, waiting for me to decide if I still want him to remove the demon.

But I never do catch anyone actually watching me, except Luke, once, when I walk past the same café I saw him at before. He waves, like he did then, and I wave back. He doesn't wave a second time, and he doesn't follow me. I am both relieved and disappointed.

The demon voice is silent.

All that week, though, it pesters me in words and thoughts, so by the end of it I hardly know which are his and which are my own. And that is what bothers me the most; that I can't tell, and I should be able to. The demon and I are so unalike that it should be simple to tell its ideas from my own.

But it is subtle and I think it uses my thoughts and feelings as a place to begin, and then slowly turns them into something uglier. Strangely, the one thing it doesn't pollute my thoughts with all week is ideas about Luke. I want him, I can't stop thinking about him, and it shames me. Not because I desire another man – that's something I came to terms with and accepted a very long time ago. No, it shames me because I am supposed to be in a committed relationship already.

No, not "supposed to be." *Am*. I am in a committed relationship.

The shame leaves me vulnerable, and I expect the demon to pounce on the weakness, but it does not. So at night it isn't Su I dream of – when I'm not reliving ghostly nightmares. Instead, I have intense dreams about Luke, but the demon doesn't try to twist them into something vile. There isn't even any sex in these dreams. We just do ordinary things. Take long walks, go to the movies, have coffee. In my dreams, night after night, we become friends, and fall in love.

In real life, night after night, I avoid him.

Until I can't. There's a staff meeting, and attendance is mandatory. It's a routine thing, with the usual not-very-useful mall news, updates on procedures, sign-ups for the company sports teams. But I can't avoid it, and somehow, the only vacant seat when I arrive at the beginning of my shift is next to Luke.

"Hey," he says, and looks at me, then away.

"Hey," I say. I want to tell him sorry, but I can't get any other words out. I sit, and try to pretend I don't notice that we're crammed so close together in the tiny staff room that our knees touch. But I can feel the heat of his flesh next to mine and I hope I don't blush. At least blushes don't show well on olive skin. And vampires don't blush much.

The meeting is torture, though not in the usual way of utter boredom. Instead, it's an agony of wanting to look at him, of wondering if every shift of his weight that presses his knee harder against mine is deliberate or accidental, of not knowing if I *want* it to be accidental. Of not daring to move lest I seem like *I'm* trying to press close. Or shrink away. Of guilt and desire, and the desire to cast aside guilt and go with my feelings. Of knowing that if Su were here I would not be having such feelings in the first place.

But you would, I think. *You'd just be better at suppressing them.* At least I think I'm the one thinking that.

When the meeting is finally over and I'm free to do my rounds I try to get up and leave without catching Luke's eye. But his hand brushes mine, and I turn automatically.

"I..." I say.

"You're sorry," he says. "You need to think," he says. "I know." He looks at me, ignoring the other mall staff filing out of the room around us. "You feel guilty," he says. "You love your girlfriend. You're not really gay."

I glance around at that, not wanting private things overheard, though I don't care who knows my sexual orientation, but the room is already empty.

"You don't want anyone to think something's going on between us." He doesn't sound angry, or even hurt. "But I've kissed a lot of guys, and no one kisses like you do when there's nothing there. You feel something. If you don't want to go ahead, that's fine, but stop avoiding the whole question."

He stares at me, chin up, defiant and glaring. "I won't hate you if you still want your mysterious overseas girlfriend. I'll even still be your friend.

Just tell me what you want."

"I want to go to work," I say. The words come out without thought. But I can see he was expecting that sort of reaction, and it stings that he thinks so little of me, and that I deserve it.

"Fuck you," he says, and pushes past me.

And then somehow my arms are around him and I'm kicking the door closed, pressing him against it, and kissing him. And this time, I can't even blame the demon. It's all me, and if we weren't at work I wouldn't stop. I wouldn't say simply, "Yes," and then open the door again and go about my rounds.

If we weren't at work, I'd say, "Yes, please do fuck me," and I'd kiss my way down his body to his hardening cock and suck it till he screamed my name.

Chapter Eight

I DON'T LET MYSELF think about what I've done – again – until I'm home with the door locked and the curtains closed. Then I sink down on the couch and start shaking.

There is no doubt that I love Su. She is magnificent. She is everything. But there is also no doubt that I am overwhelmingly attracted to Luke. I could use the excuse that I'm bi and therefore have "needs," but that's bullshit. Being bi only means I can be attracted to both men and women, not that I'm incapable of monogamy. I also don't believe that men are at the mercy of our sex drives. We've evolved beyond the instinct to fuck everything that moves and we are fully capable of choosing not to cheat on our partners.

And now I have gone and repeated the mistake of kissing Luke, only this time I can't even blame the demon. This time it was all me.

It was nice, though, wasn't it, you sick fuck? Only mild vulgarity from the voice this time. Maybe it's taking a different tack, trying to lure me into thinking I'm making it more like me instead of the demon making me more like it.

I rub my face with both hands and try to decide what to do. If I can't hole up in my apartment and wait for the demon to attack so I can defeat it, then I have to do something else. I can't just try to go on as if life is normal and hope the demon won't fuck things up worse than I've already fucked them up myself.

So what do I need to do? One, I still haven't talked to Magne about the Jinny Greenteeth, though with recent events she doesn't seem so important anymore. Still, Magne deserves some sort of explanation.

Two, I need to talk to Karasu. I have to see if I can get any more information out of him, and then I have to let him know what my decision is.

And I owe Luke something more of an explanation, too. Maybe I can't tell him I'll leave Su for him, and maybe I can't tell him I won't, not yet, but at least I can let him know I am going through some weird shit and maybe not to give up on me entirely. Though it would probably be kinder to tell him I'm bad news. If only I could tell him the truth.

So three people to talk to: Magne, Karasu, and Luke. Maybe I need to confront Jinny, too, but not yet. First I need to know she can't overpower me again. And I need to know the demon won't just put me in her power even if she can't.

So first I'll eat, then I'll call Magne. Maybe he'll have some idea what I should say to Luke, though I'm not sure I want to tell him about that. I wonder if Cara is enough of a friend that I could tell her. Maybe I'm stereotyping women – and knowing Su should have taught me not to do that – but she seems like she might be kind and good with people. Maybe she can give me advice about my suddenly messed-up love life.

And as a witch, maybe she'll have some ideas about how to contact Karasu, too, because I really have no idea how to go about that.

I'm about to pick up my phone to call Magne when I hear heavy footsteps on the stairs leading up to my apartment, then a loud knock. I go to the door and pull back the shade just enough to get a glimpse of the bright morning sun on a very hairy, very muscular forearm, bare despite the chill in the air. I unlock the door and step back several paces.

"Come in," I say.

Magne, for all his appearance of big, dumb, muscle guy, is actually very intelligent, and also cautious. He opens the door slowly in case I'm still close enough for the sun to reach me.

"Hey, Magne," I say.

He steps in, swings the door shut behind him, and deposits a large bottle of 12-year-old Scotch on my kitchen counter.

"We need to talk," he says.

"I was just about to call you," I say. I don't look at the Scotch. Just thinking about booze makes me a little sick. I don't want a repeat of getting drunk with Luke, even though the headache the next day was a result of wrenching myself free of a true dream and not a killer hangover. Probably.

Magne stares at me and I try to read him. Usually, werewolves are easy to read. They use a lot of body language to communicate with other pack members, and an observant person can learn to understand quite a lot of it. But I must be off my game because I don't understand his tense posture. Though I do understand it's strange that he's visibly tense. Magne is a master of relaxation, sprawling instead of sitting, and making the casual lean look actually casual instead of the attempt to look cool it usually is for most people.

"Has something happened?" I say.

He relaxes minutely and points at the bottle. "Glasses?" he says.

I get him a stubbly tumbler from a cupboard and say, "None for me."

He raises an eyebrow. "Nothing's wrong except you were acting very odd, you smell of... off, and then you vanish for a week."

"I didn't vanish, I was at work."

He waves my words away with one hand and pours himself a drink with the other. I put the kettle on, mostly to give myself something to do.

"I –" I say, but now that Magne is here, I don't know how to go on. I stare at the packet of tea leaves until Magne takes it from me and finishes readying the tea pot.

"Something happened to you," he says. "Something that freaked you out and sent you running to Su's place. Something that involved a pond and a woman. That about right?"

I nod and sit on one of the hard wooden stools at the kitchen island. Magne pulls up the other to avoid towering over me.

"Something that didn't just mess you up, but that's got you freaked out enough that you're withdrawing from your friends and..." He pauses and flushes a little, like he's embarrassed about what he's going to say next. "And looking for comfort from someone else."

I open my mouth to reply, but once again the words don't come out.

"I'm not accusing you of anything," he says. "But I'm your friend. Don't shut me out."

"You're Su's friend," I say. I don't know why I say it. It's not fair.

He scowls, but the shrieking kettle interrupts whatever he was going to say. He makes the tea and sets the pot in front of me with a cup and a jar of honey, then sits down again.

"I'm *your* friend," he says. "If you force me to choose, sure, I'm Su's friend first, but I don't think it'll come to that. I think I know you pretty well, after all the shit we went through."

I nod and stare into my cup. I pour the tea and watch a stray leaf swirl around in the amber liquid. "It's not easy to explain," I say. "And it's not one thing that happened, but two."

"Okay," he says. "I'm listening."

It takes a long time to tell the story, but Magne can read human body language as well as werewolf, and I have human enough expressions that there are a lot of things I don't have to put into words. I tell him about the park, the strange blood, the woman in the pond. I hesitate when I get to the part where she lured me in and violated me.

"I read the book you were looking at at Su's," he says. "You left it open to the Jinny Greenteeth page. Is that what's in the pond?"

I nod.

"I went there. Me and a couple of my pack mates. We could smell her, but we didn't see anything."

"She must come out of the water sometimes," I say. "If I followed her blood, she had to have been out in the park, maybe downtown, and got jumped by some vampires."

"Why would a group of vamps be stupid enough to hunt? Especially in the city. Especially an *other*."

I shrug. "It didn't make any sense to me, either. But she said she was in Charleston's research facility. You know they fed *others* to each other, to see what would happen."

"You think they fed some vamps her blood and then they wanted to find the source?"

"Maybe," I say. "Maybe it's addictive." I think for a moment. I'm still avoiding telling him everything. "I'm not sure she's even an *other*, though."

"Well, she isn't human."

So I remind him of what Karasu said, about how there are beings unknown to *others* the way *others* are unknown to humans. I don't say that magic is real.

He shakes his head. "Maybe there are beings we've never heard of, but wouldn't they still be some sort of *other*?"

I shrug and sip my tea.

He takes a drink from his Scotch and watches me, and I find I can't meet his eyes. He has big brown puppydog eyes, open and completely honest.

Finally, he sets his glass aside. "So you met some powerful pond woman who was attacked by maybe-junkie vampires. But that isn't what freaked you out."

"No," I say. I still can't look at him. "I... She..." Magne is my friend and I can't bear to have him think less of me. But I have to tell him why I was acting so weird.

"Like I said, it wasn't one thing, it was two."

"Okay. What's the first thing?"

"The pond woman, Jinny Greenteeth, she... she lured me somehow. Got me into her pond and..."

"Tried to drown you, like in the book?" His voice is soft and I can tell he knows it's not so simple.

"Yes. And she... she made me..."

His hand on mine is warm and strong, brotherly, and I wonder how I could have thought his touch erotic. *Oh right, the demon.* I can almost hear it smirk.

"She forced you?" His voice is beyond gentle, but full of steel, of anger. But it's anger *for* me, not anger *at* me. How could I have ever thought he would think badly of me?

"Not to... to fuck her." His hand tightens on the word "fuck." I don't swear much, and it's surprised him.

"Did she..." Now it's his turn to hesitate. "Blow you?"

I nod, and finally look up at him. His eyes are like his voice, gentle but angry. There is no contempt in them, no pity, no disgust. At least not for me.

"And then she put her legs around my neck." I touch my faded bruises. They're almost gone, but I can still feel them. "And –"

"It's okay," he says. "I get the idea." For a long moment, he says nothing. Then, "What was the second thing that freaked you out?"

"The demon is back."

I thought he would be surprised, but he only nods.

"You knew?"

"I guessed, when your creepy old vamp dude showed up at my loft."

"I wonder how he knew," I say.

"This whole thing really has you messed up," he says. "You don't talk like yourself, or act like yourself." He leans back on his stool and I immediately miss the strong heat of his hand on mine. "Is it the demon who's going after the strawberry blond?"

"You *have* been following me." My nostrils flare as a flash of anger fills me. Is that me or the demon? I never used to get so angry, but if my friend is spying on me, I have pretty good reason.

"No," he says. "I just checked up on you once in a while. You seem pretty cozy with him. I was worried."

"Worried about me, or worried I might be cheating on Su?" My voice is petulant, but I don't care.

"Are you?" he says.

I suddenly feel deflated as the anger leaves me all at once. "No," I say. "I like him. A lot. I made a mistake and kissed him, but nothing more."

"Yet," he says.

"Yet," I say.

He sighs and leans forward again, resting his elbows on the counter. "I'm not going to tell you what to do," he says. "But if you have any respect for Su, at least break up with her before you start fucking someone else."

"I love her," I say. "I love her more than I thought it was possible for one person to love another. But I keep doing stupid things around Luke." I gulp down the last of my tea and pour another cup, but then I just look at the leaves swirling in the bottom. I remember trying to learn how to read tea leaves. Me and Su. We never believed in it, not really, but it was fun to make up silly predictions based on the shapes we saw in the leaves. Like pretending the shapes clouds make can tell the future.

"When I'm near him, I just want to touch him. And when I'm not near him, I can't stop thinking about him."

"Did this start before or after the demon came back?"

"After," I say. "But I can't blame the demon for my own fuck-ups."

"Are you sure they're *your* fuck-ups?"

"The first time, the demon took me over just long enough to make me kiss him –"

"It took you *over*? I thought it was just a voice in your head, maybe made you say things sometimes, helped the pond bitch lure you in."

"Mostly, yes, but..."

He glares at me, and then I have to tell him everything about the demon, about the things it made me think and say, about how it took over my body. I almost don't tell him what it said in my head about him taking off his boxers in front of me, but he only laughs.

"I do have a great ass," he says.

"A little too hairy for me," I say, and I'm even able to laugh myself.

"Good thing," he says. "You may be pretty, but you have all the wrong parts for my taste."

It's good to laugh. Luke made me laugh, too, but that was different.

"How do you know the demon isn't cleverer than you think?" Magne says, when we're serious again. "Maybe it's making you *think* you're the one going after this Luke. I mean, I've seen you with Su, and someone that in love doesn't act like a hormonal teenager around anyone but the one they love."

"You should know," I say. "The way you carry on with Cara."

He smiles. "Carry on with Cara. I like that. I think I'll go home and carry on with her later today."

I smile, too. Why didn't I talk to Magne sooner? If I'd known I would feel this much better, I would have.

You wanted to keep your nasty thoughts to yourself, says the demon.

Magne must see my expression change. "What?" he says. "Is it here now?"

I shake my head. "It's fine. It's just putting unpleasant thoughts in my head again."

Unpleasant? the voice says. *I'll show you unpleasant. The very most pleasurable of unpleasantry.* Then it laughs.

And as I sit there across the table from Magne, my vision is filled with a small town somewhere in Europe. There is the smell of rubber burning, and wood, and paint. There are screams and people running. Soldiers. Their uniforms are plain, with no insignia, as if they are meant to be unidentifiable, yet still recognizable. So if one villager escapes they will be able to say only soldiers, and not which soldiers, did this terrible thing.

This is the place of my nightmares, the place where one insane human, believing himself to be a magician, was able to carry out the vilest of magical contrivances. How he has such loyalty from those soldiers that they would kill for him alone, would torture, rape, slaughter children for him, I can't imagine.

He hand-picked them. One by one from the most vicious of the Tsar's brute squad.

And as I watch, a soldier rounds a corner, chasing after a young woman. She runs, terrified, and he runs after her, but she is thin, malnourished probably. This place looks poor, in the midst of famine, perhaps. He barely has to jog to keep up with her.

It is a terrible game to him. She is the mouse, and he the cat. She flees, he stalks. She hides, he drags her out, lets her escape, lets her think she might get away, only to corner her again.

I see her eyes, wide, afraid, exhausted, as she runs again, and he follows. She ducks under a raised porch, scrabbles on her belly, and she is so thin she fits there where he can't follow. He only laughs, takes out his penis, and pisses on the porch so it rains down on her. She chokes in disgust, weeps in fear, but does not emerge.

She is shaking now, trembling so hard her teeth knock together. Her nose runs and her eyes weep. She is frozen in fear.

The soldier laughs again, puts himself away, and looks around. Another soldier passes by, carrying two cans of gasoline. The soldier grins, calls out, takes one of the cans. The second soldier looks at the girl, shakes his head, spits, and continues on his way.

The first soldier splashes gasoline over the porch where he had already splashed urine and the girl reacts even less. She only shakes harder and when I meet her eyes this time, I see only terror, fear so intense it is the only thing that exists for her.

The soldier calls to her in Russian, softly, sing-song, like a lullaby. At first she only continues to shake. Then as he sings, she trembles less and less, and finally she looks at him. He smiles and holds out his hand. She stares. For a moment, I think she will surrender, and take his hand, and emerge to whatever new torture he has for her.

But then she bares her teeth and growls like an animal, whimpers and tries to huddle deeper under the porch.

He shrugs, reaches into a pocket, and pulls out a box of matches. He is grinning as he lights a match and flicks it at the gasoline.

At first, it seems the match has gone out and he scowls and takes out another. But then there is a muffled "whoof" and the porch is alight.

The girl does not move and I think I will be forced to watch her burn alive.

This is not one of the memories I have experienced before, or not that I recall. Usually I live them from inside, not as an observer.

I try to wrench myself free of this vision the way I got free from the true dream with Su. I don't care what sort of headache I'll end up with. It can't possibly be worse than this vision of horror.

Then the flames reach the girl and she shrieks and scrambles out. She tries to get past the soldier, but he is waiting as she emerges, grabs her hair and flings her across the rutted track that serves for a road in this village.

She scrambles away again, but her escape attempts are less energetic, almost half-hearted. I can see now that she is spent, defeated. She only wants it to end.

Then she seems to see me. Or she sees whomever it is I am seeing this memory through. Hope blooms in her eyes and she scrambles towards me, grasps the hem of my trousers.

"Please, sir," she says, her Russian accented with rural tones. Her eyes, I see now that she is close, are grey, her hair honey-colored. She is pretty, or was once. She has a face that would look lovely with more weight on it, but is now shrunken from starvation.

"Please," she says.

The soldier laughs. "Sir?" he says.

Always before, I have seen these scenes from inside the mind of the victims, though I don't recognize this girl at all.

I've been saving this one for you.

"Please, sir," says the girl, and I see hope die in her eyes when she realizes that I am not her salvation.

She hardly even winces as the soldier grabs her hair and pulls her away, tosses her on her back in the dirt.

"Let me hold her for you," he says. His accent is cultured. He may be a mere soldier, but he grew up in a wealthy family, is probably educated and could do anything he liked with his life. Why is he here?

He liked what the mad prophet was offering. The chance to murder, maim, and fuck.

Whomever it is whose eyes I borrow in this memory steps forward, toward the terrified girl. He – I – loosens his belt, drops his trousers, crouches.

She doesn't fight, merely turns her face away, as I – as he – rips her skirts upwards.

And then there is a heavy blunt pain in my jaw and I'm falling backwards, crashing over on my stool and staring up at the ceiling of my kitchen.

Chapter Nine

MY CEILING IS WHITE, clean except for a dark smear where Su killed a mosquito not long before she left. It bit her and then began flying erratically, like her blood caused a weird reaction in it. She said she was putting it out of its misery.

The vision, or memory, or nightmare I've just had was far worse than mere misery. The demon was saving it for me. That was hardly the worst memory of the hundreds that are stored in my head, but somehow the demon knew that that one, seen from the right perspective, would wound the most.

It is much worse, somehow, seeing it from the point of view of the perpetrator and not the victim. I did not do those things, but I could not stop them. The demon wants me to feel what the soldiers felt, their bloodlust, their power hunger, their psychopathy. That is how it will try to defeat me.

I stare up at my ceiling and taste blood, my own blood, and feel a throbbing ache in my face. It is a relief after the other kind of throbbing, that which the soldier whose memories I saw was feeling.

"Ev?" Magne bends over me and I blink up at him.

"Thank you," I say, and my words sound blurred.

"I think I broke your jaw," he says.

I reach up and touch my face. Parts of it are askew in a way that would be seriously concerning if I was human. But I'm not.

Vampire science might well have removed some of the symbiont's effects, like the weres' ability to reshape their bodies, but it didn't change everything. We reborn still have some parts that reconfigure. Our fangs fold up into the roofs of our mouths like those of snakes, and our jaws can unhinge and separate to let us bite more easily, unrestricted by the tiny human gape.

My jaw isn't broken, only "vamped out" as Su would say, unhinged and partially split, as if I were about to bite a resisting foe. Or as if I just got punched in the face by a werewolf.

I close my eyes and wiggle my jaw until it pops back into place, and my face folds closed again. My fangs slide into their resting position. It hurts, but not too much.

"Ow," I say.

"Not broken?" says Magne.

"No," I say. "But I think I'll just lie here a moment."

"What the hell happened?"

"The demon," I say.

"Is that the shit you've been seeing in your nightmares?"

I open my eyes and sit up. Too quickly. My head spins, and then Magne's there, propping me up.

"You could see that?" I say. If the demon is putting visions in Magne's head, too, it is more powerful than I thought.

"Bits and pieces." He helps me to my feet and back onto my stool. I don't refuse when he pours a splash of whisky into my tea cup. It burns going down, but it takes some of the shake out of my hands, the cold from my belly.

"That was... not like the others," I say. "Before, I experienced what the victims experienced."

"You never told me that," he says. "Only that you had nightmares about the slaughter."

"I didn't want you to worry. I didn't want anyone to worry."

"Too late for that," he says. "So this time the demon showed you a soldier's memory."

I nod, and my hand shakes so hard trying to pour tea that Magne takes the pot from me, pours, and adds another splash of Scotch.

"How would a soldier's memory even exist among those of the victims?"

"I don't know," I say. "Maybe some of the soldiers died, too. Maybe they were betrayed and that betrayal is part of what makes the demon."

"Nasty," says Magne. "Fucking evil."

"And this is what I'm supposed to absorb into myself. This is the power I'm supposed to claim."

"Is there any other way?"

I sip my tea, stare at my trembling hands, sip again. Magne waits. I can sense his impatience, read it clearly in the way he leans forwards, hands only appearing relaxed on the countertop. He is nearly quivering with tension, but he waits for me to speak.

"Yes," I say.

"Then do that," he says. "No power is worth this."

I finally meet his eyes. "When you were made a werewolf," I say. "Was it by your own choice?"

"Of course," he says. "My whole family is wolves. Why would I want to stay human when I saw what they could do?"

"Even though you knew how brutal the process would be?"

Magne has never told me exactly how one becomes a werewolf, but he's said enough that I can guess. And those scars that cover his body – it looks like he was torn apart by something sharp and stitched back together.

"Yes," he says, cautiously, as if he thinks I might be laying a trap.

"Would you ever go back to being human?"

"Hell, no," he says. "I'd rather die." And then I see understanding come into his eyes.

"That old vampire," I say. "He calls himself Karasu, and I think he may be the oldest vampire alive. He said he can remove the demon."

"And?"

"The only way is to change me genetically, so the parts of me that the demon was made to graft onto are gone."

"Which parts?" But I think he already knows; he just wants me to say it out loud.

"The vampire parts," I say. "And the witch parts."

"You would be human," he says.

"Yes."

"I can think of worse things." But his voice betrays him. When he said he would rather die than be merely human again, that was genuine. Maybe he *can* think of worse things to be than human, but death would better than all of them.

"Promise me something," I say.

"What?" he asks, his voice cautious again, waiting for me to ask for something he can't give.

"If I live through this, but turn out a monster, I want you to kill me."

"Are you sure?"

"Yes."

"How will I know you're a monster?"

"If you can't tell, Su can."

"Su would never let me kill you, no matter what you became."

I shake my head. "She's stronger than you know," I say. "If it comes down to it, she'd kill me herself."

"No," he says, but he's not saying he won't do it. That's not what he means.

"No," I say. "I don't want her to have to. That's why I'm asking you." I look down at my hands. They're steady now. I know what this might come to, and I'm ready.

I look back up at him. There is sorrow in his eyes, and understanding. I know I can count on Magne.

"You'll kill me, if it comes to that?"

He doesn't speak for a moment, just stares into my eyes. Then, as if finding in them something he was looking for, he nods.

"I will," he says. "If you need me to kill you, Ev, I will."

Speaking of killing and Magne, werewolves have a strict code about forcing someone against their will. They can be violent, and sometimes it seems like fighting is as natural as breathing to them. But werewolves have no tolerance for bullies or abusers or rapists. They fight among themselves, yes, but only if their opponent can fight back in an equal match. And the punishment for one werewolf violating another is death. Once a wolf is found guilty – and it's almost impossible for one werewolf to lie to another – they're hunted down and killed, torn apart by their own pack. Magne's never told me the details, of course, but he didn't have to be specific for me to know what was implied.

So I'm not really surprised when he suggests I should confront Jinny Greenteeth. He doesn't actually say I should kill her, but the hint of it lingers in his eyes. Among wolves, they punish their own, but who knows if Jinny even has a community, let along their policies on crime. I realize I have never considered whether or not female werewolves would receive the same sentence for rape as males. I suppose it doesn't come up often, but weres are a pretty egalitarian bunch, from what I've seen, men and women treated equally. So I suppose a female wolf *would* get the same punishment.

"Karasu said I should kill her," I say, and Magne's eyebrows shoot up. "Or, that he thought it was the right response, except there are... I can't remember the word he used, but there are people who would object to someone killing her."

"Some kind of supernatural police force," he says, jokingly, except his eyes are too serious for jokes. "You know wolves deal with our own. If it was one of us who... you know, we'd take care of it."

"You offered Su the option of dealing with her own attacker, and he was a wolf," I say. I hope I don't need to add that she chose to let the wolf pack mete out the punishment.

"Only after he was found and tried."

I shrug. "I'm beginning to think the world is bigger and stranger than we know."

"I guess we've discovered how humans feel when they find out *we* exist," he says. Again, he grins, but it doesn't reach his eyes.

We sit for while, not talking, and I feel the sun slide slowly down in the sky. It's a relief to know where it is again, to not be blinded to the passage of time.

"So you think I should confront her?" I say. "Then what?"

He shrugs. "No idea. But I think you need to face her."

"I'm afraid," I say.

He doesn't answer, but he nods.

"She's powerful," I say. "And what if the demon comes back?"

"Cara has some ideas about that," he says. "She's making something for you. A talisman. It won't work forever, but it should help in an emergency."

"If I'm going to defeat this thing, I need to let it free," I say. My stomach clenches at the thought.

"Yeah, but having something to keep it at bay when you need to be free of it for specific tasks might be useful."

"Like going to work."

At that, he shakes his head. "I don't think you should go to work. Not until you've dealt with this demon and are back to normal." He pauses. "Or whatever the result is."

"I can't not go to work," I say. "I –"

He shakes his head, holds up one hand. "Already taken care of." He pulls something out of his pocket. "There are still a lot of folks around who are glad you and Su took out Charleston's facility. A lot of them were prisoners there, or knew people who were." He puts a slip of paper on the counter. A check. I can't read the amount, but the number of digits is not small.

"I can't," I say.

"You can," he replies. "I didn't tell them why you needed it, just that you had to take time off to deal with stuff, and needed to cover a month or two of expenses."

"Magne –"

"Let people help you," he says. "You may not have intended to help them, but you did. This –" he gestures as the paper "– lets them feel they've paid you back. Like they're not indebted to you any more."

"They were never indebted to me."

He shrugs. "Maybe not, but they felt like it. Now they're free of that place for good."

"Except those vamps who decided to snack on Jinny Greenteeth," I say.

He snorts. "Sure. But don't feel bad about that. She doesn't deserve the sympathy."

"Maybe not, but she might not have been their only victim."

"You deal with your demon," he says. "If you're really worried about those vamps, I'll look into it."

I stare at my hands again. They're still steady, but I feel weak. "So I'll go see Jinny, try to get some... what is it they say? Closure?"

"Last decade, maybe," Magne says. "But yeah. Do that. But wait for Cara's talisman first, just in case."

"Then after that, I lock myself up here so I can confront the demon."

"About that," he says. "I think you should lock yourself up at Su's instead."

"So you can keep an eye on me?" I say, but I can't keep the smile from my lips.

"Exactly. But also because, one, Su's place will be a lot easier to demon-proof, and two, it's not in a residential area. At least not one where humans live."

"You think I might... cause a ruckus."

"I'm pretty sure of it."

After that, Magne goes home to see if Cara has had any luck making an anti-demon talisman, while I call in to work to ask for emergency time off. I'm lucky to have a boss who doesn't ask awkward questions, not about why I can only work during full dark, and not about why I suddenly need an unspecified amount of time off, immediately. He grumbles and lets me know how inconvenient it is, but doesn't really give me any trouble. I wonder if he's got *otherly* connections, if he knows what I am. I wonder if he's one of Magne's many contacts. He smells human enough, but Karasu's comments have made me wonder how many people I assume to be human might not be.

And then I have nothing to do but wait. And sleep. I worked all night and talked with Magne most of the day, so I'm exhausted. If I am going to face Jinny, sleep is probably a really good idea.

Mercifully, there are no dreams of any kind, and I wake well after dark. The moon is up, but not too bright, so I open some curtains to let its light in. Su loves moonlight, and I love looking at her in it, seeing it slide over her skin like quicksilver on bronze, bring glints to her black hair, and make her reflective fox eyes blaze green.

It's such a perfect memory it makes me ache for her and I realize it's been what seems like ages since I was able to think about her properly, like the demon or my encounter with Jinny or both tainted every thought.

I sip a blood bag cold out of the fridge and lay on the couch, just watching the moonlight and shadows flicker on the walls. And I imagine Su as she was not long before she left, naked, hair unbound and falling around her in a flood of ink, of silk.

She stalked me across the floor, mischief in her fox eyes, and switched the great red furry brush of her tail like a playful cat. Here, alone with me, she could be her true self, fox-eyed and fox-tailed.

Then she pounced, pinned me to the couch, and licked my face. I tugged her tail in response, and we tumbled to the floor, knocking the coffee table to one side, and spilling wine on the rug.

I turn my head to see the faint stain where we didn't quite get it all mopped up because I was distracted by her wiggling backside and tossed my cleaning rag aside to grab her hips and pull her close.

I kissed her neck and heard her breathing quicken, heard her gasp as I slipped both hands around her ribcage to cup her perfect breasts, slide my fingers across her nipples.

"I love you, Ev," she whispered, and wiggled closer, so my hardness fit into the cleft between her buttocks.

"I love you my heart, my Su, my everything," I had replied, and then slid my hand down her body, parted the curly hair between her thighs, and stroked the damp softness there.

She moaned and reached around to grasp my buttocks, to pull me closer. Then for an agonizing moment she leaned away, but only long enough to shift me so I could slide inside her.

"Maybe you would fit inside my suitcase," she said.

"I'd rather be inside your body," I said, pushing into her, then sliding away so I was nearly out, pushing back in.

"Me too," she said, her voice thick with passion. "But that way you could come with me."

"I do intend to come with you," I said, thrusting harder and faster, and her movements matched mine. We didn't quite finish together, but it was close, and after, we just curled up on the floor where we were and I stayed inside her until I shriveled and went soft.

The blood bag I'm sipping empties with an obnoxious slurp, disturbing my reverie. I'm happy, and I realize how rare that has been lately. Even my stupid encounter with Luke, that seemed so jovial, had an undercurrent of wrongness.

I'm hard, now, at the memory of her, and though I want to linger, to torture myself with perfect, beautiful, erotic thoughts of Su, I have things to do. I should check in with Magne, maybe try to figure out how to contact Karasu.

So I don't linger. It doesn't take much to finish pleasuring myself anyway, I'm so stirred up by my perfect memory of my perfect lover.

When I'm washed up and dressed, and sipping another bloodbag, there's a knock and I almost fling the door open, assuming it will be Magne. Except he always makes sure I hear him coming up the stairs, and I've learned enough of caution since I was made a vampire to stop myself in time.

"Hang on," I call, loud enough that even a human visitor should be able to hear me. I toss the bloodbag in the garbage and hastily rearrange the fridge to hide the rest. At least I have real food in there. I look around my apartment to see if there's anything too obviously vampiric. The other bloodbag, empty and flat, is still on the coffee table. I grab it and toss it after the other, just as there's another knock.

"Just a minute," I call. "I'm not decent."

I make a quick tour of the place, remove a few weird items to places they won't be seen, and tidy a little as I go.

Why am I tidying? Who am I expecting to show up? If it were Magne, he wouldn't care what the place looked like, and he also would not have knocked so timidly. I'd have heard him coming. He can be silent as a shadow when he wants to be, but figures approaching someone's home loud enough to be heard coming is only polite and decent. And as much as I enjoy quiet, I think he has a good point.

Finally I leave off fussing and head for the door. There's a mirror in the hall outside the bathroom – and if it's not already obvious, vampires are perfectly visible in mirrors – and I glance at myself as I walk by. I'm not especially vain, but I'm glad to see I've lost some of the haunted look I've been carrying lately, though I now have a nice bruise coming up on my jaw where Magne hit me.

"Who is it?" I say when I get to the door, caution again overcoming my urge to fling it open.

"Someone who doesn't care if you're decent or not."

Luke. He sounds happy, cheeky. And I remember how I left him. I kissed him, as an answer to his question about whether I wanted to be with him or not – though he had not asked in those words.

I'd kissed him, deep and hard, tongue probing. I'd tangled one hand in his hair, pinned him to the door with my body, and pulled him closer with my other hand on his ass.

And he'd responded in kind, kissing back with lips and teeth and tongue, fierce and exciting. He'd wrapped a leg around mine, strong, hard, pressed back against me.

I had told him, last time I saw him, not in words, but in pure body language, that I wanted more than anything else to get him naked and fuck him, make love to him, over and over until we were both exhausted.

And he had told me the same thing back.

"Oh, fuck," I whisper, and lean my head against the back of the door. All my thoughts of Su flee like shadows facing sunrise and the giddy happiness I was feeling vanishes in dread.

And is replaced by a different kind of happiness. A raw glee. A naughty, mischievous, misbehaving delight that is so unlike the joy Su brings that it frightens me.

Could Magne be right? Could this attraction to Luke be the demon? But I can't stand here for the rest of the night, not opening the door.

There's another knock. "Alexeyevich?" he calls. "Are you going to make me stand here all night? I brought wine. And condoms."

My stomach falls, and my excitement rises. What is me and what is the demon? And how can I open the door when I know what I'm going to do? When I know what I'm going to do is unfair and cruel to Luke, who will only be hurt when I end up rejecting him again?

Except that rejection won't happen until it's too late. Either my own uncontrollable attraction to Luke or the demon's foul sense of humor will see to that.

"Evgeny?" his voice is less certain.

Finally, I open the door.

He smiles. "I hope last time I saw you is your final answer," he says.

I want to tell him no, to explain, to apologize. But I don't. I can't. And I can't tell at all if it's me or the demon who pulls Luke close without a word of greeting and kisses him, pulls him inside the door to pin him to the wall. I can't tell if it's me or the demon with my tongue in his mouth, full of hunger, of desire so strong it hurts.

I can't tell, and I don't care.

Chapter Ten

MY SENSES FILL with nothing but Luke: the feel of his muscles under my hands, the grasp of his fingers on my ass. Today he tastes like dark chocolate and smells smoky, like lapsang souchong tea.

For a moment that scent pulls me out and away and jerks at my thoughts. They say smell is the most powerful of our senses for evoking memory. But what do I remember of lapsang souchong?

Then he's kissing me again, pushing me before him until I'm imprisoned against the kitchen island and his hands are under my shirt, pulling off my clothing.

"Well hello," he says, breathy. "I'm fine, how are you?"

"Better, now that you're here," I say. Something feels off about that, tastes like a lie, but I'm not lying. Now he's here and I have everything I want in my grasp.

I will have everything I want, the voice says. My voice. How could I have thought it was anything but my own voice, narrating my thoughts movie-style, the way inner voices sometimes do?

There's a loud clatter outside, but I don't care. I'm pulling Luke farther into the house, into the bedroom. Something feels wrong about that, too, taking him to my bedroom, like it's not a space for a new lover to be in. But I push the thought aside. The bedroom is where the bed is, and the bed is where I'll fuck this man whose tongue is down my throat.

And later I'll fuck him in the shower, bent over the counter, on the couch, the floor, up against the wall.

He stops kissing me to pull my shirt over my head and I laugh.

"You okay?" he asks.

"I will be when you put your mouth on me again."

He grins and his teeth flash. "I'll put my mouth on you," he says, and tugs open the fly on my jeans, drops to his knees. And just as he's about to put his words into action the door slams open.

"Am I interrupting something?" Magne says. From behind him, Cara stares, hand over her mouth. But her eyes are hard.

Aren't these my friends? For a moment, I'm only confused, but then I feel Luke stand, straighten my clothing, even zip me up. He steps away, and that makes me angry.

"Yes, Magne. You are interrupting something," I say, and it comes out a snarl. "You're interrupting what was shaping up to be a very good night. Get out."

"Maybe I should go," says Luke. His voice is shaking a little and he smells like fear. I look at him, and he's not staring at the angry werewolf in my doorway. He's staring at me. He's afraid of *me*. That, I won't stand for.

"Yes," says Magne, to Luke. "Our friend Evgeny is not himself right now, and you really should go."

Luke doesn't seem to know what to do. Then Cara leans to Magne and says something in his ear. I should be able to hear her easily, but all I can hear is anger roaring in my ears.

Magne takes two long steps into the kitchen, not towards us where we're still crowding the bedroom doorway, but to one side to make room for Luke to get by. Cara beckons, and Luke starts towards her, hesitates.

"Don't leave," I say, trying to keep my voice calm. "We were just getting started."

"Leave," says Magne. I can see he's struggling to keep his face human, his teeth unfrightening.

"Don't tell him what to do," I say.

"Leave, please," says Magne, drawing out the second word.

"You seem like you have some things to work out," Luke says. He moves closer to Cara, carefully, like he doesn't want to startle me.

"Don't leave," I say again, but he keeps going, edging toward the door.

So I stop him, moving vampire-fast to block his way. Except Magne moves faster, and something has disoriented me, and Luke is gone, out the door to Cara, and only Magne is there, keeping me from following.

He's so much bigger than me, and an experienced wolf. He should be able to take me on. He would have been able to, easily, if I were an ordinary vampire.

But I am not an ordinary vampire, and I can destroy him without hardly breaking a sweat. Except every time I lay a hand on him, something happens to my perceptions, things go strange, and he slips away from me, lands a blow, and I can only grasp at air.

Magne should be fast, but not this fast. He seems to dance, to waver before my eyes, only to vanish and appear behind me, to club me on the back of the neck, or try to cut off my air with a burly arm. His hits are ineffectual, even if his movement is not.

But it enrages me, and that is worse for my concentration. I know this, and try to go vampire-cold, to ignore the anger. But I can't. It's as if it originates outside of me, yet wells up from deep within. It overwhelms and confuses me.

"Fuck you, werewolf," I yell. It sounds like a shriek. "I will destroy you and then I will consume the half-breed puppies you have gotten upon your dark-skinned witch-woman." The words don't sound right somehow, but they are so satisfying. And so is the look of startlement on Magne's face. Something I have said throws him off enough that I land my next swing, claws tearing rents in his shirt and scoring the flesh beneath. He falls back, trips on the coffee table and sprawls on the floor.

He is hairy and unappealing, and smells like an animal. I don't know how I could ever have found him attractive. I don't even want to feed on him, but I'm hungry, and he is there. And for all its gamey taste, werewolf blood is strengthening.

I leap on him, jaw unhinged and fangs extended. I barely get a taste of his blood when the disorientation washes over me again and I roll off of him and away, hissing.

"Fuck you, werewolf cur," I say. And then I fling the door open and fling myself into the night. I have business to attend to.

I notice the witch on the landing outside the door, and I can tell that she shrinks away from me in fear, but she does not concern me now and she and the house are behind me in seconds.

I see Luke, too, but he is also not what I am after now. Later, I will find him. And maybe I will let him live when I am finished teaching him a lesson for making me desire him. But though I am in a vengeful mood, it is an older slight I am concerned with. Somebody out there needs to know she can't make me her sex toy against my will and get away with it. Her, I do not think I will let live.

When I reach her pond, I don't have to see her to know Jinny Greenteeth lurks within. I can sense she is frightened, too, though not of me. Not yet. A group of young vampires sits on the rocks that bank the pond, as if waiting for her to come out. They are of no concern to me, but she is, so I blend into the shadows and wait to see what comes to pass.

"Hey pretty water witch," says one vampire, a white boy with his brown hair in a mohawk, feathers dangling from the back of it.

"She's not a witch," says a curvy black-haired girl who sprawls half in his lap.

"Water-bitch," says the red-headed kid next to them. He looks at her like he wants her in *his* lap.

"Yeah," echoes one of two identical looking Asian youths farther around the pond. "Water-bitch."

"What is she then?" says mohawk boy.

Curvy girl shrugs. "Some kind of fairy."

"Like fairies exist," says one of the Asian twins.

"Did you think vampires were real," says the envious redhead, "before you became one?"

"I wished they were," says a timid voice, another girl, dark-skinned, thin and hungry.

"Who cares?" says mohawk boy. "She tastes good, and gives me a boner that lasts for hours."

Envy boy scowls and looks away as curvy girl mimes a handjob.

"Three times," she says.

"I coulda gone again," Mohawk says, "But I got hungry."

"I did go again," says Curvy, wiggling her fingers. "I don't need you for everything."

They laugh.

I scowl. This bunch of ragged vampires, barely past their Rebirth, and barely of legal age in human terms, are what has a powerful old creature like Jinny Greenteeth afraid? It must simply be because there are so many.

"We could swim down there, drag her out," says one twin.

"Are you stupid?" says Envy. "She'd drown you."

"I'm a vampire, I can't drown."

"You're a moron," says Curvy. "And I'll drown you myself."

I have had enough of them. I step out of the dark.

"Whoa," says one. The stupid boy.

"That's him," says Timid.

They all stand, and Mohawk steps to the front of the pack.

"You're him," he says.

I raise an eyebrow.

"I heard you were in some kind of trouble," says Envy. "Some weres were taking donations."

"Nice scam," says Curvy.

I ignore their words. They make no sense, and these youths all smell like they have been living too close to a cheap Indian restaurant. The spices irritate my nose.

"You are in my way," I say. "Leave."

"We were here first," says Mohawk. "If you want a piece of the watery bint" – Curvy chuckles at this – "then you'll have to get in line."

"I have no quarrel with you," I say. "But I will remove you if need be."

"If need be," mocks Stupid.

Timid touches Envy on the arm. "They say his blood is the strongest. Down in the facility, the bigwigs kept him for themselves."

Mohawk smirks. "Well, then. Maybe we'll wait on our watery tart, and dine on this old man here."

I am not so much older than they are, in human terms, and even less in how long since I was reborn. But maybe it's my power they sense. Usually a vampire has to be very old indeed to have even a fraction of my strength.

It takes the barest signal from Mohawk and they are on me. For brief moment, I sense something of what frightened Jinny Greenteeth. These vampires are not normal. Something they fed on made them faster, more vicious, better fighters.

But they are still nothing to me. Not as I am now. I hardly need think about it and they are on the ground around me, not moving. One neck-broken, two spouting arterial blood, one throttled – the one who claimed he couldn't drown – and two whose still-warm hearts are like a matched pair in my hands.

"How disappointing," I say aloud, to the night. "For a moment, I thought they might prove a challenge."

There is no one nearby to see the glory I have become. No one but the pond woman, who watches now, her eyes barely above water.

She rises enough to get her mouth clear of the surface. "What are you?" she says. "You're different."

It's what she said to me before. "You're different." But she doesn't mean it now like she meant it before.

"I'm better," I say.

She smiles, but there is fear in it, in her fierce eyes and bared teeth. "You're a monster now, just like the rest of us."

It's my turn to smile. "Maybe I am, lover," I say.

"I'm no lover of yours."

"Ah, but you were," I say. "And I don't really remember consenting."

"You came willing into my pond."

"I was not myself."

"You liked my mouth on your cock well enough."

"Like I said, I was not myself."

"More than you are now," she says. "And you used your tongue on my cunny cleverly enough, though I'm glad your face weren't like *that*."

I forgot I was vamped out. I re-assemble my face, and she relaxes, but only marginally.

"I was *drowning*."

"You didn't complain after."

I shrug, and decline to point out that I didn't stay after. I fled.

"What do you want, vampire?"

"What are you offering?"

"Nothing, to you. Not today."

I toss the hearts aside. They have become cold and sticky. I lick one hand absently as I walk to the edge of the pond and I think she might cringe. But her eyes gleam and she looks hungry.

"Fancy a taste?" I hold out my other hand to her, and resume cleaning my fingers, cat-like.

"What do you want?" She does not seem inclined to come closer, so I squat by the edge of the pond and rinse my hands. She stares at me. No, at the plumes of blood curling off my hands into the water. She seems mesmerized and drifts closer, sniffing.

"Only you," I say.

She looks up at me, wary.

"Last time, you said if I came back, I could fuck you. I'd like to take you up on that promise."

She swims backwards a stroke, catches sight of the blood and her nostrils flare. It entices her, lures her the way her voice and her eyes lured me the last time I came here.

"Do you want some?" I say, flicking a few drops of blood-tainted water at her. She stares, drifts closer, closer, until she is close enough to sip at the darkened water.

"More," she says.

I wave my hand at the bodies. "All you can eat," I say.

"Give me one."

"Take them all."

"Put one in the water." She looks up at me. Her green eyes are feverish. "Bring me one, vampire."

"And you'll do what for me?"

"You can fuck me."

I lean out and grab her hair, pull her close until her face is next to mine. "I plan to do that anyway, water whore."

Anger wars with fear on her face. "I'm not a whore, bastard." She hisses. "Don't you call me that."

"And I'm not a bastard." I shrug. "I don't care what you are. I only care that you took the pathetic boy that I was when I came here last and forced him to get you off. Forced *him* to get off."

"You're crazy," she says, clawing at my hands with hers, trying to free her hair from my grasp.

"No," I say. "I am so much more." I stand, bringing her with me, and she shrieks as her full weight hangs from the hank of hair in my fist. I toss her onto the grass before her scalp can tear free.

She tries to scramble around me, back to the safety of her pond, but it is child's play to block her each attempt. She knows when she is defeated, and so she scrambles backwards, instead. I let her flee. It is easy to keep up with her, to let her think she might escape, and then show her she cannot.

There is something about this scenario that seems familiar, not quite right, but I push the thought aside. Now, there is only the night, and a tasty fish stranded on dry land, and I a hungry cat.

She almost makes it to water, to a fast-running stream. But it is not her natural habitat and she hesitates. It's enough for me to catch her again, to wrap an arm around her waist and swing her around.

"Too slow, poppet," I say, a low growl in her ear.

Her fear is tangy, sweet. I can taste it as well as smell it. I lick her neck and she trembles.

"Do you know why you are in this situation, my dear?" I say.

"I fucked with the wrong man," she says.

"You fucked with the wrong *monster*," I correct her. Then I tear off the thin t-shirt that is all she's wearing. It doesn't tear easily. The neck is especially tough, and I leave welts before I am done.

I press her wet back to my chest. "You are a frigid bitch," I say. "Flaunting your sex, but only giving when you can also take."

She starts to shake.

"Afraid now?" I say. "Do you think about how your victims might be afraid?"

"They aren't," she says, her voice shaking so much I almost can't understand the words.

"They aren't what?"

"Afraid," she whispers. "They aren't afraid. Not even when they drown.

They die happy."

"You enchant them."

She shrugs, her bony shoulder pushing against my chest.

"Well, afraid or not, you violate them, and you kill them."

"I don't kill them all," she says, defiant despite her terror. "Only the tastiest ones."

"How kind of you," I say.

"I'm a monster," she says. "It's in my nature."

"You're a thinking being. It is in your nature to defy those instincts that you do not like."

"You should talk," she says.

I laugh, but she must not hear the merriment I hear, because she shivers. "I will teach you what your victims would feel, if they could," I whisper.

"You a vigilante now?" she whispers back, but her fear must be overwhelming. It's a delicious stench that fills me with hunger and makes me hard. I grind my pelvis onto her backside and she whimpers and loses control of her bladder.

"Your piss does not disgust me, precious," I say. "It only makes me hunger more."

She's crying now, shaking so hard her teeth knock together. Something about that momentarily disgusts me, where her urine did not.

I fling her away onto the grass, and the sight of her sprawling, skinny naked body, ripe with terror and smeared with dirt and pondweed makes me forget whatever disgust washed over me an instant before. Now I just want to teach her a lesson.

"Please," she says.

"Yes, beg," I say.

"Please."

Then I realize she is not looking at me, but beyond me. I have not been paying enough attention, and someone has snuck up behind me. That should never have happened, should not be possible.

I whirl around, and something flies out of the dark at me. I catch it, reflexively. It is a small bag that smells of herbs and insects. I try to toss it away in disgust, but I can't let go. And then several things happen at once.

A dizzy feeling comes over me and I feel like my consciousness is being pulled in two. A fist strikes me out of the dark in the exact spot it hit me earlier today. And someone smashes me on the back of the head with what feels like a sharp rock.

I crumple to the ground.

Everything is blurry.

"That was inelegant," says a voice. It has an accent that is not an accent at all. It sounds older than dirt and fills me with dread, but I can't remember why.

"But effective," says another voice. Male, husky.

"I hope you didn't kill him," says a third voice, female and velvety. The kind of voice that could give a man an erection just by reciting the alphabet. Not that my body is capable of such a thing right now.

"I hope it *did* kill him," says another female. That one I recognize as Jinny Greenteeth.

"You very nearly deserved what he was going to do to you," says the old, terrible voice.

"No one deserves that," says alphabet woman. No. *Cara*. Magne's girlfriend. He's a lucky man. Wolf.

"You don't know the details of what she did to him," says husky male voice. Magne. He could recite the alphabet to me, too. But no. Magne's my friend. *Only* my friend.

But if they're all here, where is Su?

But of course, I think, my thoughts muddled and my grasp on consciousness fading. *I put her in a box on my dresser.*

I think there might be someone else I am forgetting, someone I also care about. Maybe not. I can't think. My thoughts fly apart and it all goes dark.

I hope I don't dream, I finally manage to think. Then I'm gone.

Chapter Eleven

I SEEM TO BE spending an awful lot of time staring up at my ceiling lately. Or someone's ceiling. I don't recognize this one at first, so instead I listen to the voices.

"You cannot keep him here," says the old terrible voice. Karasu. "I know a place where he will be safe – or where the world will be safe from him, until he conquers that which lurks inside his head. Or it kills him."

"Your solution is to lock him up alone, to live or die? No. No way." Magne. He's angry. Why is Magne so angry?

"You saw what that thing can do to him." The old voice is patient. "That is only the beginning."

"My charm worked." Alphabet-velvet woman. Cara. "I can make something stronger."

Karasu laughs without humor. "You have talent, yes. But your little magics only delay the inevitable, and in the end might help the demon-ghost instead of helping your friend. Separating them as you did might have set back the process that was already underway."

"So he can stay here," says Magne. "Upstairs at Su's place. We'll clear it out so he can't hurt himself. And we'll be close, so we can keep an eye on him."

I'm at Magne's. That much I gather from the conversation, and with that information, I begin to see familiarities in the high, unfinished loft ceiling. The rest of the words I'm not so sure of, so I file them away. I'm so tired of being helpless. Of having to be helped, rescued. For once, I'd like to be the hero.

A sound, like an abrupt movement. "No." Some of the patience has gone from Karasu's voice. "Even I am not certain what he will become, what the demon might do. I had hoped he would master it quickly, quietly. Now I fear he will follow his great grandfather."

A pause, a liquid sound. Are they having tea? I am suddenly thirsty.

Karasu goes on. "There is only one place for him now, and one person who can watch over him. He must go to Wolfram Gottfried on Wonder Island."

"The carnival?" says Cara, surprised.

"The tattooed dwarf who runs the freakshow?" says Magne.

Karasu laughs, and there might even be genuine mirth in it. "Wolfram, like many of is, is much more than he appears, and telling you so might bring his wrath down on me, and on you as well. He and his people prefer to be unnoticed."

"So, what, he's some kind of sorcerer?" Magne sounds dubious. Magne is not the type to believe easily in the unknown, which is amusing, because he's a werewolf.

"The less you know, the better," says Karasu. "All you need know is that he is an old acquaintance, and has the resources to ensure your friend is as safe as it is possible to be while undergoing this ordeal. It is his best chance."

"His best chance is for you to remove that thing from his head."

"And leave him human? Do you think he would forgive us for that?"

Magne makes a frustrated sound, and I hear fabric shift. Perhaps Cara putting an arm around him.

"At any rate," says Karasu, "It may be too late for that now. I fear the demon-ghost has already begun to merge with him. Now we can only hope he is strong enough to remain the dominant personality. Though what we just witnessed of him is not encouraging."

"Jesus," says Magne, and I hear him get up and pace.

"Whatever happens next," says Cara, her voice calm and reasonable.

"It has to be his choice. We can't make this decision for him."

That makes me smile. I wonder if Magne truly knows what a treasure he has in her. I wonder if he knows she's pregnant with twins. His children.

I wonder how *I* know that.

"Of course," says Karasu. "If he is coherent enough to make a rational decision. But know that whatever he decides, I will not let him harm any more of my offspring, even if those ruffians are better dead. That is not *his* decision to make."

His offspring? Did I do something while I was unconscious?

And then it hits me. First, the memory of two hot, sticky hearts in my hands. Then it all plays backwards, jerky, like I'm watching an old VHS tape rewind. Then my memory clears, falls into order, and I remember it all in terrifying detail, everything I said, how it felt to kill each of those young vampires. How I terrorized Jinny. What I was going to do to her.

Was that me? Or was the demon in control? With a sinking feeling I think I know the answer. It was the result of me and the demon joined. If *that* is what I will become, I don't want it. I hope Magne will kill me first.

But as much as it frightens me, there is one other choice.

"Karasu," I say, weakly. It is not Karasu but Magne who appears in the bedroom doorway.

"Ev, you're awake."

"Get Karasu."

He ignores me. "How are you?"

"I feel like my skull was crushed with a rock."

"It almost was." Cara, brushing past Magne to dab my face with a cool, damp cloth. It feels heavenly.

"Congratulations," I say. "By the way."

They both look at me in confusion.

"Twins," I say. "They're very tiny still. Probably invisible."

"What?" says Magne, stepping closer. "What are you talking about?"

Cara says, "I wasn't sure yet. How can you know?"

"I don't know. I just know you two are going to have twin girls." I look at their staring faces. "Sorry if I spoiled the surprise. But that's why you need to stay away from me right now."

"What?" says Magne again, as if still processing the thought. He looks at Cara and she smiles, tentatively. "Girls? Babies? Holy shit." Then he gathers Cara in his arms. He looks happy. She looks uncertain. I'm glad my friends have some joy. It will make things easier, knowing at least there is something good coming.

"Get Karasu," I say. "I need to talk to him."

"I'm here," he says.

Magne and Cara pull apart and step back to give the old vampire some room. He might have dampened the terror he carries, but he still makes people uneasy.

I can't quite muster the energy to sit up, so I settle for removing the cool cloth from my forehead.

"Take the demon out," I say. "I can't become what I just was. Not permanently. Take the demon out, and I'll just be human, disappear back into an ordinary life."

I don't say it, but I think that if I can't be with Su, then at least I could see how things work out with Luke, and not have to worry about him discovering any *otherly* secrets.

"It may be too late," says Karasu.

"Try."

"It may kill you."

"That would be better than becoming that monster."

Karasu nods. "I do not like this. I think your best chance is to lock yourself away where you can concentrate only on assimilating the demon in a way that does not destroy you. But I will abide by your choice."

I nod.

"On one condition."

I stare at him, wary. "What condition?"

"If I am unable to remove the demon-ghost, you go to Wolfram on Wonder Island."

"No," I say. "If you can't remove it, kill me."

"Only if you cannot defeat it."

I don't like it. Being that monster again terrifies me beyond words. I clench my teeth, but finally I nod.

"Try to remove it. I mean really try."

"I will do all that I am capable of."

"And if you can't, then I will go to this Wolfram. And I will try to defeat the demon. But only if you promise something."

"It seems it is a day for conditions and bargaining," he says.

"Promise me that if I become that monster, or anything that is not fully *me*, that you will kill me. Destroy me."

"That, I can promise."

"Magne?"

"I'm here, Ev."

"Tell Su —" My voice breaks and I think I might be weeping, but I refuse to lift a hand to my face to check for tears. "Tell Su I died well, but don't tell her the horrible thing I became."

"You know I can't lie to her." Even if werewolves were better liars, very few people can lie to Su. She can smell it, I sometimes think.

"Don't lie," I say. "Just don't tell her all the details. Don't tell her what I did. I couldn't bear it if she thought that was *me*. Really me."

"Okay," he says. "Okay."

"If we are to do this, it must be soon," says Karasu. "Before the demon-ghost realizes what we are to attempt. But I do require some equipment."

"Give me a list," says Magne. He's not as good at finding hard-to-locate items as our old deceased vamp acquaintance Liam was, but Magne has a lot of friends and even more contacts. If he can't get something, he'll at least know who to ask.

"While you gather these things," and Karasu hands over a slip of paper, like he's already thought ahead to this moment, "I must speak to Wolfram."

"We might not need him," I say, determined to be hopeful.

"And yet we might," says Karasu. "And if we do, we will need him immediately. So I will speak to him. This requires... diplomacy." He steps towards the door. "Upstairs, we can clear a large space?"

Magne nods. "Su doesn't have a lot of stuff."

"Good. Please do so. I will return as soon as I can."

"What can I do?" I say. I'm not even sure I can sit up.

Karasu looks down at me, concern in his eyes. Concern for me, or only for the horror I might unleash? "Rest. You will need all your strength for what is ahead. If you know any meditation techniques, practice them."

Then he's gone out the door, and Magne and Cara follow.

I stare at the ceiling again, and try to practice the martial arts breathing techniques Su was teaching me before she left. And I pray to that long-lost childhood God. I don't think he'll answer. Even if I hadn't stopped believing, what decent god would bestow grace on a vampire?

Because even if I don't become the monster I fear, I'll still be a monster. Unless Karasu can make me human.

Absurdly, what I think about as I lie in Magne's bed, waiting to try to erase everything that makes me who I am now, is the undeveloped roll of film in my camera.

Twenty-four frames of the city at night, and at the end of the roll, a series of shots of a luna moth and a splatter of dried blood. I wish I had developed them right away so I would know what they looked like. Now, I might not develop them at all. I shot them to share with Su, to show her the beautiful thing that I had found in the night. If I become human, I will withdraw from her life; I might even move to another city so I won't have to be tortured by the possibility of running into her on the street. Developing that film, making those prints, even if they turn out to be terrible, would only remind me of everything I have lost.

And, too, I don't want to think about beauty in darkness. For me, now, the night means monsters, and I am one of them. Human, I can go back to shutting out the night, living in the sun again.

Moths the size of my palm with fur as soft as kittens are just food for something larger. Some moths, I have read, don't even have mouths as adults. As caterpillars, they exist to eat. Then they transform and as adults they exist to reproduce. They don't eat, they just look for a mate, fuck, lay eggs, and die. Why waste such beauty on that?

Do moths even enjoy sex, or is it merely a mechanical process that they are driven to perform?

Depressing thoughts. I miss Su. I try to remember how she taught me to breathe. In and out, calming. My breathing is so much slower than hers it was hard for her to explain, hard to follow her instructions.

"It's not like you're turning off your thoughts by concentrating on breathing," she said. "Or shutting out the world." She had smiled, and tugged on a lock of hair that fell over my eyes. We sat cross-legged on cushions, facing each other. She could do her breathing exercises anywhere, in any position, but she said it would be easier to learn sitting down, like this.

"Just focus your conscious thoughts on breathing, the air flowing in and out, and the muscles clenching and relaxing." She took an exaggerated breath to demonstrate. "And let your other thoughts flow around you. Direct them to one side if they're too insistent, but don't try to *not* think."

I copied her breathing, but it was too quick, and made me dizzy. She laughed, gently, and leaned over to kiss the tip of my nose.

"Just breathe normally," she said. "*Your* normal, not mine."

"We could be here a very long time," I said.

"I like being here with you." She leaned close again, and this time I cupped a hand on the back of her head to pull her closer, to kiss her properly.

"You're not concentrating," she said.

"You're distracting me," I said, and pulled her into my lap. We kissed. When she began to move away, I said, "Don't," and she didn't.

"Shall we end the lesson, then?" she said, teasing, tracing the line of my collarbone with one finger.

"Let's start a new lesson," I said, sliding my hands under her shirt to feel the silk of her skin.

"What's this lesson called?" she said.

"Try to make love without moving from this cushion."

"Mmm. That could be difficult."

"Not up for the challenge?"

"I'm always up for a challenge. How do we start?"

"Like this," I said, and pulled her tank top over her head, then her sports bra.

"Like this?" She removed my t-shirt.

"Mm-hmm," I mumbled, then occupied my lips with kissing her skin. She arched her back so I could reach her breasts. I had to bend carefully so we wouldn't topple over.

"How are we going to get our pants off?" she said, when she caught her breath.

We figured it out, eventually.

I must drift into sleep, remembering, because when I spasm in climax, the stickiness in my boxers pulling me out of reverie, I sense time has passed. I don't want my friends to come back to find I've soiled myself with my own pleasure, so I feel around for the cloth Cara left, and use it to clean up. Then I stuff it under the pillow. I hate being sticky.

I try the breathing again, and this time it seems to work, bringing calm and focus. When the thoughts of Luke come, I try to squash them until I remember Su's advice.

"Don't try to *not* think. Direct your thoughts to one side if they're too insistent."

I'm going to have to confront my thoughts about Luke sooner or later. I will have to decide what I want and how I will fill him in on my messed up life so he won't hate me. But I can't decide anything until my mind is free of the demon. Too many of my encounters with Luke are tainted by the demon's thoughts that I don't know which are my own.

He deserves better, and I can't offer him better until I am wholly myself again.

I wonder if this process of Karasu's will destroy my memories, if it will not only take away my *otherness*, but also my memory and knowledge of being *other*, of the existence of vampires and werewolves and fox women. And if the process doesn't, will Karasu find a way to take those memories anyway, so I can't betray my former kind? It would only make sense.

If that's the case, then I should savor my memories while I still have them, shouldn't I?

I think of the curve of Luke's cheekbone, the way his long red-gold eyelashes lie against his freckled skin when he closes his eyes.

I should be thinking of Su, but I find my memories of her blurring, and all I can call up is her voice. "Breathe," she said. "Just think about breathing."

So I think about breathing. How my lungs speed up at the touch of Luke's lips on mine, how my breathing goes ragged when he pulls my hips against his. How *his* breath changes when I slide my palms against the hard muscles of his back.

Breathe in, breathe out. As a vampire, it goes so slow unless I am excited. Fear can do it, or pain. Laughter or joy. Hunger, bloodlust, violence. But I breathe most fully when aroused. And my blood flows less sluggishly, lets me achieve an erection.

Some vampires like to eat and have sex at the same time, and sometimes mix in violence, too. Each breath-quickening, blood-stirring action intensifies the others, makes our emotions stronger, even, as we feel more alive.

I've always preferred to keep sex – which, for me, is also love – separate. Love and violence don't belong together in my mind, and vampire feeding in its pure form is also violence. But what if, just once, I could combine them? Fucking, feasting, and a little struggle? I would never force sex, but a bit of roleplay could work. Rough sex, but consensual.

Would Luke go for that? If he knew I was a vampire? It will never happen, of course. If I see Luke again, it will be when – if – I am human again. But what if?

Breathe. In and out. Breathe.

Kissing Luke's neck. *Biting* Luke's neck. I can imagine him against me, hard, excited, then the pain of my fangs piercing his skin. A brief struggle as I pin him against the wall with my body. I feel him go soft in fear, then hard again in excitement when he realizes what is happening.

"Do it," he says. I lift my mouth from his neck and show him my vampire face. I'm a neat eater, so I don't drip blood like a horror movie vamp, but I know I am frightening to look upon.

His eyes widen, but he only pulls my hips closer, grinding against me, and moans.

"Do it," he says. "Do *me*."

I can't speak well with my jaw unhinged, so I just growl, low. Fear flickers across his face, then vanishes. He is bold, my Luke.

My imaginary Luke.

He takes my face in both hands and kisses the horror that is my vampire mouth, doesn't flinch when one fang nicks his lip and draws blood.

He kisses me, hard, tongue probing, and then swings us around, and

I am the one pinned against the door, standing helpless as he removes my clothes. He kisses my chest, leaving bloody lip prints down my body, envelops me in his crimson-stained mouth, and sucks.

I stop him before I come, pull him up, then change my mind and push him to the floor. He looks up at me and smiles. "Alexeyevich," he says. He almost never calls me by my first name. He wriggles out of his shirt, then his jeans. He has no underwear on. I stare down at him. He's pale and freckled, decently muscled, with an impressive erection.

"Roll over," I say, voice strained and awkward from trying to speak through my vampire face.

He does. He looks back over his shoulder at me and wiggles his butt. He has a fine ass.

"I'm yours, you monster," he says. That almost stops me. *Monster.*

But then I crouch, stalk him on all fours, growl.

He laughs, then moans as I stroke his skin. "Bite me," he says, so I do, on the thick muscle below his armpit. I bite him, and this time I'm not such a neat eater. This time, when I raise my head, I am drooling, blood and slobber.

"Take me, monster," he says, pushing back against me.

I wipe the mess from my face, rub it on myself for a lubricant, and then I take him.

Chapter Twelve

I WAKE UP STRUGGLING against Magne, who is trying to hold me down.

"Ev!" he says. "It's okay. You're okay."

Conscious, I don't know if I'm more aroused than ashamed, but that me in the... daydream? That wasn't me. I am not violent, bloody, crude. That isn't the kind of sex I like. Su has even teased me, once or twice, for being a prude.

Even if I were ever to be with Luke, I wouldn't want it to be like *that*. Even in my fantasies, I don't want to dominate, to subjugate. Equality is my turn on. If this is another taste of what I am becoming, I don't want it. Better to be human. Better to be dead.

I try not to picture to look of hunger I imagined on Luke's face just before I woke.

"I need the demon out of me, Magne. I need it out *now*."

"Okay," he says. "Your old vampire dude should be back any minute now."

I lie back, suddenly exhausted again. I am slick with sweat and I smell like semen. If I can smell it, I know Magne can, too. But there is no judgement in his eyes.

"You want to talk?" He sits on the edge of the bed, hand still on my shoulder like he might need to hold me down again. His strength is comforting.

I shake my head, but I say, "It's giving me nightmares."

"Like the one with the soldiers?"

"No." I look away, to where deep green curtains hide the window. I feel for the sun to determine what time it is, but I have no sense of it. I remember that being human will feel like this, so many connections to the world, to my higher senses, severed.

"I was thinking of Su," I say. "It was nice. A good memory. And then... I started thinking about Luke."

"You like him." Magne's voice is cautious.

"Yeah. If I were single. And human."

"But you're not."

"I might be again." This time I look into Magne's eyes, let him see my fear. All of it. He can read me as well as if I said the words.

"Su won't leave you for being human," he says.

"What if this... process takes even my memories of being *other*?"

He just shakes his head, at a loss for words.

"So I was thinking about what I'll do, once I'm human again. I thought, if Su... she should have someone her equal. A true partner. I won't be able to be that for her."

"Maybe you don't give her enough credit. Maybe you don't give *yourself* enough credit."

"I know she won't leave me just for being human," I say. "But I don't want..."

"You don't want to be less than her."

I let out a shaky breath. "I don't want to be less than she deserves. So much less."

He sighs, but I can see he understands perfectly. "So you'll leave her," he says.

"Leave her free to find someone better. If you weren't with Cara, I'd say..."

He shakes his head. "I missed that opportunity some time ago." His voice holds the thinnest trace of regret.

"So I started to think about Luke. He's human. I like him. If I didn't completely freak him out last time I saw him, then maybe... But I didn't intend to start fantasizing about him. Especially not right after... thinking about Su."

"The demon?"

"Maybe. But the things I was imaging. They weren't nice things. They weren't how I would treat a lover."

A little smile quirks the corner of his mouth. "We don't always know what's going to turn us on until we find the right partner for it," he says. His eyes are soft, and I can't help but wonder what he and Cara have been getting up to.

"Not this," I say. Then we sit quietly for a while, until Cara pokes her head in the door.

"He's back," she says, and I don't need to ask who she's talking about.

Su's loft looks like the set of a *Frankenstein* remake, which seems appropriate – we already have the monster, after all, and it is even one stitched together from disparate parts.

Only I hope this will make me human, and not even more monstrous.

Obscure chemical apparatus clutter makeshift tables around a hospital bed fitted with restraints. I feel myself pull back, away, as that bed brings back memories I'd rather not have. At least it looks more comfortable that the cold metal table I was strapped to in the research facility.

"Ev?" says Magne.

"I'll be fine." But it's hard, even with his help, to walk across the floor to where Karasu waits.

"I realize this seems somewhat primitive," he says, waving his hand at the apparatus. "But vampire science grew out of alchemy, and I haven't the resources your old friend Mr Charleston had."

"Close enough," I say. "As long as it works." But it is too close for comfort. It may be a good thing I'm too weak to run. Because I might. The thought of being experimented on again is almost too much to bear.

I opt for bravado, because fear will get me nowhere. "Let's get this over with," I say, and try to hoist myself onto the bed. I can't manage it, and in the end Magne has to lift me like a child, which is comical, because I may not have his bulk, but I'm not so much weaker than he is, normally.

"I need you to not fight me," says Karasu, and he holds up a syringe. I nearly lose it then, as memories of all the needles Charleston's lackeys stuck me with flood back. I can't stop myself from snatching for it, to stick it back in its wielder. Fortunately, Karasu is old and powerful, and very very fast. He seems hardly to move, and I miss my grab, and the syringe has emptied into my shoulder before I can even blink.

"Sorry," I say.

"It was expected," says Karasu. "I recall that your past experiences in a... medical situation were not happy ones. You will relax now, and with luck, you may not even feel anything.

"With luck?" I say, drowsiness stealing over me already.

"I don't want to worry you unduly," he says. "But you must be prepared. I warned you this would likely be unpleasant."

"Yeah," I say, the word slurring as the objects in my view seem to slide sideways and melt.

Karasu fastens a restraint around my wrist. I feel Magne tighten another at my ankle. For a moment, I'm afraid I might piss myself in fear.

"I told you I would have to remove parts of your DNA," he says. I am unable to form a reply. "Perhaps you will feel nothing, but I fear your body will respond by unmaking and remaking itself." He looks down at me and fades from the edges in until I see nothing. "I am afraid it could be excruciating."

At first I think he must be mistaken. The haze I float in is pleasant, like relaxing in a warm bath, or one of those sensory deprivation tanks.

I feel my own limbs, but nothing else. No movement, no sounds, no pressure. It's nice. Comforting. I could stay like this forever, if the lack of stimulation didn't send me into my own head for something to entertain me. I don't want to look inside my own head. There are ghosts in there, and a demon. And memories of the things I've done.

Some of them, like terrorizing Jinny Greenteeth, I did while the demon was in control. But others I did all on my own, even before I had a demon in my head. I have killed a lot of vampires. Yes, most of them were trying to kill me at the time, but that is still a lot of sentient lives ended by my hands. The vampires who hunted Su, before I even remembered who I was, I was so newly reborn. I killed them with hardly a thought, because they were following her and she had been kind to me.

Now I wonder if they had followed her because they were nasty people as I had always assumed, or if they were under orders from someone else, henchmen trying to make a living in a world that does not make it easy to be a vampire, even if most of that world doesn't even know we exist.

There was a vampire woman who pretended to be my long-lost girlfriend to trick me, to bring me into the hands of Charleston and his vampire council. I had almost believed her, until she said something bad to Su and revealed her vampire nature. I snapped her neck without bothering to find out if she was really a threat.

And then there was the gang of vamps who pursued me and Su into the park. While Su fought off two of them, I had killed the rest. I hadn't known how many there were at the time, but I know now. Thirty-two. I had left only one alive to report back to their boss.

I can see each face now, feel each life ending. They weren't innocents, of course, but they didn't deserve to die simply for doing what they were told.

I don't know if this is the demon taunting me with my own crimes, as he did with the memories of the dead ghosts who linger in my mind. And it doesn't matter. I am guilty of each death, of each murder. I have killed thinking beings when disabling them might have been enough. I have put my own life – and Su's life, some part of me insists – before the lives of others. I deserve to feel guilty and much more.

Perhaps I should have asked Karasu to just kill me now instead of making me human. It would have been just.

As I remember the dead, the water or air or whatever I am suspended in grows warmer, and at first it is nice. It is comforting, and though I don't deserve comfort, I enjoy it. But then it exceeds my body temperature, exceeds human body temperature, climbs past hot bath temperature to scalding.

There is nowhere to go. I imagine it is like being boiled alive, unable to even thrash about, except there are no bubbles. Wouldn't there be bubbles if it was boiling? Would the bubbles provide pinpricks of relief, or would they make it worse?

I expect to feel the flesh fall from my bones, cooked or roasted or broiled, but I do not. I only feel each nerve ending shriek and sing and frantically tell my brain in is *too hot* and my brain does nothing, can do nothing.

And then it stops and the breath rasps in my throat and I realize I have been screaming. The heat fades and the pain with it, leaving only rawness in my windpipe. I can hear now, but the only sound to hear is my own gasps. Sobs. I feel things now, too, beyond heat. There are tears on my face, mucous in my nose, my tongue sticks to the inside of my mouth.

I feel the bed I'm lying on, but I am not conscious. I feel the restraints. I can see nothing at all save dim grey. Like the in-between place one sometimes visits in true dreams, but there is no one here to talk to.

No one but myself, and my demon.

Tickled you, did he? the voice says, and I am alarmed by how much it sounds like my own voice. The demon voice used to be different from mine, didn't it? Now it is so alike we could be brothers.

We are brothers, he says. *And soon we'll be one.*

"Leave me alone," I whisper.

Can't, he says. *You trapped me here. Made me feel all your unnatural lusts for other men.*

Is that why it made my fantasies of Luke cruel? Because it's *homophobic*? Or were those thoughts not the demon's at all, but simply my own darker desires?

At least your granddad knew that real men fuck women, it says. *Even if he turned out to be too weak to join with me.*

"You sick fuck," I say. "I won't miss you."

It laughs. *No you won't, because the old scare-vamp's plan won't work. It's too late.*

"Leave me alone."

And anyway, who's more sick? An honest demon trying to complete the task he was created for, or a sissy-man who wants to stick his cock up another man's ass?

"Being queer does not make me sick."

His words are nothing I haven't heard from others before, even now in an age when people are less close-minded. It isn't anything that I haven't heard even from members of my own family.

But hey, at least you can appreciate a fine woman, and you and me will have that pretty fox chick of yours in every way you can imagine, and some ways you probably can't.

"Hurry up," I whisper, not to the demon, but to Karasu. How long have I been out? Why aren't I free of the demon yet?

He'll torture you, you know. He knows this won't work, but he'll keep going anyway. He likes to hurt people almost as much as you do.

"I don't," I say. "I don't like to hurt anyone."

Not yet, maybe, but once you and I are properly assimilated, you will.

Then it fades and I think I can feel it struggling. Maybe Karasu's procedure is working after all.

I read once about how people in the Arctic become shamans. They learn how to contact spirits, and in order to gain their full powers, they have to surrender to those spirits, to let them tear the shaman-to-be apart. Then they have to put themselves back together again. If they survive, and if they're still sane, then they become a full-fledged shaman, and a mediator between the spirit world and the human world. And from then on, they can also change shape, at least in the spirit realm, by taking themselves apart, down to the skeleton, and then dressing in a new shape, new flesh.

I used to think that story was an *otherly* tale, a mythologized description of becoming a were. But whether it is or not, when the demon leaves my mind, it feels like I am assaulted by a host of otherworldly spirits, except there is no one else there but me. I come apart, it seems, bit by bit, piece by piece.

It feels as if each hair is pulled slowly from my skin, one at a time. First my head, then my face, and so on down my body. The hairs on my testicles hurt most coming out. Then my finger and toenails go, and my teeth — those who've ever had a tooth-falling-out dream will know a fraction of the horror of this, though not the pain. Then my skin peels off in strips, and my muscles, tendons, veins. And finally my very bones seem to dissolve and I am nothing.

Except I am not nothing. I'm screaming again, and intact, and every nerve is on fire. Then it fades and I relax, float in the grey haze, only the echoing memory of pain buzzing in my body.

Still alive? says the demon, and I want to weep. I thought surely this time Karasu succeeded, and my body coming apart and reassembling was the sign of his success.

'Cause I am. It chuckles. *How about we jerk off to pass the time? Oh, no motor function? Pity.*

No, a mercy. At least it can't do that to me. Not again.

But I'm wrong. It can, after a fashion. It plays memories in my mind, a mix of ghost visions of horrific death and every terrible thing I've ever done to another person, however trivial. And it mixes in memories of lovemaking with Su, with that girl next door so long ago, with the young woman I almost married in college. I expect memories of kissing Luke, of my first gay fuck, the abusive boyfriend I was so crazy in love with, but he spares me that much, and shows me only women, his own bias coming out at last. The demon, somehow, produces an erection for me, sends pleasure through my body even though I can't move, and taints that pleasure with the suffering of others.

"Stop," I say.

Surrender to me, it says.

"Fuck you."

So it brings me to the edge of climax, but won't let me finish, and then it vanishes as Karasu's next attempt to remove it begins.

This time, there is no pain, only a feeling of weakness. It's familiar, this weakness, and I remember now what I was like before I became a vampire, before I knew I was a witch.

Normal, ordinary, human. I can't smell all the things I smelled as a vampire, or hear as well. I feel dull and sluggish, small and unimportant. And I know, for sure, that Su will not want me like this. Even Luke might not want me.

I feel tears again, and this time they are sorrow for what I've lost, for the speed, the heightened senses, for the best lover and companion I could ever ask for, for power. But I also cry in relief. I am human again.

Perhaps I fall asleep inside my sedation, because I dream. Not a true dream, but a dream of the life I can now have.

As a vampire, I could never have children. The original form of the symbiont did not interfere with its host's reproduction – werewolves can have children, though their offspring are human – but the altered forms of the symbiont, the form that now makes vampires, renders its host sterile.

But if Karasu has remade my DNA, I will be all human. I have never thought of being a father, never really wanted it, but now that there is the possibility I can be one, I want it desperately.

And in this dream I dream I am in the sun, in a park, meeting the woman who will be the surrogate mother of my child. Mine and Luke's. She and I will produce the child, and then Luke will adopt. A family. He is beaming and the woman is kind and the sun feels unbelievably good on my skin.

After our meeting, Luke and I walk hand in hand, and though a few people scowl and turn away, most smile at us, like they would at any two people in love.

And we have an apartment in a tall building with big windows, and we lie in bed in a pool of sunlight and make love. There is no undercurrent of violence or domination like I had in my other dreams of Luke. It is all sweetness. We joke, and wrestle, and kiss, and though we are enthusiastic, neither of us tries to hurt the other. Our bodies strain together and by the time the sun fades we are exhausted, and satisfied.

Later – days later, perhaps, because who can say how time passes in a dream – I pass Su on the street and she nods to me, hugs me, asks how I am. There is no guilt in either of us, only happiness at seeing an old friend. She looks good. Wild and fierce. I ask if there is anyone special in her life and she smiles a secret smile and says there might be, but she's not sure yet. She makes me promise to let her know when my child is born, and I tell her Luke and I have decided she should be its godmother and Magne its godfather, though none of us is really religious.

I meet Magne and Cara, too, and they are busy with two adorable little girls with kinky dark hair and toffee-colored skin who growl and nip at each other like puppies. They seem to have something of Magne's strength and something of Cara's kindness, though really they are too young to tell.

Magne looks like fatherhood really agrees with him, and Cara looks like she might be pregnant again already and doesn't appear to mind.

And one night I meet Karasu on a dark street corner and he looks sad. "I'm sorry," he says.

"For what?" I say. "I'm happy. I have everything, I'm going to be a father. Luke loves me and I don't have to be guilty because Su is happy. My friends are happy. I can walk in the sun again. Thank you."

He shakes his head. "I'm sorry for this," he says, and he puts his hand on my forehead, like he did that day he showed up at Magne's loft, and just like that day, it burns.

Pain rushes through me, and if I thought the previous agonies he inflicted were the worst I could feel, I was wrong. This is worse. Far worse. So awful I can't even scream. I can't even vomit and I want to, badly.

It is a pain unmeasurable, and no metaphor I can think of comes close. I can't bear it, and yet I have to, and it goes on and on but at least I'll still be human at the end. At least I'll be free of the demon.

And finally, I lose even the semblance of consciousness I had here in the world inside my head and there is nothing at all.

I wake still strapped to the table, throat raw and nerves singing. But I'm alive. Karasu is a shadow with his back to me, tidying up apparatus and putting things in boxes.

I smell fear and bodily fluids – both probably mine. And I smell sorrow.

"Hey," I say, and Magne is suddenly by my side. When did he get so fast? But then I remember I'm human now, so of course he would seem fast to me.

"Evgeny?" he says. He hardly ever uses my full name, and he sounds uncertain.

"Who else would it be?" I say.

He glances up at Karasu, then back at me.

"How long was I out?"

"A few hours."

"That's all? It felt like days." I swallow. It hurts. "Why is my throat sore?"

"You were screaming." Magne sounds subdued. Perhaps he doesn't know yet that it worked. That I'm human. Or maybe that's *why* he sounds subdued. Because I am no longer *other*, no longer his equal.

"Sorry," I say. "It hurt." I smile, try a chuckle.

"I'd ask if you're all right," says Magne, "but I don't see how you could be."

"I am all right," I say. "I mean, I feel slow and stupid, and I ache, but I feel pretty good."

Again, Magne glances uncertainly at Karasu.

"What is it?" I say.

"Ev," says Magne. "It didn't work."

"Of course it worked. I'm human. I feel human." I look at him, at Karasu. "I know it worked."

Karasu finally turns from his cleaning and puts a palm to my forehead. I can't help flinching, but his touch is cool, pleasant.

"Regretfully," he says, "I could not remove the demon, or the symbiont, nor alter your genetic makeup. You are too far blended with the demon, and too fully developed as a witch and a vampire." He sighs. "The weakness you feel is not your humanity returned, but the exhaustion of your body fighting off every attempt I made."

I shake my head, confused. "No, it worked, I felt it working. I feel human."

Can you feel me? says the voice in my head. *'Cause I can feel you.*

Chapter Thirteen

THAT, I THINK, is the cruelest torture of all. To believe we succeeded, to see the things I could have had if we succeeded, only to have it taken away. It hurts more, if in a different way, than all the tortures Karasu could inflict on me.

Did you like the dream I made for you? Of your perfect, happy life?

I am stricken. There is nothing to say, nothing to do.

"Kill me," I whisper, and Magne bends close to hear. If I were not bound to the bed, I would grab his shoulders, shake him so he can understand. "Kill me," I say again.

This time he hears. "Ev," he says. "I can't."

"You promised." I say this through gritted teeth, fighting back tears. I am so sick of tears. Magne would not cry in my place. But then, he would not ask for death, either. Not until he had fought with everything he had.

"*You* promised," says Karasu, "to go to Wonder Island, if this did not work."

"Why do you want me to go there?" I say, turning on him. Anger rushes in and I no longer care to hold it back. "Why is it so important I go there?"

He shrugs, a subtle, elegant motion in him. "My only concern is to ensure you don't endanger the rest of us."

"You have your own motives," I hiss. "You never cared about me."

He looks down at me, face impassive. "You interest me, as your great-grandsire did. But I derive no pleasure from your struggles. You asked me to attempt to remove the demon, and so I attempted it."

"Did you really? Did you try so hard? Did you even want to succeed?" I'm trying to bait him, I think. To make him angry so he will reveal his true motives. But my questions have no effect on him.

"My word is good," he says, simply. "I tried everything I know to fix this, to remove the demon-ghost. You nearly died. More than once. There is no more I can do. And now you must prove that *your* word is good."

He turns away, tucks more equipment in boxes. "Your only hope now is to do as I have asked. Let Wolfram close you in a neutral space, where nothing that happens can touch those of us outside, and face your demon."

He turns back, eyes bright, and the feeling of threat he carries floods over me. "And if you fail, your friend will have no need to kill you, because I will give you death myself, as I did for Alexei."

It turns out that going to see Wolfram Gottfried at the famous Wonder Island Carnival isn't as easy as getting on the ferry with the tourists and carnival-goers and buying a ticket on the other side.

I am considered a "special visitor" – an especially dangerous visitor, I suppose – and will have to wait while the ferry comes and goes in order to have the boat to myself. Well, myself and my entourage – my friends who are now also my captors. I gather Karasu has to pull considerable strings just to get me permission to go to the island.

We wait to one side of the dock, in a spot where deep shadows hide us from the bright and garish lights that decorate it. Under a huge neon sign that spells "Wonder Island Ferry" in art deco style letters, a thin man in a top hat and tails directs visitors down the gangplank and onto the boat. The vessel itself is as garish as the sign, and its crew wears uniforms as out of place in normal city life as the top hat.

"I always thought it was Wander Island, with an 'a'," says Cara. "Isn't the river the Wander River, because it meanders?"

The mundanity of her question is both comforting and infuriating, and I feel like I'm going to my execution, only nobody wants to admit it.

"It is, officially," says Karasu. "But it is called Wonder now, for the carnival." He stands on one side of me, my arm in his grip in case the demon decides we need to make a break for it.

In my mind, I get the strong impression that the demon is looking forward to the coming ordeal as much as I am dreading it.

"Although," continues the old vampire, pensively, "the carnival, or what became the carnival, has been here for a very long time."

"Since the city was just a clear spot on the river bank," says Magne. His voice sounds light, but I can hear the tension in it. He stands on my other side, his hand only resting behind my elbow, not gripping, like he doesn't want to make me feel trapped.

"Indeed. Though briefly, the island was the location of an insane asylum. And then a prison, though I confess I never saw much of a difference between the two, either in the people they put there, nor in the way they were treated."

Cara shudders. "And the carnival just went on, next to the crazies and the murderers."

Karasu chuckles. "It was bad times for the carnival, and some said the folk who ran the midway would have been just as much at home in the institution next door."

"When it was a prison, or when it was an asylum?" says Magne.

Either one, says the demon, just as Karasu shrugs. The vampire looks at me closely and I wonder if he can hear the demon, or if I've made some move that betrays its presence.

We stand and watch the man in the tailcoat swing a gate shut behind the passengers and then the boat pulls away from the dock, lighting the waters of the river with its blinking red and yellow lights. I can hear music drifting over from the island, laughter, the clunking sound of midway rides. I smell hot dogs and cotton candy. I feel like the island still is a prison, for all its gaiety. It certainly will be for me.

"Who is this Wolfram Gottfried?" I say. It isn't the first time I've asked, but Karasu doesn't seem inclined to give me a straightforward answer. "Besides the world's only fully tattooed dwarf, or however he bills himself."

Karasu looks pointedly at Magne and Cara.

"Someone we shouldn't know about, I'm guessing," says Magne. "But we know more now than most of our lowly kind. Why not tell us?"

"I do not consider your kind lowly," says Karasu. "Nor do I think any of us should think the same of humans. It is merely safer if you don't know. You may already know more than certain parties would be comfortable with. They don't even like that *I* know of them."

"I thought you were more than an ordinary vampire," says Cara.

"Perhaps. But I am still less than a god."

I hope that doesn't mean we're about to meet a bunch of figures out of mythology. I don't even believe in the Christian God I was raised to worship, let alone the gods of old myth. On the other hand, most humans don't believe in the monster that I am.

Magne snorts, and Karasu raises an eyebrow.

"I am not taking you to meet the Allmighty," the vampire finally says. "Only someone very old and very powerful." He stares off after the bright lights of the boat. "And, oddly, probably one of the most human of beings I have ever met."

He looks back at us. "You two." He nods at Cara and Magne. "Will likely be asked to wait in the carnival. You may even be sent home. Do not ask questions, and say whatever goodbyes you wish immediately. There will not be time for more." Then he stares off into the dark again, and stays that way until the boat returns. We wait some more while returning passengers disembark, then a little longer while most of the staff leave, too, climbing up to shore to wait with the next batch of carnival-goers accumulating in the queue for the next trip.

Finally, the thin man in the top hat approaches us. He bows slightly to Karasu, formal and old-fashioned. "They're ready for you now," he says, and I recognize a faint trace of Russian in his accent. He stares at me, hard, as I pass by and mutters "koldun," while making the sign of the cross.

"Really, Dmitry?" says Karasu. "I thought you gave up that faith after they tried to drown your mother in the town duck pond."

The top-hatted man only mutters and scurries ahead to hold the gate open for us, and close it again after we've passed.

"I feel like we're taking you to your execution," mutters Magne.

"Let us hope it does not come to that," says Karasu.

And then we're on board, the brilliant lights flashing around us. The boat's motor churns and we're away, the river current catching us and pulling us downstream until it seems as though we'll miss the island entirely. But the little boat purrs and rumbles and soon the opposite shore is approaching, far faster than I would like.

I have never been to Wonder Island before. I always meant to go with Su, to have a night of eating junk food, riding rickety rides, and looking at sideshows. And since it is open at night – noon to midnight, except Sundays and Mondays – it is a place even a vampire could feel comfortable. Su and Alex went once, I think, but I never did.

Now I step off the dock, Karasu on one side, Magne on the other, and Cara trailing behind as if uncertain where she belongs, and it is nothing like it would have been had I come with Su. Instead of being surrounded by happy crowds flocking toward the ticket booth, we are met by a strange group who seem to keep a buffer zone of empty space between themselves and the carnival-goers. No one of them is especially odd, but together the light seems to glance off them in a strange way.

One steps forward and I can't tell if they are male or female. There is something compelling about their gaze, though, and I find myself blushing. I brace for the demon to say something, but it is silent.

The person, slender and pale, with an almost bluish cast to their skin, looks me up and down, then nods sharply.

"The witch and werewolf cannot come where we are going, but Wolfram extends the hospitality of Wonder Island. All rides, amusements, and concessions are free of charge for tonight."

Magne stiffens. "We don't want –" but he stops when Cara puts a hand on his arm.

"Thank you," she says, and holds Magne's hand tightly. She looks at me. "You're stronger than you realize Evgeny. Be the man you know Su thinks you are."

I nod.

Then Magne grasps forearms with me, looks like he wants to say something that refuses to be put into words. For a moment, I think he's going to hug me. "Kick that demon's ass," he finally says.

I nod again, too full of conflicting emotions to form words.

"Come," says the pale person, and Karasu draws me forward into the midst of the group. Though surely they stand out in the crowd, all dressed in shadow colors and walking silent as monks, no one pays us any mind, and people swerve out of our way.

"Where is Wolfram?" asks Karasu. He still holds my arm, but loosely, like he is no longer worried the demon will try to flee. Or perhaps he knows its attempts would be useless.

"He is finishing his show. He will join us shortly."

Karasu snorts. "I have never understood why he must put himself on display like that."

The pale person shrugs. "He says he wishes to make an honest living. We believe he also seeks to remain more... human."

I think I hear one of the others mutter, "Ridiculous," but it is so soft I can't be sure.

"We do not question him," says the pale one.

They take us through the very middle of the carnival and I can't help but look around, and think sadly how Su would have enjoyed coming here. She would have made me go on every ride and sample every calorie-filled treat she ate – and she would probably try to eat one of everything.

Past the midway and the food stalls we make our way through a maze of colorful sheds and tents. "The Bearded Twins," says one over the door, and there is a large, bright painting of two curvaceous and very beautiful women with long, full brown beards. "Wolfram's Cabinet of Peculiarities," says another, with a smaller sign reading, "Featuring the World's only Fully-Tattooed Dwarf."

"This Wolfram is a sideshow himself," I blurt out. I knew, of course, but somehow seeing it on the sign surprises me.

"We all do our part," says our guide.

"What do you do?" I'm finding it hard to care, but I can't help think it's something Magne would be curious about, so I ask.

"We run the Goblin Market and Fairy Fair," they say, gesturing ahead.

"Finest strange goods from all corners of the Earth," says one of the others in the group.

"And a very dangerous place, indeed, should you find yourself there outside of regular visiting hours," says Karasu drily.

"Good reason not to visit when you shouldn't," says one of the group.

"Are you —" I'm about to say, "fairies," but a sharp pinch from Karasu's hand on my arm stops me.

"Best not to ask questions here," he says.

We pass by a building that says "Troll's Menagerie" and promises two-headed animals and other oddities of nature, and beyond that an unassuming door marked "Staff Quarters – Keep Out."

And then we pass between two tents and I think we may be getting closer to the site of the old asylum and prison and I begin to feel afraid again.

There's an archway we must pass under that advertises the Wonder Island Goblin Market and Fairy Fair, and then we are in a courtyard full of colorful tents and awnings. On the far side is a row of old-style caravans just as bright as the tents.

As we cross the courtyard, our entourage disperses. Here it is quiet, as if few visitors come this way, though there are some tourists wandering the stalls. But maybe it is only a slow time of night. By the time we reach the far side of the market, there is only our guide left to lead me and Karasu on.

We squeeze between two caravans and stop in front of a blue door set into a stone wall.

"Here we wait for Wolfram," our guide says.

"I had thought," said Karasu, "That we would use the quiet room in Troll's place."

Our guide shakes their head. "Wolfram said to wait here."

"He thinks the quiet room is not enough for this," says a new voice, definitely female.

We turn, and another pale, dark-haired person in dark clothes faces us, but this is a woman who would never blend into a crowd. She's slender and muscular and tall, and probably the most beautiful woman I've ever seen. There's a touch of cruelty around her eyes and a look that says she fears nothing.

"Thea," says Karasu, taking her hand and kissing the backs of her fingers.

"You know I detest you, you creepy old bloodsucker." She wipes her fingers on her trouser leg.

"Enchanting, as always." Karasu seems amused rather than insulted and Thea scowls.

"I believe you had an Ichneumon Queen in Troll's quiet room recently, did you not?" Karasu's voice is sharp, like he's making more of a point than his words suggest.

"And she only stayed in there because –" Thea glances at me, then decides I'm safe to hear what she has to say. Or perhaps she doesn't think I'll live long enough to tell anyone. "Because my brother exerted his considerable will to keep her there. He slept for three days after."

"Surely you exaggerate," says Karasu. "But this is your place, and I am only a humble seeker of favors."

"Precisely," she says. The two glare at each other, but it is an oddly companionable animosity, as if they have been sparring like this for a very long time. But Thea looks barely forty, so surely she can't have that much experience with Karasu's bickering.

"And your brother is displaying his fine physique again?"

Thea snorts. "As he does several times a night. I think he does it as penance." She doesn't say for what, and Karasu doesn't ask, so I assume this is an old conversation, as well.

"He'll be here shortly." She laughs. "He didn't think it appropriate to greet our... guest in a gold lamé G-string and sparkly velvet cape."

Karasu laughs, too, and I think it might even have been startled out of him. I am beginning to like this Thea, even if she terrifies me.

"So this is your baby vampire with too much power," she says, turning to me. Her eyes are clear gray – too bright to be human – and when they meet mine I realize she is far older than forty. She might even be older than Karasu. I can't quite suppress a shiver, and she lets a toothy smile raise one side of her mouth.

"Born a witch, made a vampire, infested with a demon-ghost created from the suffering of innocents," says a new voice. My voice, though I have not chosen to say anything.

"So, it speaks." This voice is also new, but deep, rough, a little earthy, yet also elegant and cultured. The speaker is short. Very short.

Even knowing Wolfram Gottfried was the tattooed dwarf of the sign,

I somehow did not expect him to be so short. He walks with the slightly awkward gait of genetic dwarfism, but every step is powerful. Physically, he is muscular, perfectly toned, though his proportions aren't quite the same as those around him.

Like his sister he has pale skin – tattooed everywhere I can see, except his face. His hair is dark like hers, but shorter. His eyes are the same too-intense gray, and he is strikingly handsome. Like Thea, his eyes are ancient, though he doesn't look too many years older than Magne.

"Wolfram," says Karasu, nodding in respect.

"Karasu." The dwarf returns the nod, with no less respect.

"This is Evgeny Alexeyevich," says Karasu, gesturing to me. He finally releases my arm.

I don't know what to say – assuming the demon will let me have my voice – so I just nod, too.

"Alexeyevich? Indeed?" Wolfram walks around me, inspecting me as Karasu did in the true dream, however many days ago that was now.

"Indeed," says Karasu. "Unlikely as it seems. I investigated his bloodline, and even tested his DNA."

I stare at him. "You what?" I say.

"I had to make sure you were the real thing, Evgeny," Karasu says. "And not merely a lucky break in one of Mr Charleston's less tasteful experiments."

"Descendant of the old Tsar himself," says Wolfram, something like awe, or maybe just respect, in his voice.

"The only known family to produce male witches since ancient times."

"In Europe," says Thea, impatiently. "You are aware that many African witch families produce primarily male practitioners, and there are some in South America, and east Asia as well."

"Of course," says Wolfram. "And it will be interesting to see how those bloodlines mix as the world becomes a smaller place."

"You two speak of people as if they are merely statistics, or lab rats," says Thea, hotly. "Are you responsible for this experiment, vampire?" She glares at Karasu, and gestures at me.

"I believe I answered that when I said I investigated him."

"All you really said, old friend," says Wolfram, with an odd emphasis on "friend," "was that you discovered he was genuine."

"I did not unleash the demon-ghost on him," he says. "Nor did I impose it on Alexei, as I have told you many times over the years. And I am not responsible for turning him into one of my kind. I have no wish to unleash a *koldun* upon the world."

A cold feeling grows in my gut, penetrating the vague fears already there. "Did you bring me here to kill me?" I say.

They all look at me, and I want to vanish into a hole in the ground, but I tilt my chin up and glare back at them, meeting each of their eyes in turn. Wolfram's I hold last, and I find I can't look away. Something there tells me I can trust him.

He shakes his head finally, and breaks eye contact. "That is only a last resort," he says.

Thea smiles, a softer smile than I would expect on her cold face. "I like him," she says. "I hope he lives. Too bad he's a boy, though." She leers and laughs at what silly expression I must have.

"Enough," says Wolfram. "If the demon-ghost dares speak to me as it just did, then we can delay no longer." He removes a large, ornate key from his belt and steps toward the door. As he fits it into a keyhole – not in the door, but in the stone wall beside it – he turns to me.

"I would ask if you're ready, Evgeny Alexeyevich, but I do not think this is the sort of thing one can ever be ready for."

Then he steps inside and gestures for me to follow.

Chapter Fourteen

WOLFRAM STOPS Karasu from following me inside.

"Just me and the boy from here," he says.

Thea scowls.

"I need you to look after the carnival, sister," he says to Thea, smiling. "And I know you're only here out of curiosity, anyway."

"As if this island needs our help to keep its affairs in order," she says, but she turns to go. As she does, she catches my eye and winks. "Good luck, vampire-witch boy."

The name is so close to what Su called me just before she left that my stomach clenches in sorrow.

Oh, this is going to be fun.

Karasu frowns, too, but doesn't look surprised.

"There are things beyond this door only island folk know," Wolfram says. "I hope you know how big a favor you have asked."

Karasu inclines his head. "I thought the quiet room would be enough," he says. "I am grateful." Then he looks at me, eyes unfathomable. "I cannot tell you for certain why Alexei failed to assimilate the demon-ghost, but I suspect it was not merely a matter of strength. He was young, and inexperienced, and had not known real love since his family was executed. Even your great-grandmother was not a love-match, but a suitable bride chosen for him by that filthy monk. He was barely old enough to father a child, let alone be made a vampire or given a demon. And such a horrifying creature the demon is."

The sorrow on his face, I think, is genuine. "I believe he was already half-mad even before Rasputin inflicted the first part of a *koldun's* nature upon him." He reaches through the door and grasps my shoulder. "You are not so young, and you have known love."

Perhaps I look surprised that he knows anything of my love life. "I met your fox woman, do not forget. You have known real love, and you are not insane."

Not yet, promises the voice.

"I believe you may very well survive this intact in your own mind." Then the old vampire turns, and leaves, and just for the barest moment he unleashes the full force of the terror that surrounds him and even the demon cowers inside my head.

"Show off," mutters Wolfram, apparently unaffected. "Let us hope he's right."

Then he shuts the door behind us, leaving us in the dark.

"*Licht*," he says, in a language I don't quite recognize, but which sound a bit like something I've heard Su mutter under her breath when we were reading old fairytale books, and light blossoms around us, in a tracery of Viking designs, twisting serpents and dragons, geometric shapes, curves and angles. It spreads out from him, almost like he is the source of the illumination, and leads off down a hall.

"Do not tarry," he says, and sets off. "Some parts of this island are meant for Islanders only and may resent it when others step foot here. You are my guest, and safe so long as you are with me, but get left behind and getting lost is only the best you can hope for."

I follow close behind him, resisting the urge to touch the lighted designs as we pass. "What is this place?" I ask.

He glances at me, and away. "A place you never would have seen if you were merely a vampire or a witch," he says. "And this is only the outermost edge of the heart of Wonder Island."

"Karasu said there are things the *others* know nothing about the way humans know nothing of *others*."

"Did he?" He sounds uninterested, but I get the distinct impression that there is nothing in the world that does not interest him to some degree. "And what did he tell you of me?"

"Only that you're very powerful." I pause, watching his back as he strides ahead of me. And there is no other word to describe how he walks, though he doesn't even come up to my collarbone in height. The farther we walk into this maze of halls, the less awkward he seems, almost as if he is becoming more himself, more real somehow.

"And also that you're the most human person he knows." I can hear the doubt in my own voice. The farther we come into this place, the *less* human he seems. Outside, he appeared merely a dwarf, now he seems something much more.

He laughs at that. "Then I have achieved something of my goal in life. Though I would bet under other circumstances old Karasu might also say I am the *least* human person he has ever met."

We walk in silence for a time, and I begin to wonder how big this building is, or if it is only deceptive because of the twists and turns and intersecting corridors.

"Would it mean anything to you if I said my mother was *svartalfar* and my father was *dvergar?*"

"I've read a lot of mythology books," I say. "My – My beloved didn't know what sort of *other* she was when I met her."

"And what did your mythology books tell you?"

"*Svartalfar* – that's dark elves? And *dvergar* is dwarves. Two of the mythical peoples of the old Norse and Germanic tales. Only maybe not so mythical." He looks, now, like he might be comfortable wielding an axe, and some of the tattoos on his arms glow like the designs on the walls. Twin wolves decorate his forearms in glowing lines of blue artwork, and I think I see the beaks of two big birds by the bends of his elbows.

"Are you a... a fairy?" I say. "Or a god?"

He laughs again. "I am what I am. It doesn't matter."

We keep walking.

"So your sister takes after your mother?" I say to break the silence.

Laughter again, and I feel oddly privileged. Wolfram doesn't seem like a man who laughs a lot. He seems like someone who takes on too much responsibility for others.

"I like you, boy," he says. "Though it makes me profoundly nervous that a new *koldun* might arise in the world, I do hope you make it."

"Can you tell me what a *koldun* is?" I ask.

Pure power. I ignore the demon.

"Did your mythology books not tell you?"

"Only that they're evil sorcerers. Most of them seem to be tricked into destroying themselves by little girls," I say. "In the fairy tales."

"Indeed. Never underestimate the power of a little girl," he says. "Some of them are extraordinarily clever. And fearless."

I laugh, but I don't feel very jovial. Every step takes me closer to my doom, but now I just want to get this over with.

I like little girls.

"He's talking to you, isn't he?" says Wolfram, abruptly stopping to push open a door in the wall and step through. Nothing about it looks any different from any other door in any other corridor we walked past, but I follow.

"Yes," I say. "A little."

"And sometimes he speaks through you."

I nod.

"Has he taken over your body?"

"A couple of times."

"Do you know what allows him to do so?"

"No," I say.

"You might find it useful to figure that out."

We walk out of a hall into a courtyard, stone walled, stone flagged. There is a broken fountain in the middle of it, with a statue of an old man in a big hat, leaning on a staff.

"Move over, old man," says Wolfram, and he pushes a raised design at the feet of the statue. It slides to one side, revealing a spiral staircase twisting down the center of the fountain base, down into the ground. "Almost there," he says.

And that's when the demon decides to run.

He whirls me around, heads me towards a random door, and forces me through it.

"Stop," I yell, but no words come out.

Fuck this, says the demon. *The nasty dwarf is going to kill us.*

"No," I say, yelling only inside my head. "He is going to keep us from hurting anyone while we... merge... assimilate. Whatever."

Nice words, pretty boy, but you heard him. He doesn't want our kind to exist.

We flee down one corridor and into another, running blind, in near total darkness. Being a vampire doesn't help much, what with the lousy night vision. At least my other vampire senses keep us from crashing into walls. Most of the time.

"Stop. Just for a moment."

I don't think he wants to, but a locked door gives him pause and we take time to catch our breath.

"Listen," I say. "Let him lock us up. I won't fight you if you agree."

Of course you'll fight me. I intend to rip your mind apart from the inside out.

"I mean... I'll... I won't try to destroy you. I'll absorb you, like Karasu said."

Not much of a bargain, considering that's your only option anyway.

"Just go back."

No. You're mine. You were always mine. Even when you thought you were alone with your hot Chinese love bunny I was there, watching you fuck, feeling you come. I'm pretty sure you had bigger hard-ons because I was there.

"You can't taint my memories of her," I say.

I already have.

I'm afraid he might be right, but I will not let him know that.

"Take me back, or we'll end up fighting it out here in the dark in this weird building that doesn't want us here."

You believe that twisted old dwarf? Do you believe in fairy tales, too?

"I have good reason to believe in fairy tales," I say. "And so do you."

Well, too bad, he says. *I can't take you back.*

"You can."

Nope. I'm lost.

"Then how did you expect to get out of here?"

Hope. Faith. Charity. Who the fuck knows? I just wanted to get away from that tiny Viking nightmare.

"You're afraid of him."

More than I ever was of that dried up vampire Jap.

"Take us back."

Wish I could, he says.

"Wait, you do?" His tone has changed so fast it leaves me confused.

Hell yeah. That dwarf might be scary, but those fucking things are terrifying.

And then I see what he's referring to. Or rather, I see their eyes. Two pairs of glowing, electric blue eyes. Then a flutter and two pairs of gleaming black eyes, higher up, visible only because of the blue glow glinting off their wetness.

"The first time he frees us in ages, and it's only a tiny mortal," says a voice out of the dark. It's a deep voice, growling, a bit like Magne when he's full wolf. I flare my nostrils, expecting to smell werewolf, but I don't smell anything beyond damp stone, only an ozone after-odor, like lightning leaves behind but much fainter.

"Not a mortal, but not much better," says a second voice, almost identical to the first, but softer. One pair of icy eyes blinks, turns to look at the other.

"Oh, but it has a demon inside," says a third voice, harsher, with an odd bell-like echo to it.

"And oh so many ghosts." Another harsh voice, just a little higher pitched.

"And we mustn't let the house have it," says the bell-like voice.

"And we mustn't let it find the house's secrets," says higher voice.

"Nor let the house's inhabitants eat the poor child for lunch, demons or no," says softer voice.

"But we can chase it," says growly voice.

Fuck, says the demon. *I don't know what those are, and I don't want to find out.*

"Take us back, and we'll be safe."

"Oh yes, safe as you can be, little sorcerer-to-be," says bell voice.

"Or else as bedlam-crazy as the rest of those who dwell within these walls," says high voice.

"And then he might let the boy just live out his days here," answers Bell.

"I still say we chase it," says Growl.

"Teach, if not touch," says Soft.

Fuck this, says the demon, and we run.

More doors, more corridors, more corners, and more bruises. The demon is so mindless it gets harder and harder for me to use my vampire senses to avoid running into things, but the demon makes full use of my vampire speed anyway. I'm surprised we're not knocked senseless over and over.

"They're toying with us," I say, when a particularly hard collision with the end wall of a corridor forces the demon to pause us in our flight to figure out which way is up. "And you're doing a lot more damage than they would."

Fuck you know, the demon says. *Do you even know what those things are?*

"Do you?"

I don't want to.

"They could have caught us several times over, you dumb fuck!" I finally yell. I don't swear much, but the demon deserves it.

Finally, I'm starting to like you. You're much more interesting when you're not whining or crying.

"It's talking to itself," says Growl, and the demon takes off running. Only a few pounding steps later it stops us as a pair of cold eyes appears in front of us.

"It's talking to the demon inside," says Soft, and I realize that I have been able to speak aloud again, though for how long I'm not sure.

"Same thing," says High.

"Or not," says Bell. "I vote for not."

The eyes are all around, leaving only one path clear. The demon runs for it, grabs a doorknob, wrenches a door open and flings us through, slams it behind.

It's another courtyard, much the same as the last one, stone walled and stone flagged, with a statue in the middle. We look around wildly for something to block the door, but there is nothing. I do not even hear our pursuers trying to follow us.

There don't seem to be any other doors out of this courtyard. The demon takes us on a circuit of the place, testing the walls. The only windows are a floor up, too far to jump. Or maybe not. With vampire agility, I could probably climb the rough stone. I hope the demon can't hear that thought. I am tired of running, so sick of using my speed I want to vomit, or to just lie down in a corner, and let whatever owns those cold eyes eat me.

With nowhere else to go, the demon takes us to look at the statue, a detailed carving of an old, gnarled tree. There is a squirrel on its trunk, and a serpent winding among its roots. I recognize the image from somewhere, but I can't think where. The statue looks very old. Maybe too old for this place.

What the fuck is that?

"A tree," I say, too weary to care that I'm stating the obvious.

Who the fuck makes a statue of a tree?

"I like it." I reach out and put my hand on the trunk, near the lifelike squirrel. It isn't stone, as I thought, but wood, silvery-grey with age. It's a real tree. The squirrel twitches its nose and the serpents winds slowly around the root it clings to. I snatch my hand away.

Fucking hell. I don't like this place.

I don't think the demon noticed that I touched the tree, nor even that I pulled my hand away so suddenly. I say nothing. Now that I'm not touching it, the tree has gone back to being a statue. I reach out again, brush my fingers against the bark and smile when the squirrel chatters at me.

Jesus fuck.

I like that the demon is afraid. For so long, I was afraid of it, of him. Now it has been chased by monsters and terrified by a tree statue that is not a statue, yet is, and I am less afraid.

The door opens and we spin around to face it, the demon fully in control again. What comes through terrifies him further, and I can't help but smile.

First, a black bird, bigger than any I've ever seen, flies through, circles overhead, and lands in the branches of the tree-statue. The squirrel scrambles around to the other side of the trunk and the snake hisses.

"This is not a place for your kind," says the bird, Bell-voice.

The demon backs away, trying to keep both door and bird in sight. As second bird flies through, as black as the first, and just as huge. It circles, and perches.

"The old bastard will be cross," it says, and I am not surprised to learn it is High-voice.

Then a wolf steps through the door, bigger than any wolf ought to be, grey-brown and grizzled. Its eyes glow blue even in the light of the courtyard.

"You chased it here," says Growl.

Another wolf, huge and grey. "We all chased it here." Soft voice.

The birds – ravens, and I should know, since there is one tattooed on my body – regard me from the tree, and the wolves from just inside the door.

"What now?" I say.

We run again, says the demon, but he doesn't. The wolves are between us and the door.

"Will you come quietly, now that Greedy and Ravenous have had their fun?" says Bell-voice. I think the bird must be referring to the two wolves.

"I will," I say, "but I don't seem to be working my legs right now."

"Is it fear sets it off?" says the wolf I've been thinking of as Growl. I wonder if it is Greedy or Ravenous.

"You can conquer fear," says Bell.

"And if you don't," says High.

"You might as well die now," says Soft. Or is it Ravenous? Or Greedy?

Fear, my ass.

"It's afraid," I say. "The demon." I look at the tree, touch its bark, and both wolves growl, both birds hiss. I understand, then, that it is a sacred symbol, okay for magical birds to perch in, but not okay for an abomination like me to touch. It is *their* symbol, and I am something profane in a divine place. A devil in church. But the tree feels good and right, and gives me courage.

"I think I can walk now," I say. I look up at the ravens and see faint blue light, like electricity, like the light that lit the designs on the walls when I walked with Wolfram, tracing the edges of their feathers. I look over at the wolves and some of that same light flickers on the ends of their fur, burns in their eyes.

"Well then," says Bell and launches itself from the branch to circle the courtyard.

"Let us go," says High, and follows.

The wolves move, one to each side of the door and the ravens swoop through. I follow. Inside, it is no longer dark, but softly lit with designs and traceries of light, paler that when Wolfram was nearby. No dragons or monsters comprise the images now, but wolves and ravens instead.

The walk seems longer than the original trip from the blue door to the courtyard with the fountain. How long and how far must I and the demon have run?

I'm so tired, now, but he stays quiet and lets me put one foot in front of the other. Sometimes I'm so slow the ravens have to wait, and eventually they give up flying to walk along the floor. You'd think a big bird built to soar would be awkward on the ground, but they seem quite comfortable there, like they're only out for a nice evening stroll.

Finally, one more turn, one more door, and we are back in the courtyard with the fountain and the statue of the old man.

The ravens and wolves vanish as I walk through the door, as if they never existed.

Sparks seem to flicker in Wolfram's eyes as he looks up at me. He's sitting at the feet of the statue, leaning back, ankles crossed.

"Did you have a fun adventure?" he says.

"Not really."

"Did you learn anything?"

I almost sit next to him, but I don't think I will get to rest for long.

"A few things."

"And?"

"The demon can be afraid."

"Of you?"

I shake my head. "Of your wolves and your ravens. And a tree."

He laughs. "Anything else?"

"I know who you are."

He shakes his head. "You may think you do, and you might even be partly right, but don't assume you know all."

I nod. I don't really know anything, I just wanted to see what he would say.

"Do you know the nature of those wolves? Those ravens?"

I shake my head.

"Did your mythology books not teach you that?"

I frown, try to remember. Su doesn't have any Norse heritage, though it is closely related to German, so we didn't read much Norse myth, though we did read a little.

"Odin's ravens were called Huginn and Muninn," I say, probably pronouncing the names wrong.

"Thought and Memory," says Wolfram. "And his wolves?"

I shake my head, "I can't remember." But I do remember something that one of the ravens said. "Greedy and Ravenous," I say.

Wolfram nods. "Close enough. Geri and Freki. Desire and Hunger work, too." He climbs to his feet, seeming more human again.

"Remember that your demon fears thought and memory, hunger and desire."

"And a tree," I say, following him to the edge of the stair.

"Not any tree," says Wolfram. "Yggdrasil. The world-tree. " He smiles sadly. "Life itself. Your demon fears all the things that make a person a person." Then he steps onto the stair and begins to descend, and I follow him down into the dark.

Chapter Fifteen

DESIGNS LIKE THOSE that lit the wall in the building above flicker on the walls of the stairway, too, but fainter. Instead of running far ahead and staying lit behind us, they crowd close, only lighting enough of the stair for us to be sure of our footing.

I wonder if the lighted designs are not merely responding to Wolfram's presence, but are somehow powered by him. I wonder if he is tired, or if this place drains him, suppresses him.

"Those wolves," I say, and my voice echoes in the dark, but dies away quickly. "Those birds... What were they?"

He doesn't answer at first, and I wonder if I have even spoken aloud. But finally he speaks without turning, and I have to keep my footsteps quiet to hear him.

"They are something you never should have seen," he says. "Something very few have ever seen." He descends in silence for several more steps. "I'm surprised they allowed you to see more than their eyes in the dark."

Questions crowd my thoughts. "Do you see through their eyes? Are they part of you somehow? I thought you said they were Odin's wolves?" I snap my mouth shut, realizing my flood of words must sound childish.

Wolfram laughs, but it sounds like more than half sigh. "Dangerous questions, vampire boy," he says.

"I'm not a child," I say, but it sounds petulant even to my own ears.

A laugh again. "Compared to me, you are," he says. "May I call you Evgeny, then? Or do you prefer Alexeyevich?"

He pauses just long enough for me to assure him that "Evgeny" is fine.

"I suppose it's a distancing mechanism. I knew your great-grandfather, though not well. I liked him, for all his illness. Many of us liked him, Karasu included. Many of us learned not to offer friendship so easily the day the demon was created for him."

He falls silent again, and I am left to ponder just how old Wolfram is. Except for his eyes, he might be in his forties. Fifty at the oldest. At first glance he looks late twenties, barely older than me. But if he knew Great Grandpapa he must be at least... I try to do the math in my head, but fail. My ears are ringing too loudly to concentrate.

"But the wolves..." I say.

We reach the bottom of the stairs at last and step out into a stone chamber. The blue flickering light strengthens, brightens, burns steady, and spreads across the floor to reveal a dry, dusty space. Square, with a closed door on each side save the one we just stepped out of, where the stairway is, instead.

"Evgeny," Wolfram says. "At this moment, the less you know about me, or wolves, or ravens, or trees, the better. Right now, you need to focus on yourself. Who you are, who you truly are in your deepest heart. Hold everything you most value about yourself close and safe. Choose who it is you want to be, and be that so thoroughly the demon cannot penetrate your depths. If you are still *that* Evgeny when I return to fetch you, then perhaps we will speak of Odin's ravens and Odin's wolves."

"Okay," I say. I can't think of any better words, though that one hardly seems adequate.

We've stopped just beyond the stairway's opening and I stare around me at the lights, the designs. I spot wolves and ravens, but also serpents, dragons, deer, horses, trees, and twisting vines. When Wolfram steps to the middle of the small space, they momentarily become blinding in intensity.

I shade my eyes with one hand. "Why are my ears ringing?" I say. That, too, has increased until I feel I must shout to be heard.

"It is time," Wolfram says. "We were almost too late." He says no more, but walks to each of the three doors in turn, laying a palm on the ancient wood and tilting his head, as if listening. The first door is green and bears a pattern of leaves and branches, grass and flowers. The second is blue and decorated with waves and fishes, waving kelp and seashells. The third is pale yellow, almost golden, and has cloud patterns, birds and butterflies, a sun and moon.

Wolfram looks at me, considering, then nods sharply, and opens the third door. Sunlight floods out and I dart for the safety of the stairwell, peer back. There's no light at all beyond the open door.

"Sorry," he says. "I should have warned you." He indicates the doorway. "In you go, Evgeny. Good luck."

I step out of the stairway cautiously. "Was that sunlight?"

"It was the illusion of sunlight," he says. "It would not have harmed you."

"Is there more? Is it still in there?" I don't know if I'm more terrified that he might be wrong, and the light might burn me to cinders, or excited that there could be such a thing as sunlight that *won't* burn me, that maybe I could bask in it.

The ringing in my head is so loud now I have to guess his answer from the shape of his lips. "Your best chance is to face the demon in darkness, so it has nothing but your own thoughts to use against you."

Considering the content of my thoughts lately, that seems quite frightening enough.

"In you go," he says again.

I try to stand tall as I walk past him and through the door, but I'm afraid I probably slink. His hand on my arm is warm, strong. For a moment he reminds me of Magne.

"You are strong," he says, and the words somehow penetrate the incessant noise in my skull. "Karasu might be right; you just might be strong enough."

I stop just inside the door, staring into the dark, resisting the urge to turn back.

"It is just a simple empty room," says Wolfram, and I wonder why none of the brilliant blue illumination penetrates beyond the door. "That is its real power."

I nod, not really understanding. "What do I do?"

"Only stay strong," he says. "Good luck. I'll be back when it's over."

I don't ask how he'll know when it's over. I have a feeling it is another one of those things I am better off not knowing, according to whomever decided what things people should and shouldn't know.

"I'm ready," I say, though really I'm not. But I won't get any more ready, and anyway, I can feel the demon creeping in, marshalling itself from whatever crevices of my brain it was hiding in. It's time to face it at last, and see which of us comes out the victor.

"You're not," says Wolfram. "You can't be, but maybe you'll survive."

I take a deep breath, hold my shoulders square, try to ignore the roaring in my head that makes thinking nearly impossible.

"You can absorb it," he says. "And still remain yourself." He doesn't say how I am supposed to accomplish that.

He closes the door softly, and all at once the roaring in my ears stops. There is no sound, nothing to see but darkness. If not for the stone floor under my feet, the faint odor of dust and earth in my nostrils, I might be in the nothing place of Karasu's demon-eradication attempts again.

I wait for the demon to speak, to taunt me, to try to take over my body, but there is nothing. Only silence.

I might as well be utterly alone.

It's impossible to tell how much time is passing. My ability to sense the sun is gone again – even at night I should know how it is moving through the sky. Or maybe it is this place that blocks it.

For what feels like a long time, but could be merely minutes, I stand just inside the door, staring into the dark, waiting for the demon to speak.

It does not.

I felt it creeping up on me as we descended the stairs, as I waited for Wolfram to choose a door, felt it mustering itself as the ringing in my ears grew, felt it recoil as the illusion of sunlight flooded out of the door. But now, nothing.

After a time I take a step farther into the room. What am I supposed to do here? Wait? How can I battle a demon if the demon won't show up to the fight?

I turn in place, reach out, take a step, and feel stone under my fingers where I expected to feel wood. With one hand on the wall I walk along it and only a few steps brings me to a corner and the next wall.

I turn around, put my other hand on the wall, and walk back, past where I figure the door should be, and meet another corner.

Is the door gone, or did I get turned around?

Wolfram said it was only an empty room, but I am still hesitant to follow the wall all the way around, in case somehow it changes while I walk and I am lost in infinite blackness. In a tiny square room underground.

Finally, I return to where I think the door should be and take off my shoes, leave them next to the wall. Then I walk again, one hand on the stone. Clockwise, because I am feeling superstitious and anti-clockwise is supposed to be unlucky, to rouse dark forces. It occurs to me that maybe I *should* try to rouse dark forces, to provoke the demon into coming out where I can fight it. If I knew how to fight it.

I walk, turn, walk, turn, walk turn, walk, turn, walk, and trip over my shoes. Each side of the room is six long paces wide, and there is no door.

On a whim, I pull off my socks, too, instead of putting my shoes back on, and feel the cool stone under my feet. It is not exactly smooth, but it doesn't have enough texture for me to tell what sort of rock it is, or even if it is natural bedrock smoothed for a floor or stone flags fit together so cleverly I can't feel the seams.

I wish I had a source of light. Su used to carry a Zippo lighter. Not because she smokes, which she doesn't, but because she likes having a source of illumination like a little lantern in her pocket. But once her powers began to manifest, she carried it less and less, because she didn't need it. Doesn't need it. But even Su would not be able to see in this blackness.

I wonder how Su is doing. I wonder if she's worried that I have sent so few texts, or if she's too busy with German witches to notice. All at once, I miss her so much I feel weak, nauseated, and I have to sit down.

The floor should be uncomfortable. It is stone after all. But it's nice to sit on. I lie down and roll so I can press my face to the cool and my nausea eases. Then I lie on my back and stare into nothing again.

No door. I have to trust that a vanishing door is simply a part of the magic of this place, and that somehow Wolfram will know when to open it, and that it *will* open, will reappear when his hand touches the knob on the other side.

I wonder what significance the colors and symbols on the door have. Surely they mean something. Su would have asked before stepping through, would have gathered information, wanted to know why *this* door and not one of the others.

Sunlight to contain a vampire? In case the demon prevails and I become a monster? A room that could become filled with sun would be a convenient way of getting rid of me, were that to happen. But then, Wolfram said it was the illusion of sun and would not harm me. Except, maybe it *could* harm me, if he needed it to.

But what of the other doors? Green and trees and leaves. Nature? And blue with fish and waves. The sea? It feels like a puzzle, and with the demon not making itself felt, I don't have much else to do. And I can't help but think that Su would have seen the answer immediately.

Green, blue, yellow. Three doors. Earthy things, ocean things, sun things. Clouds and moon. Sky things. Earth, water, and air? But then where is fire? The stairway takes up the fourth wall. Unless that is magically changeable, too.

But four elements is Greek, isn't it? And not all folklore, not even all Western folklore, is based on the Classical model. I came here with a man bearing Viking tattoos, who claimed to be descended from beings out of Norse and Germanic myth. The designs that lit the halls and walls were Germanic, too. So maybe the Greek model of four elements doesn't apply. I remember that a lot of Northern European folklore uses threes, not fours. Three wishes, three sisters, three times lucky, third time's the charm. So three elements?

The darkness makes a better canvas against which to imagine things than the inside of my eyelids. I picture the three doors, try to tease the meaning out. If I had known I would be facing this Viking stuff, I would have read up more on Norse mythology.

Earth, water, air. But those are the Classical names. I narrow my eyes as if it will help me think — it certainly doesn't help me see. What other names might they go by?

I think of Su reading fox myths. In European stories, foxes are mostly tricksters, and not often the hero of a tale. But she found one tantalizing mention of an Irish Celtic fox goddess, something she could never confirm in any other source, though we paged through all the books from Papa Vamp's library that might have mentioned her.

And in the Celtic research there was something. Not three elements, but three *realms*. Land. Sea. Sky. I wonder if Celtic and Germanic myth might share that idea, as they share similar forms of twisting, half-abstracted art and decoration. I wonder if this place might have Celtic as well as Norse connections. If so, I have been locked in the realm of Sky.

It may be an answer to my puzzle, but it doesn't really tell me why Wolfram chose this door over the others. What might Sky symbolize? Is it meant to neutralize me or help me?

"Why don't you just come out and get this over with?" I say aloud. My words are muffled by the small space. The demon doesn't answer.

I lie there and stare into nothing and practice breathing like Su taught me to. I let my thoughts swirl around me, deflect them gently aside until my mind is as empty as I can make it.

"Come get me," I whisper.

Still no answer.

Anxiety crowds around the clear space I've made in my thoughts and I know I won't be able to push those worries aside forever.

"If you can't keep the negative thoughts away," Su said, when I asked her once how she could always find calm, no matter how stressful the situation. "Fill your mind with positives instead, so there's no room for bad thoughts to fit in your conscious mind."

"Think positive," I said, half mocking.

She grinned, showing me her sharp fox teeth. "In a manner of speaking," she said. But she hadn't really meant "think positive" in that sense, in the sense of coming up with reasons why the crappy things that happened might have positive effects.

Instead, she meant fill your thoughts with things that make you happy — good memories, a favorite poem, fun or exciting ideas for new projects.

Things entirely unrelated to whatever was causing the bad thoughts.

Of course, one always has to face the negatives eventually, but her mindfulness techniques were a way of coping with unhappy thoughts short term. I guess they worked for her.

So I think about her, about Su, and without the demon lurking right on the edges of my mind, I can really think of all the things I love about her.

Not just physical things, of course, though she is beautiful and sexy. She smells good and tastes better (as long as I don't try to taste her blood). She was always fantastic, and she was as enthusiastic as I was. *Is.* I refuse to think of Su in the past tense.

But more than that, she's smart and brave and kind. She found me as a newly-reborn vampire, with no memories yet of who I had been before Papa Vamp woke me to my new life. She could have killed me, easily. In that state, with no parent vamp to watch over me, I was dangerous to everyone. She even told me it had occurred to her to put me out of my misery, especially since she had just killed Papa Vamp, leaving me orphaned.

But she didn't kill me. She took me home, fed me, and kept me safe until my memories returned and I ceased to be a mindless, hungry monster. That was the first time Su saved my life.

The second time, she infiltrated a high-security underground lab to rescue me from being experimented on. She had also, in the process, rescued a sizeable number of *others*, probably including the monstrous Jinny Greenteeth.

And then, time three, she and Alex had worked together to save me from the demon, dissolving it back to memories before it could take me over. That the demon's dissolution turned out to be temporary doesn't diminish her heroism.

That is what Su is. She is a hero. She is the knight in shining armor, and I have always been her damsel in distress. Maybe I should wear skirts and grow my hair long. I have certainly been letting my life be about Su for long enough. I can be the princess and she the prince.

I *am* disdainful of gender stereotypes after all. Why not own what I am? I am Evgeny Alexeyevich and I am the princess in the tower, the dragon's sacrifice, the sleeping beauty. That is who I have been. Evgeny. Witch. Vampire. Always in need of rescue.

I am hers.

But if that is all I am, how can she respect me? And isn't thinking of myself as a princess in skirts just another way of fitting myself into the gender binary? Why can't I be rescued and still be no less of a man?

And there, that has been my greatest fear. That Su will grow tired of having to save my life, that she will think me weak and unworthy.

And maybe, too, that thing Magne said about having a life outside of Su, things I can do without her, is about that, too. How can she stay interested when all I do is exist for her?

And so I need to find what it is *I* am. Maybe that is the core of self Wolfram was talking about, that which I must keep safe from the demon in order to defeat it.

But what is at my core? What am I?

My name is Evgeny Kostas Alexeyevich. I have a demon in my head, though he is currently reluctant to make an appearance.

I am last in a bloodline of rare male witches. I was made a vampire, which should have killed me, but it didn't. It did make certain my bloodline ends with me, however. It made me unable to produce children to carry on my legacy.

I am an abomination in *other* lore, and maybe in all lore. I am a thing which should not be.

Other witches tried to destroy me. Other vampires tried to use me.

But that is only *what* I am, not who. It is my shell, not my core.

I am Evgeny. I am twenty-five. I love to cook, and take photographs. I am attracted to women, and to men. I refuse to be what people tell me I must be.

Su loves me, so there must be something in me to love, because she is extraordinary, glorious, magical. If I lost Su, what would remain? Who am I with Luke? More forceful, more dominating, but still me. What is that "me"?

Who am I? I am Evgeny, and I refuse to be what people tell me I am supposed to be.

Pretentious hipster asshole, the demon says. *You'll be who I want to be.*

Chapter Sixteen

O R MAYBE I SHOULD *say, "You'll be me."* The demon snickers.

I continue to lie flat on the floor, arms outstretched, eyes open to the dark. I force my body to stay calm, my muscles relaxed.

"Do your worst," I say.

Already have done, it says. *You just didn't notice.*

I nearly panic. Is the fight over before it has begun? But I refuse to react. I am still in control of my body. I lie on the floor, stare at the dark. To test myself, I slowly make a fist with one hand, relax it. Then the other. The demon is not in control.

"Whatever," I say aloud.

I thought you wanted a fight? it says. He says.

"I thought you'd give me one." I don't know if Wolfram meant I should hide what I'm feeling from the demon, when he said to bury my truest self deep inside where it will be safe, but maybe if I seem not to care, the demon will… What? Get bored and leave?

Not much of a strategy.

Meh, he says. *I'm good.*

"I don't suppose you'd just get the fuck out of my head, then?"

Oh, listen to you, all swearing and everything. I have been a good teacher.

"Fuck off."

Too easy, he says. *It* says. It is not me. It is not a person, it is a *thing.*

I do like to fuck, though, it says. *And as soon as we get out of here, that's just what I'll do. I might even let you hang around, sentient and conscious, just so you see what I do to your life.*

My first worry is not for Su, who is safe in Germany for now, where the demon can't reach her. For now. It's for Luke, innocent and unaware of what I even am.

The demon laughs, suddenly. *Don't worry about that, it says. You might enjoy your perversions, but I'm looking for pussy. And if I fuck an asshole, it'll be a nice, tight, virgin* female *ass.*

It's harder, this time, to lie still, to continue to feign nonchalance.

I thought I'd start with our old friend Jinny. She's got a few places I'd like to stick the ol' rod.

I cling to Su's breathing techniques, her thought re-direction, and I barely keep myself calm.

"You'll have to defeat me first," I say.

You're a pushover, it says, and I feel it try to creep into my limbs.

"Not this time."

I have you figured out. You'll slip, you'll get scared, you'll be distracted, and you'll be mine. For good this time.

"No," I say. Then I sit up, to prove I can , pace back and forth across the room. I'm afraid I won't be able to keep still much longer, and pacing means I don't have to. I can hide my fear in motion. Because I *am* afraid. I know it's right. It *can* take me over, because I still don't know what allows it to do so, and what allows me to push it back sometimes.

It took over when I was drunk, and when I was lustful. It took over when I was afraid. And I took myself *back* when I was afraid.

Give in, it says. You've already lost. He put you in here, in this particular room, so he'd have a quick and easy way to dispose of you if you fail.

"So if I fail," I say, "we both die." I stop pacing, stand in the middle of the room, and let it feel me smile. "I can live with that."

You can die with that.

"Exactly."

Psycho.

"Get out," I say. "If you win, we both die. The only way out is to leave my body, or be destroyed."

I have no intention of leaving, it says. *Even if I could. Which I can't, since I was created just for you.*

"You were created for Grandpapa." Or Great Grandpapa. I can't remember, if I ever knew for sure. And it doesn't matter, anyway.

My hand waves in the air, dismissively, and I realize I've allowed the demon to take over, just a little. I jam both hands into my pockets and hope it didn't notice.

I was made for your bloodline. Alexei was too weak. Sickly and crazy before I even got there. If that wizened old vampire and the nasty dwarf hadn't set us on fire, I would probably have burned Alexei from the inside out after a few years.

I suspected Karasu had something to do with Great Grandpapa's death, but I didn't know Wolfram was there, too. And though I know they did what they had to, I can't help being angry.

"You were mad," I say.

Alexei was mad. I just got caught in him. I'd have become different before too long.

"After you killed half the world, maybe."

I don't see the problem in that.

"Get out," I say.

Can't. Besides, you're supposed to assimilate me, remember?

"Or destroy you."

If old vamp dude couldn't detach me with his magical vampire alchemy, what makes you think you can do it with brute force?

I suppose he – it – has a point. How can I expect to succeed where Karasu failed? But didn't he say I could destroy it? I try to push aside the sinking feeling, not wanting to give the demon any advantage, show it any weakness. Karasu said I could destroy it – by absorbing it.

"Fine," I say. "I will absorb you and make you just like me."

It laughs. *I am already like you,* it says. *I am your darkest desires and most tortured lusts.* It pauses and I can almost feel it thinking. *Except your boners for man-ass. That's just not natural.*

I shrug, let it feel how it cannot wound me with its outdated notions of queerness.

"You are nothing," I say.

I am everything, it replies, and then it takes my body.

"I am so going to enjoy this," it says, in my voice, aloud.

I try not to weep, assuming I still *can* weep. I pretend to be unconcerned. I will not show fear. I will be my own hero this time. I'm all I've got.

How do you expect to escape? I say, no longer able to use my voice. *If you win, we die, we burn alive and you get imprisoned in my ashes again.*

"Not if the dwarf thinks *you've* won."

You think you can fool him?

"If I can let just enough of you remain intact, I can."

I'll tell him, the moment I'm in control.

"You won't," it says. "Because by then, you will want more than anything to be me. I will teach you to lust for what I lust for."

Good luck with that.

"I don't need luck," it says. "Only time. And here, in this one place on Earth, I have all the time there is and ever was."

What are you talking about? Can the demon known more than I do about Wonder Island? It knew more about Wolfram.

"Why do you think we were brought here? Why this room? The green door: realm of earth, endless land, endless area. The blue door: realm of sea, endless water, endless depth."

I get it. I don't need the demon to finish, but it does.

"And the yellow door: realm of sky, endless air, endless time."

Three realms, I say.

"Three dimensions," it says.

Space-time.

"See," it says. "We do get along."

Fuck off.

"Like I told you, you're already like me. Every day I was in your head, once your genetic quirks managed to re-assemble me from the mess your fox woman made of my parts, every day I infected you a little big more.

No.

"Little by little, I let you share my anger, my language, my tastes in sex. Lucky for me, you were fucking your China doll and not your boy toy.

But overpowering him was kind of fun, too."

Don't call her that.

"China doll. A little too butch for me, really, though. But I bet she'll put up an excellent fight when we see her next. I *am* looking forward to that."

You will never touch her.

"Oh, I *will* touch her. And I'll hit her. And I'll fuck her till she stops moaning. And after, too, because why waste a good wet cunt just because it's gone cold?"

No! And suddenly, I am in control again. I pace back and forth across the room again. "I will defeat you in here, and you will never leave this room," I say, more grateful than I could have before imagined just to be able to speak aloud.

You forget, it says. *As long as we don't die here, I leave when you do.*

"No."

You keep saying that. I think you have forgotten its meaning.

"If there is any trace of you left that can ever hope to have an individual existence, I will have Wolfram kill me rather than leave here."

Martyr.

I ignore it, try to think of some way to attack. I have no idea how to fight something that only exists inside my head. Do I *think* at it?

You want so much to be the hero, it says. *You're afraid your precious fox bitch won't suck your dick anymore if she keeps having to rescue you. That she'll start fucking your friend the hairy wolf cur instead.*

They are not the words I would use, but the demon has hit too close to the truth for comfort. Except with the part about Magne. If Su is going to love someone else, I'd rather it were someone else I love than a stranger.

"Are we just going to stand around and talk at each other, or are we going to get this fight over with?" I hope, if it attacks me first, I will know how to fight back. Because I sure as hell don't know how to make the first move.

You might want to lie down for this, it says.

"Why? Do you think you'll sweep me off me feet?"

I just thought you might like to get comfortable while I show you everything you could have if you surrender quietly.

"That will never happen."

Suit yourself. But don't blame me for the bruises later. Oh, and you might want to unzip. I'm probably going to get a raging hard-on from this.

And then it doesn't take over my body, like I'm expecting. Instead, it shows me the memories that created it.

I do feel the crack of my knees hit the stone floor, but not for long. Because I'm too busy struggling against the torrent of ghosts it throws at me.

It begins with the lesser brutalities, though I say "lesser" only because they are the least horrible of a great many horrible things.

Like the nightmares I've had these last weeks – or is it months? – I experience the atrocities as if I am the victim reliving his or her own death. Because they all end in death. These are the ghostly memories I have been carrying around with me and they are no less horrifying because they are familiar.

First, the simple deaths. The ghosts whose lives ended relatively quickly. These memories are all much the same, but each is fresh and raw. An early-morning awakening, noise, soldiers.

At first, each villager is brave. He asks what the soldiers want, tells them to leave, stands between them and his family. And he is shot for his trouble. Some die mercifully swiftly. A bullet in the brain that hits with a punch, and then nothing. These deaths are sad and senseless, and each piles on the others to add up to more than their sum.

That is where the demon begins.

Some men are not so lucky. They are shot in the gut, maybe, and die slowly, watching or hearing their loved ones murdered, unable to do anything to help. They add sorrow, frustration, and anger to the pain and fear. Some take many bullets to die. A few even manage to injure a soldier first, but in the end, they all die.

The men not shot to death are beaten or tortured, and as their memories play through me, I am beaten or tortured. The beatings are easier to bear. There is pain and fear, of course. More than any human or animal or feeling being should ever be subjected to, but eventually it ends and there is blackness, dullness, and then death comes.

The torture, though, goes on and on, as torture is designed to do. I learn what knives feel like on every part of my body, and cigarette burns, what being poked and hit and burned and pinched feels like. Only the fact that the soldiers are given a single day to accomplish their task means each torture has an end. And the end is relief. Death is relief.

The children are harder to bear. Many of them are simply shot as if perhaps the soldiers aren't quite as monstrous as they could be. The fact that many of the children are too young to understand makes their deaths more tragic. They would be unbearable if I had any choice *but* to bear them.

The ones who are tortured and beaten don't last long and bore the soldiers, so few suffer that fate.

The women, as seems to be the case through history, get the worst of it. None are killed so quickly as a simple gunshot. A few – the elderly and crippled, mostly – are beaten until they stop moving. The young, the healthy, the beautiful – they suffer the most.

They watch their men die – their brothers, husbands, fathers, son, and lovers – they see them shot and beaten, tortured, and burned. And then they see their children die. Sons and daughters, cousins, grandchildren, neighbors. Some lose the will to go on then, and when it is their turn, they die quickly. They don't give the soldiers any sport, so they are strangled barehanded, crushed under rifle butts or underfoot, tied to house poles and burned with their homes. In their ghostly memories, they are already gone, and the final pain is just a formality to get through.

But those with fight left in them, those few women – and I am so glad there aren't many – those the soldiers play with. These men gathered by the mad monk are inventive. They rape, using their own members or whatever tools they have to hand. They hit and torture, too, but it is the sexual violation they seem to enjoy most. And it is with these memories the demon lingers.

He – it – can't slow the memories down, or I'm sure it would. But it can pause after each one, savor it, make me feel the erection it has forced on me, laugh at my sorrow. It cannot linger too long, however, because it wants me overwhelmed. It does not want to give me any chance to recover.

So I live through each violation – in memory, I am violated. I feel each woman's terror and fear and pain and shame. And I feel the demon grow and form until finally it's a real and tangible thing, a force, a dark shadow that hangs over the smoking ruins of the village.

And then the memories pause, the demon savors a little longer, strokes my hardness until I want to scream – not from pleasure, but from revulsion.

"Not a single pansy among them, you'll notice," it says, satisfaction strong in its voice. My voice, stolen and perverted. "Hand-picked, every one," it says.

I am capable of making no reply.

Then one final memory. It is the one it showed me in my kitchen, when Magne had to punch me to make it stop. But unlike last time, now I am seeing the evil deed through the young woman's eyes. I feel her terror, I run with her, flee, hide under the porch. I feel the yank on her hair, feel the earth hard under her, look up to the face the man who will steal my – her – innocence and leave her only pain and death.

And I look into my own face, or one so like mine it hardly matters.

The demon's laughter is rich. "Oh god," it moans, tugging at my erection. I want to vomit. "You are fucking hilarious," it says, between breathy pants. "You really fucking believe that's you."

But of course, it is not me. It is Great Grandpapa, Alexei Romanov. He is dressed in the same dark, plain uniform as the other men, but he looks pale and delicate next to them, and so very young. He can't be much older than sixteen, if that. And yet by this time, he must already have fathered a child – my grandfather, I think – and have been made a vampire, and come into his witch nature, at least a little bit.

Grandpapa, I say, or try to, but I am the girl in this memory, and she only whimpers. She doesn't even make much more sound when Great Grandpapa takes her. He is awkward, and fumbles, but makes up for it with anger. When he's done, the girl looks up again and this time I – she – meets his eyes. There is nothing in them. None of the anger he seemed to display at his own awkwardness. No evil, or lust, or sorrow. No fear or remorse. Nothing but a lurking madness, a disconnect that almost makes me more afraid than the things done to the girl whose body I inhabit in this ghost memory.

I barely register the rest of what happens to her. When she dies, Alexei's hand on her throat, the demon pauses again and I am relieved it is the last memory. Maybe it will show me them all again, but now I am prepared.

"Did you like that last one?" it says. Its breathing – my breathing – has gone short and sharp as it brings us to climax. But I am barely aware of my own thrusting, arching body, of the spurt of jism that lands on my bare stomach. I am still lost in Great Grandpapa's vacant eyes.

"This next one's my favorite, "the demon says. "I should have waited to come, maybe." I do not reply. Would not, if I could.

"But here, we have all the time in the world. It's just too bad we don't have any water. I'm going to dehydrate with all the jacking off I plan to do."

I try to flex my fingers, to move my hand to wipe away the stickiness, but I can't.

That one wasn't enough? I finally think at it, not caring if it can hear me or not.

"It was a good one, but I'm not so fond of being in a girl's body, in these memories. I want to do the fucking, not get fucked, no matter how deliciously it hurts."

And it shows me that last memory again, or rather, the one from the kitchen. It is worse, somehow, knowing I am Great Grandpapa Alexei, watching the horrors unfold around him – because this time, the memory starts at the beginning, with entering the village and hearing the first gunshot. He watches each death, and he feels the demon accumulate, and by the time we reach the end of the deaths, sees the girl die – the only one he raped personally – he can sense the demon's shape, and he welcomes it.

The only thing I can't quite understand is how his vampire bloodlust is not awakened by all the free lunch. Vampires are like humans in that our physical natures do not automatically make us evil, but we do get hungry when there's so much blood. And Alexei does not.

I can sense his witch powers, like electricity running just under the surface of his skin, and they, I think, are why he can feel the demon forming so clearly. But I can't feel any vampire strength, or heightened senses. And I realize that all this has been happening in full daylight.

"Can you guess what happens next?" says the demon, intruding on the memory.

You enter into him and drive him the rest of the way mad, I say.

He laughs, genuine amusement pouring out of him, though I can't tell what I've said that is so funny.

"You're still such an innocent," it says. "No, I took him faster than I took you, but it was still a lengthy process. It was months before your old vampire set us on fire to save his precious world."

He falls silent as the memory plays on, as Great Grandpapa watches his monk prophet direct the soldiers to dig a mass grave and pile the bodies in. He watches them covered over, and says nothing as each and every soldier pisses on the grave. One even drops his trousers and shits in the middle, and the other soldiers laugh and pat him on the back.

The soldiers march away, leaving only Great Grandpapa and Rasputin, looking over the grave and the burning village. Darkness falls slowly and the stars appear in the sky, and still they wait.

Why can I see this memory? I ask. *This is not a ghost memory.*

Again, it laughs, but more softly. "It is so, you poor innocent child. It is so."

Finally, at full dark, when Alexei stomps his feet from the cold and complains to the monk that he doesn't want to wait any longer, a third figure joins them from out of the fields.

At first, I think it is the demon, taken human shape, as it did just before we imprisoned it in my head. I can feel it lurking. But then, terror and an overwhelming sense of threat washes over me and I realize who it is.

The demon's amusement almost drowns out his words.

"Are you ready to die and be reborn, Alexei?" I recognize the voice, too.

"And then I can have my demon?"

"And your power," says the mad monk. "Then you will be ready for it."

And Karasu steps out of shadow and into the smoky light of the burning village, tilts Alexei's head back, unhinges his jaw, unfolds his teeth. And Alexei, Great Grandpapa, I, die in pain and terror, to become the last element of the watching demon.

Chapter Seventeen

K ARASU MADE ALEXEI a vampire. *Karasu* made Alexei a vampire. He told me he had nothing to do with the attempt to create a *koldun*. But he lied. What else did he lie to me about? Did Wolfram lie too?

If that is so, then maybe there is no hope, maybe everything up to this point has simply been aimed at making *me* a *koldun*. Maybe that was the plan all along.

No, I say, or try to, but this time I don't believe it. I know the demon lies, but the ghost-memories do not. They are true, lived experience.

"You actually trusted him," the demon says, disbelief touching his voice. My voice. *Its* voice. "You could feel his evil, but you trusted him anyway."

I could feel that he was threatening to a lesser being such as I, that he exudes terror like other creatures perspire, but evil? He didn't seem evil to me. Too impersonal, too unfocussed. Danger, yes, but Karasu never felt evil.

Then again, maybe I don't know what evil is.

There doesn't seem to be any point in fighting now, even if I had any idea how to go about battling the demon. I can only hope that Wolfram, at least, was genuine, and that he will destroy me and the demon when he comes back. If he comes back.

Failing that, Magne will kill me, and if he can't, Su will.

I try not to think that the thing I could become is supposed to be so powerful it even makes gods afraid.

Why, then, would Karasu want to create such a creature?

"I see you're coming to your senses, finally," the demon says.

I don't answer.

"You just lie there and let me show you the fun we'll have when we get out of here. Then I will consume you, or most of you, and we'll be the first *koldun* since who knows how long.

I still don't answer. I have no words.

"Don't worry, boy, I'll leave enough of you to get us out of here. Enough to give me someone to talk to who really *gets* me." It laughs.

"Now, where to begin? Oh yes, the delightful water-bitch Jinny."

What he shows me now is not the same as the memories. Those were inescapably real, and they were – despite me living them from inside the victims – things that happened to other people.

These… visions… are what the demon *wants* to do. Wants to make *me* do. And he shows them to me as if we are really doing them. I can't stop him, but at least they're not real. Not yet.

First, Jinny. Thin and fragile, but monstrously strong. I expect him to torment her, to play cat-and-mouse, like he made me do when he took over my body at home. And this fantasy of his can't help but remind me of that, remind me that I wasn't even aware that he was in control.

"Oh, yes, we almost joined then," he says. "We could have been one sooner, if not for your friends, and old vamp's alchemical meddlings."

And why did Karasu meddle, if his plan all along was to create a *koldun*? Because he needed a controlled space to make sure I didn't end up like Alexei?

No, the demon doesn't toy with Jinny in this fantasy. Instead he takes us to her pond, wades in, swims and dives, and grabs her by the hair to drag her out.

I can feel her fight, physically and mentally. She's strong, stronger than any *other* I've met, but the demon, I, *we* are stronger.

We throw her to the ground and violate her in every way a man can violate a woman – I refuse to acknowledge the details the demon shows me, though I can't help but feel them, live them, remember them. And when we've finished and she lies broken and defeated on the shore of her pond, her feet still in the water, we simply snap her neck and move on.

"She deserves that, you know," he says. We have an erection again, but he doesn't make me touch myself. Not yet.

Nobody deserves that, I say. I am at least in control enough that tears stream from my eyes, and I feel sick. I have to roll on my side to vomit, and the demon lets me, even lets me wipe the mess from my mouth.

"Pussy," it says.

Fuck you.

"You'd like that."

Just take me over and have done with it, I say.

"Where's the fun in that?"

Please.

"Ooh, begging. I like begging. But no, I'm not done with you yet. I want you to really want me inside you." It snickers. "I want you to really want what we can be together, joined equally into one being."

I thought you wanted to take over, to only leave a little of me intact, but separate.

"Only if I have to," it says. He says. "I think I will so much more enjoy what we can be as one. That's where the power is, vampire-witch boy. That's where the *koldun* comes into being. Thank you for reminding me of that."

And if we stay separate?

"One of us is dominant. Maybe we go mad. But we don't get all the juice of the *koldun.*"

Why tell me this now?

"Changed my mind. You reminded me of what it was like to almost be joined with you. *That's* what I want."

I reminded him. By remembering how my real encounter with Jinny was different from what the demon imagines. *I* reminded him. If I weren't already weeping, I would cry.

"You can't lie to me, Evgeny. You liked it, too."

Don't call me that.

"It's your name, Evgeny. *Our* name."

It will never be yours.

"Whatever. I'm bored. Let's move on to your man candy."

For a moment I think he means Magne, but then I realize he's talking about Luke. *I thought you didn't like gay sex*, I say.

"I don't. And that's why we'll do this."

"This" turns out to be following Luke home from work and dragging him into a dark alley to beat the crap out of him. And when he's little more than a bloody pulp, we drag him under a streetlight so he can see who has hurt him.

"That's what you get for trying to get into my pants, faggot whore," we say.

"Alexeyevich," he says around broken teeth and swollen lips. "I thought you liked me." Hurt in his eyes, betrayal.

We just laugh and tear his throat out with our teeth and suck his veins dry.

I suppose I should be grateful the demon's fantasy didn't include raping Luke. His homophobia is good for something, at least.

But it's terrible enough how our blood pulses with lust from the violence, and the terror.

"Having fun yet?" the demon asks.

I refuse to answer.

"Well, how about this?"

Now, the demon goes back through my life, through every lover and crush. The women he imagines us violating, and the inventive things he comes up with are worse than anything Alexei and his soldiers did.

I want to close my eyes, to shut the demon out, to scream. But I can do none of those things. He is in control, and I can only watch the fantasies he plays out in my head, and wait for him to slip up, to make a mistake. I don't know what that might look like, but I wait.

The boyfriend I had before I met Su, the one who abused me, the demon imagines being fed naked to hungry dogs. He saves the final death blow for us, though, and we wade into the fray, tearing dogs apart until there is carnage all around, and then we slit my ex from throat to crotch with the sharpened nails of one bare hand and watch the light die from his eyes.

The shy young man I met at the library, we simply drown.

My first real girlfriend… we kill her two young children in front of her, beat her husband to death with a tire iron, and use the same implement on her, but not for the same purpose. After that, I vomit again, heaving and puking until there is nothing left inside me. And still my body maintains its erection, turned on by the demon's control, his violent lusts.

I want to die now.

I don't even know if that first girlfriend *has* children, or a husband, in real life.

My first crushes, the neighbor girl and her brother, we force at gunpoint to fuck each other, and then shoot them each in the head. I have nothing left to vomit, no tears left to shed. Even the mucous running from my nose has dried to nothing.

"Having fun yet?" the demon says again, sounding happy, fulfilled, almost. He makes me look down at myself, and the hard penis that pokes up from me. "I sure as fuck am." He makes me watch as he strokes us. Coming is painful, and there's not much fluid. I am empty.

You cannot make me like you.

"I don't have to," he says, with a contented sigh. "Once we are merged we'll both want the same things, anyway."

So you'll want men, I say. *That'll be nice.*

He jerks his hand away from our crotch.

"No fucking way," he says.

We'll both want the same things. I have hit a nerve, but don't know how to press the advantage.

If you're going to make me want violation, I'm going to make you want men.

He hits me in the face with my own hand. "Don't forget who's in control here," he says, lifting our head and cracking it back onto the stone. I don't even try to stop him. If he knocks us both out, so much the better.

"How about we think about your pretty Su, now? I think I can overlook her beastly side."

I force myself not to reply, not to react. Then, carefully, I say, *Whatever, I'm ready to move on.* I imagine my love for her locked tight in my heart like a treasure in a safe, a booby-trapped temple, a strongbox on the bottom of the sea.

"Liar," he says. "Just her name makes you breathe quicker."

He imagines her for me, and I struggle to forget every detail as he calls it up, but I can't. She is too much a part of me.

She's on the tall side of average, for a woman. Too tall and too pale to look "properly Chinese," she used to joke. Slender, toned, but with perfect curvy hips and breasts that fit exactly right in my hands. Her lips are curved with a smile or with mischief, asking to be kissed, and oh, how she kissed. She always seemed to be able to sense when to be soft and pliable, and when to be harder, aggressive. Or maybe our moods just always matched.

Her hair is a curtain of black that grows back quickly when she cuts it, so quickly that she could cut off a few feet and donate it to a wig charity for cancer kids, almost whenever she felt the whim. She could wear nothing but her hair and still be covered neck to knee.

And her eyes. They were always amber, but since she discovered her fox nature, they've got slit pupils. She can make them ordinary again if she needs to be inconspicuous, just as she can make her fox tail and her fox teeth vanish or reappear. When her eyes catch the light just right, they glow green the way a cat's do in headlights.

Her voice is soft, a little throaty, unless she's angry, which happens seldom.

In my mind's eye, she stands naked, fox tail swishing, fox eyes burning, hair swept back as if by wind. She is comfortable in her body, not shy. She stands straight, looks me in the eye and I can imagine the disapproval, the disgust when she realizes the demon is present, is in charge.

Except that's not right. She would never, has never, looked at me with disgust, no matter what terrible things I've told her.

I don't know whether to try to hide the memory of her from the demon – though I don't think I can – or whether to embrace it, cling to it, and hope to somehow borrow her strength, even though she is in reality far away.

"Oh, she is a pretty one, isn't she?" the demon says.

I don't want to watch him imagine violating her, but I can't look away. Even if I could physically wrest control back from the demon, I don't think I could banish her from my thoughts. She seems too real, and for a moment I fear we have called her into a true dream somehow.

"What I'd really like," the demon says, "is for her to *want* it." And he imagines her turning around, getting on all fours, and wiggling her backside at us.

She has a perfect ass, tail or no tail, and though I've never had anal with her – neither of us was ever that interested in it – the sight of her is arousing, even with the things the demon has already shown me, and the things he will no doubt show me soon.

She arches her back, crouching her arms farther down and I can see the deep pink moistness of her, waiting for us.

Oh god, I can't help but whisper. I want her, like I always want her, but I don't want the demon near her, even if this is only an imaginary Su.

It is almost worse that when we approach her, in this fantasy, it is gently. We run our hands over her buttocks, her soft skin, slide a hand between her legs to touch her, tease her, even wait for her to start to come before entering her. It is almost lovemaking, and it is nice, like something Su and I might really do, like something we have done. It would be sweet, if not for the fact that demon is in me, controlling me, touching her.

"Did you think I'd just fuck her ass and bludgeon her to death right away?" he says. "I intend to savor this sweet piece of tail."

As it is a fantasy, Su and I don't need a break before we're ready for more. He has her suck me off, and he has me lick her until she screams in pleasure. Then we fuck her hard and fast against the wall. Then she rides me, sits on my face, gets me off with just her hand.

The demon does everything Su and I have ever done together, sweet or energetic, gentle or rough, vanilla or a little bit kinky.

I suspect he is trying to lull me, to make me forget he's there, to relax into enjoying endless sex without tiring, without getting sore, without need of sleep or rest. And to my shame it works. It works so well that I hardly react when I slide into her ass instead of her cunt.

In the fantasy, she doesn't mind. In the fantasy, she urges me on, moaning and pushing back against me, even when there's blood. And it's not like I don't enjoy anal, haven't enjoyed anal, with other men. Of course I do, of course I have. But with Su, this would never happen. Not in real life. I don't think.

The demon is trying to change me subtly, by gradually changing what is acceptable with Su, but having me do things that are acceptable with a different lover. And I almost don't catch it.

The next time, we are – he is – less gentle. The next time, she says "stop" and we do not. He does not. The time after that, she tries to fight. We hit her – he hits her – until she stops fighting.

"That's enough ass fucking," the demon says, finally. "It's getting a little too gay for me."

The Su who is in the demon's fantasy is not my Su. This woman is bruised and broken. Her lip is split and her eyes are huge. She has the same look as the girl in the ghost memories. I cling to the fact that this is not real, and I am not the one doing these things. I feel the burn of her love, or my love for her, held safe in the deepest part of my heart.

And the demon makes her say, "Please Evgeny, fuck me again." And the demon makes her spread her legs. And he makes me take her, this imaginary Su, again and again. We bite her, spit out her terrible-tasting blood, bite her again.

When the demon is done with her, he simply tosses her aside, her body flopping limp to the ground.

It's only a fantasy, I remind myself again. *Only the demon's sick, twisted fantasy.*

"But it will be real," it says. "It will be real, and soon. And you're going to like it."

I do not respond. I can't stop staring at the limp woman on the ground. She is not even there in real life, but I can still picture her. Broken, probably dead, but still beautiful. Still my one true love.

"Now *that* has got me in the mood," the demon says, and the fantasy finally fades away to the complete darkness that is my actual reality.

"I could use a good fuck for real," he says. "Hurry up and absorb me so we can get out of here and I can get laid."

We will die here, I say, finally. *And I will have no regrets.*

"We're not going to die here," says the demon. "You have too much to live for. Now just relax and do whatever it is you need to do to make me properly a part of you."

I don't know how, I admit.

"Of course you do."

I don't.

"Well, fuck."

We lie in silence for a while, staring into the dark, trying to ignore the smell of vomit and sex that smothers the dust and earth scents that are the proper odor of this dungeon.

"You didn't have to puke so much," the demon says, shifting us so we are farther away from it.

That's all on you, I say.

"You're such a poof," he says.

So go find someone more manly.

"No choice. But you'll do, once you've got me inside you good and proper."

You'd like *to be inside me,* I say.

"Fuck you."

You'd like that, too. Don't you know that homophobia is frequently a sign of repressed homoerotic longings?

"Fuck off."

It's true. That's what all the psychology books say. I don't think this taunting will help me at all, but it feels better to be able to land a blow, however small.

"I don't want to fuck men. I want to fuck that sweet Chinese piece of ass you call 'my heart' or whatever sissy nickname you have."

She is my heart, and you will never have her. Her love, my love, *our* love is a soft glow in the center of my chest. And there is another love there that I'm too nervy to look at more closely, but it blends with Su's and mine, protects it, somehow.

"I can at least imagine her again while we wait."

And he does. She reappears, still limp and dead, and in the fantasy, he goes to her, rolls her over.

You like to fuck corpses, and I'm *the sick one?*

"Why waste a tight, wet pussy?" he says. "Vampire cunts are cold, aren't they? How's that any different?"

I've never been with another vampire. And they're not dead. And we're not corpse-cold.

"You know what I mean."

We get warm when aroused.

He looks down at Su's body. I remind myself that this is not real, she is not real, none of this is real. He opens her legs.

"See, just as fine and fuckable as when she was alive. Though I will miss the fight."

I wonder why he doesn't just imagine her alive again. But this is for my benefit, after all, not his satisfaction. He wants to taint my every thought of her. I breathe in and out and try to deflect the fantasy from my conscious mind the way Su taught me to deflect thoughts when I'm trying to be still.

It works, almost. I hardly notice when he takes his penis in hand and tugs, to prepare to violate the imaginary corpse of my beloved.

Then he swears and breaks my concentration, bringing my thoughts back to the fantasy. He's staring down at the member in his hand. *Our* member. *My* member. It is limp and flaccid and unresponsive.

Guess we're tired, I say.

"This is *my* fucking fantasy," he says. "And I am *not* tired." He pulls viciously on our member – *my* penis – over and over until it hurts, and still he keeps going.

"Oh yeah, a little pain will get me hard," he says. "Works every time."

But it does not work.

I laugh. *You've killed us,* I say. *Nice.*

"Fuck," it says. "Fuck, fuck, fuck."

I think I'll take my body back, I say. And I do.

Chapter Eighteen

I KNOW THAT DEFEATING the demon can't be as easy as that. I have never yet been able to simply take back control.

And he's still in there. No, *it* is still in there. I can feel it, like a dead thing, or an abscess, festering and waiting to burst out.

I need to absorb it to defeat it, Karasu said. Karasu was telling the truth about that, I'm pretty sure.

I stink. The room stinks. I strip off my t-shirt and clean myself up as best I can, mop up the vomit and other messes without actually being able to see if I've got them all. Then I crumple my shirt into a ball with the mess inside and shove it next to the wall, weight it down with my shoes.

Then I sit, back to the opposite wall, near where I think the door will be when it opens. I don't know how much longer this is going to take, and if this room contains endless time, then I can't even guess how long it has already taken. But I don't know if I can stand another mental assault. If the demon forces me to watch those memories again, if he forces me to imagine doing all those horrible things to the people I love – things I would never do, would never imagine doing myself – I think then it will break me.

I might already be broken. But at least I am alive, and sane, and still fighting.

The demon struggles, weakly, and subsides again. It is exhausted, too, but feels triumphant. It knows it has wounded me. It knows it only has to wait. So it slips away to whatever part of my mind it hides in, to bide its time, to gather its strength. I must not let it grow strong again.

But how do I stop it? How do I fight it? Panic and doubt crowd my thoughts, so I force myself to relax, concentrate on breathing.

"Don't fight the negative thoughts," Su said. "Let them come, just deflect them, direct them away from the center of your concentration. Let them sink slowly in and they won't seem so bad."

I laughed at what seemed like pop-culture psychology, but I also did as she said. Whenever I was feeling angry, or lost, or helpless, her lessons helped.

"You can learn from your negative thoughts," she said. "Think you aren't good enough at something? Don't let it defeat you, instead let it fuel your determination to become better."

Magne said, "I like to hit things. And run. But spite is a good motivator to get better at stuff." The thought of Magne adds to the warmth of the thought of Su. I have friends who are rooting for me.

"My old teacher used to say, 'Sometimes the best way to fight is not to fight.' I told him he sounded like a fortune cookie." Su chuckled at the memory. "He said there's a reason fortune cookies became so popular."

"It kind of does sound like a fortune cookie," I said.

"Or the sayings they print under the cap of a bottle of Jones Soda," said Magne.

"Racist," said Su. But she grinned.

"You said it first, my heart, not me."

"He used to say stuff like that all the time. Sometimes he'd even put on a false Chinese accent, which was funny, because he grew up in London."

I smiled and tried to kiss her, but Magne was there, so she stepped away and said, "Fortune cookie or no – or Jones Soda wisdom – he was usually right."

I banish the memory before it goes any farther, because then we did kiss, ignoring poor Magne, and the demon's fantasies are too fresh.

"Sometimes the best way to fight is not to fight."

"Defeat the demon-ghost by absorbing it."

So the answer is to give in, to let it take me? How will that be any better than letting it take me over?

Wolfram – assuming Wolfram was more genuine than Karasu – Wolfram said to find the core of myself and keep it safe, where the demon can't touch it.

I don't know how to do that, but I can try. I think of all the qualities I most conceive of as *me*. What I look like in the mirror, the way Su looks at me. The way *Luke* looks at me. And the way Magne looks at me, the strength he said I have. My love of my friends, of art and life. I assemble all those in my mind, and I make a package of them, and I imagine locking them away in my heart with my love. And then I push all thoughts of them aside.

Now what? Wait for the demon to emerge, or try to dig it out?

Maybe I can *lure* it out.

I do something I have not yet dared to do, not even when the demon was first imprisoned in my mind and dissolved back into the memories it was made of.

I call up those memories willingly.

Always before, they were inflicted on me, either in a nightmare, on by the demon calling them forth. Now I set out to remember them on my own. I expect the demon to make itself known, lurking in the periphery, mocking and taunting, but it doesn't. It stays quiet, hidden.

I'm afraid to look at those terrible things again, and not only because they are unpleasant, full of pain and horror. I am also afraid that the demon has changed me enough that I will enjoy some part of them, feel a thrill at replaying the beatings and violations.

So when I consciously call up the first memory, of a man awakened in the early morning by soldiers in unmarked uniforms, I hunch over, hug my knees, and examine it only tentatively.

I feel no thrill of power or enjoyment of pain when the man whose memory I view is beaten and shot. Instead, I feel remorse, sorrow, anger at the senselessness and cruelty of his death. And as the memory ends it feels different, somehow, from all the other times I experienced it, whether in nightmare, or demon-inflicted. *I* feel different. It is as if, by choosing to experience the memory I have laid it to rest. It's not gone, vanished from my mind, but it's something that cannot wound me any longer.

The first time, I think I am only imagining this because I *want* to, because I need something to be different this time. But it happens again with the next memory, and the next.

It is as if, by choosing to face those horrors, the things my Great Grandpapa did and made happen, by acknowledging them instead of hiding from them. I am… not banishing them, but allowing the ghosts to rest. I am choosing to remember them as individual people, and not as horrible ingredients in a larger evil. And I realize that I know their names, each of these ghosts, and I know how each is related to the other, to make a village.

When the last of the men dies again in my mind, I pause and stare into the dark, deflect my thoughts again as Su taught me. Still, the demon is quiet, and I wonder if instead of absorbing it, I am strengthening it by choosing to look at these memories again. I wish I knew. I wish I had some indication of how this is affecting the outcome of this fight.

There is nothing else for me to do but continue. So I take a deep breath, hug my knees together, and call up the memory of the slaughter of each child, one at a time. They are quicker. Weakened by famine and more delicate than the men to begin with, the death of children plays through my mind. And though each one is quick, they hurt more.

The children were truly innocents. They had no conception, yet, of the evils of the world, and not one of them understood what was happening. So though their deaths are over sooner and they suffered less, the sorrow each brings is greater. When I have remembered the last child's passing, and pause again to stare into the dark, tears flow freely down my face and my breath heaves in sorrow.

I didn't think I had enough moisture left in my body to cry, but for what feels like hours, I can't stop.

Through it all, the demon is silent.

Finally, the women. By now, I have seen enough of these memories that the physical differences of inhabiting a woman's body isn't disorienting at all. The horrors inflicted on the women, though, are much worse. First, they watched their loved ones suffer and die, and then they were violated over and over. For many of them, death was a relief.

When the last memory ends, I fell hollow, bared, scraped empty with a rusty spoon and left to dry in the sun. My face is crusty with shed tears and snot and I scrub weakly at it with the heels of my hands.

But I feel almost at peace. There is no fear left in me. I have experienced the worst, I have *chosen* to remember the worst, and while I will always mourn the passing of those unfortunate people, I am free of the terror of their suffering.

Almost.

Because there is one last memory I have not yet called up. I have not yet remembered that last woman whose death I experienced just now a second time. The memory of her through Great Grandpapa's eyes. *That* I still fear. Because what if I *am* like him? The demon was made for him, for the DNA he carried and passed on to his descendants. To me. What if that last memory, *his* last memory before being made a vampire, and before the demon invaded him, is the one that finally lets the demon become me?

Yet, if it is, at least this will be over, one way or another. Either I will have faced all parts of the demon, exorcised and absorbed them, or I will have let the demon take me over, and Wolfram will see to my death.

My other fear is that, because Alexei was a willing participant, because he enjoyed the carnage, I might somehow be tainted by that and turn into the monster that the demon wants me to be, even if it *doesn't* have control over my body.

There is no choice, really. Either I can sit here in the dark until I rot, waiting for the demon to make a move, or I can call up this one last memory and hope it will make a difference. So I take a deep breath, hold it, let it out. And then I call up that memory.

I, Alexei Romanov, last prince of a great line of Tsars, left orphaned by a mob of mindless obedient soldiers, now have my chance for revenge. As those trigger-happy fools forced my family from their home and slaughtered them, I and my men will drag *these* dissenters from *their*

homes. And we will show them what defying their betters does for them. Only unlike my family, this village will have no survivors.

It does not matter if these particular dirt toilers were not the ones who held the rifles, who shot so enthusiastically that they didn't even bother to aim. It was "the will of the people," and these are the people, so they will pay.

And when I am *koldun*, I will take back the palace, and my country, and the rest of "the people" will pay the price for their treason.

I would slaughter every last peasant myself, but the monk tells me I should not soil my hands. That others should do the work – they were chosen for it, trained for it. I think he does not believe me vicious enough. He thinks me kind and fragile. But soon I will have left all gentleness behind. I welcome the demon that will make me stronger.

And so I walk among the soldiers, stroll through the village and watch them work. Some of the men are full of anger, hatred, and violence, and I think they may someday be difficult to control, though they are also perhaps the most loyal. We have given them leave to act out their strongest and darkest desires, and in return they will do anything we want.

The cold ones, the ones who torture and maim with dispassion, they are enough in control of themselves that they can be directed, given precise instructions. But they are also the ones who will be loyal only as long as it suits them. They will need to be closely watched.

It is exciting, at first, to watch the soldiers perform their duties, to see the peasants paid back for their treachery with beatings and bullets. But after so many, it grows dull. When it is the women's turn, that is more exciting. They squirm and cry and wail, and my hands shake with waiting. I want to tell the monk to leave me be so I can have a turn. I want to watch a woman's face turn bloody at my hands, watch the light die in her eyes as I take her over and over, but my prophet knows what he is doing. I will not ruin this ritual with my desires. I will have the demon properly made, and when it is time, I will join with him and become strong.

I am so tired of being the weak boy.

Maybe when this is over I can return to the house in the forest where we hide and try some of the soldiers' techniques on the woman I was forced to get a child on. The boy I fathered is still a babe, but he won't need her much longer.

Too soon, the day draws to a close and the last few women die, and there is only one girl left. Blonde, skinny, filthy, she has somehow lived longer than the others. Stupid bitch, she turns to me and asks for my help, asks me to save her, and I smile. She has recognized me, thinks she has found a champion.

"I will hold her for you, sir," a soldier says and the hope dies from her eyes and I have to laugh.

Then the monk puts a hand on my shoulder and says, "Yes, it is time. This last death should be yours, my prince."

For a moment, I can forget my weakness. What matter if I am hurt or scratched or cut now? If I bleed, if makes no difference, because as soon as darkness falls, I am to die and be reborn as a vampire.

"Your last memory will be the core of our demon," he says. "It is only fitting."

And so I take the girl right there in the mud of the road. She hardly struggles as I fumble and I think she is mocking my inexperience. But what does she know? I have fathered a child and she is but a virgin. I know, because I take that from her. I feel the barrier inside her as I plunge in, feel it break as I fuck her. And I take the life from her with my hands around her neck, feel her last struggle as I find release.

And when I get up, meet the eyes of the soldier who caught her and held her for me, I see only respect. But I feel nothing.

I feel nothing as the bodies are tossed into an open grave pit and covered over with dirt. I feel nothing when the men soil the grave with their piss and filth. I feel nothing but impatience as I wait for the vampire.

When he appears, finally, I feel joy. And a little fear.

I know I should be terrified. The creature is so old he carries danger about him like a cloak. The monk feels it, and it frightens him so much I can smell the fear in his sweat. But I feel only a little afraid.

Even when his face opens up and his jaw unhinges and there is a gaping wet maw with long needle fangs descending towards my neck it is mostly gladness I feel. And lust. I get hard as he bites my neck, feel something very much like an orgasm as he drains my blood, and I think I may even ejaculate into my trousers as the life flows out of me.

I am gasping as the memory reaches its end. Retching, but there is nothing left in my belly to come up.

I have to touch my crotch to make sure I haven't come like Alexei did. But I didn't. At least this time I didn't soil myself.

Even though this is not the first time I have seen this memory, I still can't fathom what Karasu was doing there. He was the one who destroyed Alexei when the demon proved too strong, and Alexei too weak. He told me he had no wish to unleash a *koldun* on the world. He offered to take the demon from me, if he could.

So how can it be that he was the one who made Alexei a vampire in the first place?

It makes no sense and I won't get any answers until I can confront Karasu. Assuming I make it out of here alive, and sane. And myself.

I expect to feel the same sense of peace, or completion from this memory as I did from the others, but I don't. It's as if some part of the memory is missing and I can't lay it to rest yet. But Alexei died, so how can there be more?

Stupid boy, the demon says, finally breaking its silence. It sounds weary, diminished, and yet it does not seem worried. *He didn't stay dead, did he?*

Of course not. I had assumed the memory ended there, where the demon stopped it last time. Alexei died prior to being reborn, and I thought it was his death – his first death – that mattered.

But apparently not. Because Alexei was reborn a vampire, and eventually would regain his memories. And then the demon, and madness. And finally he would die for good, burned alive so his ashes could be used to contain the demon.

It was a nasty, glorious death, says the demon.

"It was a necessary death," I say.

I would have gained control eventually, it says.

"I thought you *had* control," I say. "Isn't that why he had to be destroyed?"

No, he says. *I had some control, but mostly he just went the rest of the way crazy. I wasn't yet a proper sentient consciousness. It was years in the jar of ashes, being used a a focus for hexen magic, that gave me my own identity.*

I don't want to admit that I don't really understand, so I say nothing. Anyway, I'm too occupied with trying to figure out how to call up a ghost memory I haven't experienced yet. I need to do it now, before the demon realizes how much I have weakened it.

If I really have weakened it.

I was not much more than a collection of memories, it says, though I didn't ask for clarification. *The only thing I had that was almost an identity was fear, hate, rage, pain. Negative emotion. And the final memory of Alexei's. His lust for power.*

"The witches made you real?"

The demon laughs. *They could feel the power in that jar of ashes, they could feel the collected evil. They thought they could use it to boost their will.*

"They could."

They could, yes. But when they used it on you, they awakened that final memory of Alexei's, and I was truly born.

"It's my fault you exist." It's not a question. I am beginning to understand. And I think I know how to defeat it, to absorb it fully and take away its independent existence.

You and a coven of ignorant hexen. *And Rasputin and Karasu. They all turned me from a crazy, grieving kid who wanted his family to return to greatness into —*

"An evil, sick, disembodied thing."

It laughs again, its chuckle drowning out the other thoughts in my head.

Exactly, it says. *I am Alexei, in all the ways that matter. And soon I will be Evgeny.*

"You will never be me," I say, and direct my thoughts away from that core of who I am that I have locked up tight in my heart. Or I *hope* I have locked up tight.

Then I'll just be Alexei wearing Evgeny's body, it says. *Either way works for me.*

"You're not Alexei, either. Alexei was human, at least, and you are a monster."

Alexei was never human, any more than you are. He was born a witch, like you. Then he was made a vampire. Like you.

"How did he survive that?" I need to keep the demon distracted until I figure out how to pull forth that last bit of memory. And I have to admit, I *am* curious. It shouldn't have been possible, especially since he was never very strong to begin with.

How did you? the demon says.

"I don't know. Maybe because I was fed with witch blood right from my first feeding."

Your father vamp fed you the blood of your own family.

I've always been grateful I don't remember that actually happening, though I know it is true.

Rasputin did the same with Alexei.

"Alexei's family was already dead."

Another laugh, rich with mirth. It makes me nauseated to hear it.

One other survived for a time. The youngest princess.

There is nothing for me to say, but I try to find something, to keep the demon distracted. As it turns out, I don't need to.

Now don't you want to relive his final moments? So you can prepare in case it ends up being your fate, as well?

And he shows me the rest of the memory, and I don't resist. I don't fight it. In fact, I welcome it.

Chapter Nineteen

THE MEMORY OF Alexei's rebirth passes quickly, not quite like fast-forwarding a movie, but close enough. It is familiar, somewhat, because I went through the process myself. There is a memory gap – I don't think any vampire remembers the actual awakening from death to new life. And it is a new life, because unlike in fiction, vampires aren't really dead – or undead. We die briefly, the symbiont remakes us, and we return to life. Without the symbiont, we just stay dead. Sometimes that's true even with the symbiont, if the host is too weak.

The first few days of new life are blank. A new vampire is mindless, merely a body that feeds. It is why we are so dangerous, and so vulnerable, during the first part of our new life. It is why new vampires without a parent to care for them seldom make it to the next stage.

Alexei did make it, but he has no memory of feeding on his own sister, assuming the demon was right about that. For several more days after that, he is full of hunger and lust, but he is also thinking, conscious, regaining his pre-death memories.

Karasu does not seem to be around, but instead Alexei has the monk to care for him, to feed him and to encourage him to remember who he once was.

I did not have a parent vampire at this stage, either, except at the very beginning. Instead, I had Su. I carefully set thoughts of her aside. My own memories have no place here, and that one is precious and I don't want it tainted.

He remembers in bits and flashes, but his thoughts never settle into a coherent whole. He is conscious and sentient, but his mind is fragmented. Sometimes, he is Alexei, and sometimes he is a blank slate, a being without identity. Sometimes he believes he is the demon, though the demon had no separate existence then.

The monk paces back and forth in front of the cell he has locked Alexei in. Metal bars make up the front of it, thick wooden walls the back. Through Alexei's eyes, I can see that the cage is the back half of a one-room cottage. The tiny windows are covered in heavy blankets. A dark-haired, haunted-looking woman in clothing that looks to have been brightly-colored, once, sits in a rocking chair next to the open fireplace, nursing a baby.

My grandfather, I think, if I have the dates right. I know nothing about him. Dad never said much about his family, but there he is, my father's father, hair as black as the night sky. I realize with a shock that the woman who holds him so tightly – my Great Grandmama, she must be – is chained to her chair by a metal cuff around one ankle. Her leg is raw and sore-looking, as if she has tried to escape more than once.

The monk paces and rants, but I don't understand his words. I recognize Russian, but I am trapped in Alexei's thoughts, and there is something broken in his mind, something that turns his native language into gibberish.

I roar in frustration, and the woman winces, hunches into herself. She does not try to put herself between the vampire and her child, though. She looks as if she both loves and hates the tiny boy, like part of her can't help nurture her offspring, but another part of her wants to reject him. And when she looks up at me, at Alexei, the flash of hatred and terror in her eyes tells me why.

Time passes in flashes and fragments. Alexei grows stronger in body, more fragile in mind. The monk grows more ragged-looking, thinner, he never seems to stop pacing. The woman, too, grows thinner and more haggard, but the fear and hatred only grow stronger.

The child grows bigger. He is quiet and solemn, and stares at me with bright blue eyes. He has no fear.

And then, a chain of memories that almost form a coherent whole.

Something sets Alexei off, and a fireworks show of anger and frustration explodes behind my eyes. I grab at the bars of the cage, roar and scream. I am barely aware of the woman, on the floor, scrambling backward, dragging the chair behind her. The child, just old enough to stand on his own, stares at me, unmoving from where she has pushed him, near the door.

The monk tries to placate me and I reach through the bars, grab him by his filthy hair, and smash his face into the metal. He gurgles and I lick at his blood.

"*Niet*," he says, barely coherent, and for a moment I am startled into inaction because I understand him. "No." It did not sound like gibberish.

But I smell his fear and it makes me hungry. His head doesn't fit between the bars of my cage, so I make it fit. He stops gurgling but now I can reach the artery in his neck and drink my fill. He tastes strange, but good.

When I am finished I no longer hunger for blood, but I have a different hunger. I see the woman on the floor.

"Wife," I say.

She whimpers, tries to scuttle farther backwards, but the chair catches on the bricks of the hearth and traps her.

"Nikolai," she says, not to me, but to the child. "Go now. Run."

The boy glances at her, at the door, then resumes staring at me.

"Wife," I say.

"Run," she whispers.

"I want to fuck," I say. "I need to fuck." I rattle the bars of my cage, testing them. I am stronger now. Stronger than any witch, any vampire.

I am a *koldun* now, I remember. I am powerful.

"Come here, wife." I think I could probably rip this cage apart with my hands, but the woman crawls forward, dragging the chair. She is saying something under her breath, but I do not know the language. She sounds like she is cursing me, even as she is forced by my will to do as I say.

In the monk's pocket, she finds keys. She unlocks the manacle from her ankle, and tries to flee, to run, pushing the boy ahead of her, out the door.

"Wife," I say again and she stops in the doorway. The boy has vanished into the dark.

She tries to fight me, but she can't. She turns, and the hate in her look nearly overwhelms her fear.

"Even before the demon," she spits out, "You were no proper husband."

I ignore her words. So long as she does what I want, I do not care what she says. I make her unlock the cell, get on her knees and open my trousers. The stench of my unwashed body is overwhelming, even to me, and she gags when I put my hand on her head and push her to my crotch.

"Do your wifely duty," I say, and she takes me in her mouth, still gagging.

My stench is too much for her. She vomits and can't suck properly. I pull her away by her hair, look down at her. Her hate is almost a physical force, but my lust is stronger. There is a table in the cottage, so I bend her over it and take her. Halfway through, she stops struggling and I think I may have broken her. It doesn't matter. I am satisfied, and I leave the house behind. She may live, she may not. It does not matter to me.

I think about hunting the boy. He is young, and would taste good. He is like me, a witch, and will make me stronger. I have forgotten, if I ever knew, how terribly witch blood affects vampires. How it is poison.

I follow his trail for a few moments, but then I stop. I can't say why, exactly, but I have a feeling that even though the boy is somehow *mine*, he is not for hunting.

Then the memory fragments again. There are flashes of fire, of dark caves, of blood and violence. I am at the center of countless scenes of destruction and it is glorious. To Alexei.

I feed and fuck and maim, and grow stronger, but the moments of clarity grow farther and farther apart. Whatever sense of self, whatever consciousness had begun to return after my rebirth seems now to be crumbling, disintegrating, breaking up. I have memories of dying, of being beaten, raped, tortured, that are not my memories. I can no longer tell what is me and what is not. And I don't care. I just want to feed my hunger.

Then one clear scene, like a bright drop of dew in a spiderweb mess of thought strands: a lean, straight man of great age who carries danger around him like a cloak; and a short, muscular man who seems only a dwarfed human, but feels somehow more deadly even than his companion. They stand in front of me, blocking my path, but they are not looking at me, they are facing each other.

The small man bares his teeth a little as he speaks, as if he is very, very, angry. "You said you would save the boy, not make him… this."

The taller man, a vampire like me, but nothing like me, replies. "I did save him."

"And made him a *koldun*. And mindless."

"Giving him rebirth was the only way to save his life." He holds out his hands, like he's pleading, but there is nothing contrite in his posture.

"You let the magician have him first, and you let the magician have him after. *You* brought this into the world." And when he says the word "this" he gestures at me.

I growl, but they ignore me.

"Could you have killed him?" the vampire asks.

The dwarf's anger softens, but only a fraction. "Alexei, no. Not before the monk got to him. Rasputin should never have been allowed to grow so powerful."

"No one knew he *was* powerful. No one thought a human could wield magic at all."

"Then we all failed." The dwarf's anger is nearly gone.

"So what do we do?" Now the vampire looks at me. So does the dwarf. The small man's gray eyes burn, and faint traces of light flicker across his skin.

"He is not Alexei anymore," says the dwarf.

"I don't think he has been more than mere fragments of Alexei since his rebirth."

"I'm surprised he survived it at all."

The two of them contemplate me, like I am an animal in a zoo, or a specimen in a jar. Whatever tentative sense of self I have remaining feels fear, but it is soon overwhelmed by mindlessness. I lunge for the dwarf.

A merc flick of his fingers holds me still. A flutter of wings and a raven lands on each of his shoulders.

"No, little one," the dwarf says, and something in his voice makes me very cold. "You cannot drink of me."

He turns to the vampire. "This is your mess, old friend." The way he says "friend" gives the word a meaning I don't understand, would probably not understand even if I was in my right mind. Even if I still *had* a right mind.

"The boy we all loved is long gone," he says, and the ravens ruffle their wings, settle more firmly on his shoulders.

"Don't make me do this, Wolfram," the vampire says. The name "Wolfram" sends a flutter of recognition through me, but I don't know why.

So that's why he scared me, says the demon, so quiet, so faded, I barely hear it.

"You made this mess," says the dwarf. "You will clean it up."

"I won't," says the vampire, suddenly. He jerks his chin up, like a child defying a parent. "You can't make me."

"I *can* make you," says the dwarf. Out of the shadows two wolves emerge to lie at his feet. They are each bigger than he is. "You know very well I can, though I would rather not have to."

"Don't use your pets to threaten me."

The dwarf shrugs and the ravens launch from his shoulders, circle once, and vanish in a swirl of blue light. The wolves melt back into the dark, leaving only tracers of light on the backs of my eyeballs. "I hardly need them for that," he says.

They stare at each other for a long moment, while I struggle against the invisible force that holds me still.

"Alexei is gone," the dwarf finally says. "And in his place we have a mindless monster. This creature you hoped would be a *koldun* is only a force of destruction."

The vampire's shoulders slump, but only a little. So little that one would have to be very observant – supernaturally observant – to notice.

"He has killed and maimed not only humans," the dwarf waves a hand, as if to indicate the surrounding countryside, "but your own kind as well."

The vampire's nostrils flare.

"You know it is true," the dwarf says. "He has drained other vampires, werewolves, even witches. And though he has not yet killed any of *my* folk, he has come far closer than I like."

"So you do it," says the vampire.

The dwarf shakes his head. "I can make you," he says. "But I won't. I know you well enough to know you clean up your messes, old friend." This time, "friend" seems to mean exactly that and nothing more. "And I know you look after your own."

He pauses, and they look into one another's eyes, as if some unspoken communication is going on.

"This is your mess," the dwarf says again. "And this creature is *not* Alexei. You killed Alexei with your own teeth."

At that, the vampire gives in. He does not move; not even his shoulders slump any farther. But it is apparent that he has accepted the dwarf's words as fact.

"I know," the vampire says. "I was … hoping to spare him this."

"You were hoping to spare *yourself*."

"That, too."

The dwarf turns to go, and I am free to move again, but only until the vampire grips my arms with a hand like steel cables and looks into my eyes and says, "Stay." I have to choice but to stay.

"Wolfram," he says, and the dwarf turns. "You are a harder man than ever your grandsire was."

The dwarf snorts. "You never met the old one-eyed bastard."

"Neither did you."

"I like to think he's keeping track. Of Thea at least. Everyone loves my beautiful sister." There is bitterness in his words that the vampire seems to understand, but I do not.

Holy fuck, the demon says quietly in my head. *It's true.* I almost remember that I am not this creature I inhabit, but I don't understand what he means, so I ignore him.

Then fragments again. The vampire builds a great pyre on the bank of a river, while I stand still, unable to do anything but wait. I no longer care to do anything but wait. My belly growls, but I do not know why. My stomach hurts, and my member grows hard, painful, then sags again. It means nothing.

I wait.

The pyre grows.

The vampire pours something on the wood that stings my nose. He is very careful not to splash the liquid, or to touch it with his bare hands.

When the pyre is ready, he stares at it, scowls, and shakes his head. "No," he says. "No."

Then he takes my hand and leads me along the river. We walk and walk and every now and then we pause and I wait while he stares at a stretch of gravel or a patch of sand.

Finally, we reach a place where there is a sand bar in the river, not too far from the bank. It is clear of anything, of leaves, branches, detritus. Only clean, pale sand with some gravel and rocks along the outermost edge.

"Here," he says, and he directs me to lie on the sand bar, exactly in the middle.

"Stay," he says. "Wait."

So I do.

I don't see where he goes, but I can feel him nearby, his feeling of threat, of danger, his cloak of horror barely diminished from when he was right next to me. I did not really feel it as fear before, but now I do. Now the scattered pieces of my mind seem to come together into something like a thinking person and I am afraid.

This is it, Evgeny, says the demon.

Who is Evgeny? I wonder as I stare up at the night sky, watch the thin clouds scud away, leaving the stars bright above me. The Milky Way is so white it hurts my eyes, and I feel the stars like tiny pinpricks of heat on my exposed skin.

Am I Evgeny?

"I'm sorry, Alexei," I hear the vampire whisper from wherever he is hiding.

Am I Alexei, then?

To the east, the sky is no longer as dark as it was. I can sense the sun, just below the horizon, and that fills me with something. The need to flee, to hide, to find a dark place. But I don't know why.

Why do I fear the sun? As a child, I remember it on my skin. I spent too much time indoors. As a royal, I was sheltered anyway, but as a hemophiliac, and delicate, I had to take extra care. Running about wild outdoors was not for one like me, even if the sun were plentiful in Russia, which it was not always, especially in winter.

But I do remember it, streaming in the big windows of one palace or another, casting shadows. Sometimes my sisters would make shapes of those shadows with their hands, tell stories of magical rabbits, or the witch Baba Yaga, or firebirds and dragons.

Yes, Alexei. That *was* my name. I was a prince, and happy, even when my sisters teased me, even when I was confined to my bed by illness.

And I loved the sun.

I watch the glow in the east spread, turn the sky blue, as blue as… whose eyes were bright blue? Mine?" No, a quiet little boy. I push the thought aside.

The first rays of sun knife through the trees, gloriously bright, and I smile, eager for the brilliant star to make its way higher so it can touch me, warm my skin.

Because I am cold. So cold. I am in the deep forest somewhere, in the middle of a river, and there is a chill in the air, early spring, perhaps. It bothers me that I can tell what season it is, though I couldn't say why it should matter. I am lying on cold, damp sand, and I can feel the temperature of the water nearby. I wonder if the cold will kill me. My nurses always warned about dressing properly for the cold. It bites and weakens and kills, the cold.

Why am I not properly dressed for it? I wear only ragged cloth, dark, but so filthy I can't tell what color it once was. And I stink.

Nurse said one should bathe, at least once a week. I think it has been far longer than that for me.

I struggle out of the dirty clothes and toss them aside. They land in the river and float away before I think about keeping them to put back on when they are clean. Now I am naked in the wilderness, with nothing to cover me.

Too late now. Surely there must be someone around with a coat, spare clothes, a hot drink. We never went anywhere without servants, and food, horses and dogs, a carriage. Beds. Even hunting, there were spare horses, and tents, and bedding. Not that I was allowed to actually hunt.

I crawl across the sand to the water. It is so cold it numbs me, but I splash myself, scrub with the sand, until I am clean enough even my old nurse would approve. Then I crawl back to the middle of the sandbar and lie back down. I am to wait here, and I do not question why.

Someone will find me soon, I am sure of it, and in the meantime, I will watch the sun rise and enjoy the feel of it on my skin.

The sky is nearly all blue now, like summer, except for the temperature. I can almost see the bright disk through the trees, but it is not quite high enough yet to reach me. It lights up the trees on the far side of the river, crawling slowly down their length.

When it strikes the water, it dazzles my eyes and I smile. It is so beautiful.

Then it crosses the sandbar and touches me, slides across my skin. For the barest moment, it is gloriously warm and I bask and stretch and grin foolishly. Finally, I am warm.

And then it burns. The heat grows so slowly I don't realize it at first. It is simply uncomfortable, like a sunburn. Then it grows scorching and I scream. My skin blackens and curls and I cannot describe the agony.

There is a moment when it stops. The pain stops, my nerve endings burned away, maybe. But it just moves deeper, burning away flesh and muscle and I can't scream anymore, because I have no throat. And then there is only blackness.

The demon flutters in my mind, weakly, like a moth in a jar, and then it curls like smoke and vanishes. I do not quite hope it is truly gone, but it feels like it might be.

For a while, I can't remember who I am. Alexei? Yes.

No. I tentatively reach out in my thoughts and touch the place I imagined hiding my deepest self. My heart.

I am Evgeny.

And I am crying again, though my body feels dry as a husk.

I am Evgeny, but for a moment, living that memory of death by sunlight, I was Alexei. Alexei was still trapped inside the monster, and right at the end, he came to himself again.

Right at the end, it might have been possible to save him.

Chapter Twenty

MY THROAT IS RAW from screaming, and I'm sobbing again, heaving, but have no tears left to shed.

But there are strong arms around me, and a kind voice murmuring words I don't understand. I curl towards the warmth of the person who holds me, seeking comfort with the instincts of a child, not caring that I don't recognize whomever it is.

I don't feel the burn of the sun, of my own flesh glowing with heat like coals in a dying fire, but the memory of it is raw and I know it will struggle to the surface if I dwell on it. So I listen to the murmuring voice and gradually realize that it's not that he's speaking too low for me to make out words, but that it's a language I don't know.

It reminds me of one time Magne stubbed his toe – his name brings feelings of safety – and he swore in a language that sounded like it was *Beowulf.* This isn't quite the same, but the rhythms are similar, the way the consonants and vowels fit together. I try to cling to the memory, but it slips away. Then I realize I *do* recognize this voice, though it isn't especially familiar.

I pull away, to regain some composure, and he lets go.

"So you survived," he says. The blue designs flicker up his forearms and make his eyes glow ghostly. There is a faint, warm glow from elsewhere in the room, like sunlight filtered through many, many layers of clouds, only it can't be, because I don't feel heat.

"Did I?" I say. I'm honestly not sure.

He smiles, puts a hand on my shoulder, and squeezes. "You did."

We are sitting on stone, me next to a wall, and he crouched in front of me. This must be the same room, but no longer dark, and there is a heavy wooden door standing open, next to me, set deep in the wall. Across the room are my soiled shirt and my shoes.

I can't say anything else for a while, but Wolfram doesn't seem to mind. He hands me a glass bottle.

"Drink this. Troll says it's good for restoring fluids and nutrients."

The liquid in the bottle looks like tea, smells like herbs and honey, and tastes like nothing I can describe. I sip tentatively, feel the liquid soothe my raw throat, and then gulp the rest down, greedy for moisture.

Then I slump back against the wall and meet the dwarf's eyes. His look is kind and curious, but he waits for me to speak.

"At the end," I say. "Right before he burned, Alexei was… he was himself." I swallow, throat suddenly dry again. "Was that real, or was that the demon?"

I think I see sorrow shadowing his eyes, turning them a deeper gray.

"I don't know," he says. "But I don't think the demon was capable of manufacturing memories."

"So he didn't need to die," I say. My emotions are raw, unbalanced, and I have to choke back a sob. "He didn't need to burn alive."

Wolfram shakes his head. He shifts on the floor to sit next to me. "Even if he was himself for a moment, at the end, Alexei was never strong enough." He leans back, head turned to watch me. "More likely, it was the demon's final revenge on whomever it would possess next, allowing Alexei to awaken for a moment. To wound them, as it has wounded you, with the thought that maybe we were wrong, and made an innocent young man suffer a terrible death.

"But don't forget, Alexei wasn't so innocent, by then. He did some terrible things in full awareness of what he was doing, before he was ever haunted by a demon-ghost, before he was made a vampire. He was not innocent of the crimes of his army of torturers.

"Karasu gave him rebirth," I say. "Why?"

"He was interested in your family, in the possibilities of… what he called *elevating* the beings we call *other*. Of making an essentially non-magical – if extraordinary – being into a creature of true magic."

"He told me he had no wish to unleash a *koldun*. It's why he agreed to help me. I thought."

Wolfram sighs. "I have never known Karasu to lie outright, at least not to me, but he does not always tell the full truth. And he has reasons of his own for everything he does.

"Back then, many of us – *others* and not – were interested in that family. Your family. Alexei, sick as he was, had the potential for great power as a witch, and it is not unknown for witches to learn true magic." He pauses, frowns. "As it is not entirely unknown for vampires."

"Like Karasu can become mist, or take the form of a wolf."

"He showed you that? Yes, he believes all *others* once possessed true magic, and he's spent his life trying to learn how to get it back. One of his aims in the work he did to divide his kind into two – into what became vampires and werewolves – was to divide the magic from the symbiont. Back then, he believed it could be done with alchemy."

I rub my face with my hands. I feel like I could sleep for a week, but I also feel like I'm just waking up. I never have woken up easily.

"With Alexei, he thought he would try using magic to beget more magic."

"Did he have anything to do with creating the demon?" It's a horrifying thought, that I could have entrusted my life to someone who would do such an evil thing.

But Wolfram shakes his head. "He didn't know, I think, how the monk intended to create the demon. He didn't think the monk was even capable of it. Rasputin was merely human, after all."

He shifts his position on the floor again, and I wonder if he is uncomfortable physically, or if it's only the discomfort of memory.

"He did, however, do nothing to stop the slaughter once he knew about it. It is not something I will ever forgive him for."

"*Could* he have stopped it?"

"Not without creating bloodshed of his own, but he could have tried.

He could have attempted to dissuade Alexei. He was the only one apart from the monk that Alexei might have listened to. And the blood he would have had to shed to stop the slaughter himself would not have been that of innocents."

"Instead, he helped Alexei. Made him into a vampire."

"And disappeared into the forest so he wouldn't have to watch what he had unleashed."

"Couldn't *you* have stopped him?"

"To my shame, I believed he was guarding Alexei, keeping him safe, not trying to make him into a sorcerer."

"It's so senseless."

"It was."

We are silent for a while, and I feel around inside my head for the demon. It is quiet.

"Is it gone?" I say at last. "The demon?"

Instead of answering, Wolfram leans towards me and puts his hands on either side of my face. I meet his eyes, and suddenly I can't look away.

"Let me in," he says. "I don't want to make you."

I don't know what he means until I feel a force push gently against my mind. For a panicky moment, I resist. I've have enough other consciousnesses rummaging around in my head. I didn't like it when the *hexen* poked around in my mind, and I didn't like sharing a brain with the demon. But something makes me trust Wolfram. And something tells me he *could* force his way in if he wanted to.

So I dampen my witch-defenses, open my mind to his. I can feel him sifting through my thoughts, but he's subtle and I wonder if he could even do this without me being aware of his presence at all. He doesn't linger, and though I don't like that he can see anything in my mind, let alone my private thoughts and memories, he is somehow not as invasive as I would have thought.

When he leans back and drops his hands, there is a hint of relief and sadness in his expression. "It's gone."

"I expected more of a fight," I say. "It almost feels anti-climactic."

He smiles. "What you went through wasn't hard enough?"

I can't help but smile back, though I don't feel very jovial.

"Why do you look so sad, then?" I say.

He looks briefly startled, like I've seen something he thought he was hiding from me. "The demon is gone, but it has left you changed."

"Changed how?" I feel cold settle in my belly.

He shakes his head. "That will be for you to discover."

When I open my mouth to protest, he holds up a hand. "I can tell you that when you arrived here, I sensed a gentleness in you, much like Alexei had before the monk corrupted him. There is very little of it left."

"That doesn't seem a big loss."

"Maybe not. But I'm sure you'll find you've changed in other ways, too."

"Will I… will I enjoy the things the demon liked?"

Another smile. "The violence and pain? I don't think so. That much of yourself, you kept safe. But be cautious when you return to the world. You are still you, but you will have a new perspective, and that can make you seem a very different person."

"So am I a sorcerer now? A *koldun*?"

"Well, you are neither dead nor insane."

"So am I?"

"I suppose you are. What exactly that means, we will have to wait and see."

"We?"

"You have the potential to be more powerful than any *other*, perhaps more powerful than some of those who shelter here, on Wonder Island. So I plan to keep tabs on you."

"Will I be as powerful as Karasu?"

He laughs. "Do you want to be?"

"I'm not sure I care."

"Good," he says. "Now let's get you a bath and clean clothes and food before we send you home. I believe your friends will soon be tired of cotton candy and Ferris wheel rides, which they are only pretending to enjoy in the first place to be polite and not offend their hosts."

"They're here? Magne and… my friends?" Because of course Su is not here. She's in Germany, and doesn't even know I came here.

"They never left. The big werewolf was particularly unhappy to be banned from coming with you."

"How long was I in here?"

"By their reckoning? A couple of hours. By yours? Very much longer."

"How much longer?"

He sighs. "Time is meaningless in this room. Just be glad you didn't age physically for the apparent time you spent here."

I'm too weary to pursue the questioning further, so I get to my feet, gather up my shoes without bothering to put them on, and follow Wolfram out the door and back into real life.

I feel the eyes of Wonder Island's denizens on me as I follow Wolfram back through the market to a door marked "Staff Only." Su would have looked around her, curious about these people, who they were, *what* they were. She was not always very social, but she was interested in everything, including people.

Something in the feelings that come up in me when I think about her has changed. I can't really figure out what, and I'm afraid to examine it too closely, not here with strange people all around me. My love for her has not diminished – I can feel it burning strongly in my heart. But something is different. It frightens me.

I don't linger over bathing or food, and Wolfram does not seem offended when I don't want to talk. His expression tells me he probably understands what I'm going through better than anyone I know.

As we leave the staff area to walk back to the ferry to meet Magne and Cara – not surrounded by a flock of thin, pale, silent Islanders this time, I finally say, "I don't want to see Karasu."

Wolfram nods. "I told him you probably wouldn't."

I almost trip. "You knew there would be a memory of him killing Alexei?" I don't specify *which* killing I'm referring to, but I suspect Wolfram will know it was the first one that was the real betrayal. Though the fact that Alexei was lucid at the end is no small matter, either.

"I had no idea what your confrontation with the demon would be like. If I had, I could have prepared you better. But I suspected that you would learn the full story of Alexei's making and unmaking during the process." He walks quietly beside me for several steps.

"You will have to confront him eventually," he says. "If only to clear the air between you."

I shake my head. "I don't need him."

He smiles. "I understand how you feel. More than you might suspect. But Karasu knows more about *koldun* than anyone else alive. You may need his expertise in the days ahead."

"I don't feel as if I have become something else. Will I change?"

"Probably. What this ordeal has done is create potential. Maybe your full power – whatever that will be – will hit you all at once. More likely, it will develop slowly. The more you use your abilities, the more they will grow."

We walk the rest of the way in silence. Magne and Cara are waiting by the dock. Magne leans casually against a gate post, finishing off a caramel apple, while Cara stands next to him, looking uncomfortable, picking at a cone of purple spun sugar.

Suddenly, I want to run the other way. I don't know what to say to them, and seeing them again, normal and solid and loyal, I feel utterly changed, like we no longer have anything in common and I don't know how to act around them.

Magne doesn't say anything, but he tosses the stick from his apple – he even ate the core – into a garbage can and grabs me in a hug. I realize with surprise that when we came to this island, I would have felt his hug as bone-crushing, even a bit painful. But now, though it's the same not-aware-of-his-own-strength embrace it would have been before, it is no more painful than the hug of a child. Magne feels somehow… smaller.

Or I feel bigger, stronger, forceful. I'm not sure I like it.

He pulls back, grinning, then grabs my face and shakes me. "You made it."

I pull away, and see his eyes darken a shade in surprise, the grin fades. He steps back.

"Sorry," he says. "I got carried away. I should have asked how you are."

"No," I say. "I'm sorry. I thought I felt exactly the same, but I don't. Things have changed, and I don't know how yet."

His smile creeps back. "Don't worry, we'll cut you some slack."

"The next boat will leave shortly," Wolfram says. He doesn't tell us we should be on it, but I think that for all his generosity, we've probably outstayed our welcome. Or maybe he's nervous about having magic around that doesn't belong on the island.

"Yeah," I say. "We should go. I should sleep." Though I don't really feel sleepy. Just bone tired.

"If you need anything, Evgeny," says Wolfram, "you have only to ask." He hands me a business card and I'm surprised, though perhaps I shouldn't be, to see both a phone number and an email address on it. There's even a website URL.

"Thank you," I say. On impulse, I add, "And please thank Huginn and Muninn and Geri and Freki for me."

Wolfram blinks, smiles, and nods, and then he's gone into the crowd.

As we board the ferry I have to suppress the urge to tell everyone around me to shut up. They're all so noisy and it's not until we're out on the river that I realize that not all the noise is in my ears. A lot of it is in my head. I wish we had the boat to ourselves the way we did on the way to the island.

I find the quietest corner I can and it's not until I turn and find Magne behind me that I realize I didn't say anything before walking away. Is this one of the ways I've changed? Become rude and inconsiderate?

"Sorry," I mumble, and Magne just shakes his head.

We stare over the water, watching Wonder Island recede. Magne watches me while trying to pretend not to. His concern is touching, but it's getting irritating. Cara seems to be trying to hide behind him. She still hasn't said anything.

Finally, I say, "What's wrong with you?"

She flinches. "Nothing," she says. I know instantly that she's lying. Perhaps it is one of my new abilities.

"Please don't lie to me," I say. I think my voice is reasonable, but Magne frowns.

"Jesus, Ev. Some tact might be in order."

I bite back the reply I almost snap at him. Something seems to be worrying him more than just my sudden descent into assholery. And I can't deny I'm being an ass. I just wish I could see it *before* the words come out.

"Sorry," I mumble. Then, "But there's obviously something wrong. She's avoiding even looking at me."

"*She* has a name," says Cara. "And she's standing right here."

"You're afraid of me," I say, and I can hear the astonishment in my own voice as I realize it. "Why?"

She takes her time answering and I can almost hear her thoughts as she tries to find the right words. She's a witch, and has good mental defenses, so I can't *actually* hear her mental processes, but I think maybe I could, if I pushed. But I don't. I refuse to let the demon change me so.

"Mathilde," she says, and I must sneer, because she flinches again, but hides it better this time. "When she had us – all the *hexen* – use… Well, when she wanted us to destroy you, she told us what you might become." She stares at me, nostrils flaring like it's a real act of bravery to face me. And maybe it is.

"She told us what a *koldun* was. And now you are one."

I laugh, a brittle sound. "I would never have become whatever it is I am now without her meddling. It was your use of Great Grandpapa's ashes that gave the demon true consciousness. And it was your use of it on me that let the demon into my head in the first place. Whatever I have become is your fault."

The words come out cold and I think that might be worse than if I was angry. Is this the loss of gentleness Wolfram mentioned? I'm not sure I like this person I have become.

"*Not* her fault," says Magne, putting himself between us. He's big, but he no longer seems so huge to me. "Blame Mathilde, but Cara was on our side once she found out."

I shrug, then turn away. "Whatever."

"Ev…"

I turn back to face him.

"We are your friends," he says.

"I know," I say. "I do know that. But whatever happened back there, it made me different. I'm not being an asshole on purpose. And I'm trying to stop being one. I just… I have to get used to this."

"Will you tell us what happened?" His voice is soft. It's always been a deep, smoked-whiskey sort of voice, and with the quieter volume, I just want to relax into it and listen to him, let his voice, and his arms, shield me from myself. "Not right now, but eventually?"

"Yeah," I say, "Maybe sometime." But I when he says "us," I think of him and Su. Cara is too new, even if she has been here since I first met the demon. I don't think I will ever trust her, and I'm certain she will never trust me.

I look out at the river without really seeing it. The ferry slows and swings around to approach the dock, and I can feel every change in the engine and in the current. There is too much information flooding into my head. Too much crowding my senses, too many threads of other people's thoughts, too many traces of strange magic. Only Magne is like a solid block of comfort. I feel him next to me, but he's like a foundation rather than something poking at my brain.

Then a tickle of something else. Beyond Magne, but closer that all those other thoughts. I look at Cara, and I see more of her than she is likely aware of. My mouth opens on its own and my voice speaks, but at least this time I'm not being a dick. Not entirely.

"Oh God, Magne," I say. I don't know why I speak to him and not Cara. Maybe because I barely know her, and Magne is my friend. "I'm so sorry."

He looks confused. "It's –" I think he starts to say it's okay, though he doesn't know what *it* is.

Then I look at Cara again. "Your witch blood," I say. "It's fighting them, the werewolf in them." It doesn't make sense. Werewolf children are born human. The symbiont isn't transmitted, even mother-to-child except in very rare instances, so how could Magne's children even be werewolf? It's not genetic, like witch heritage is. And these two clumps of cells inside Cara aren't yet even anything that could be called "children." But that's what my new sense are telling me, it's what Cara's magic is whispering to me.

"You're going to lose the twins," I say. And then I throw up everything Wolfram fed me.

Chapter Twenty-One

THROWING UP BLOOD makes the people closest to us back away in horror, like maybe I have one of those diseases that eat you alive from the inside.

One man insists he's a doctor and tries to help, and only Magne's assurance that we're on the way to the hospital – and him picking me up bodily and carrying me off the boat – can get the man to leave us alone.

I suppose it's nice that a stranger cares.

When we reach my apartment, Magne doesn't want to leave me alone. Cara, I can tell, would like nothing better. But I can't be near people right now. Too many of their secrets are whispering at me. Not their actual thoughts so much as what their bodies know that their minds don't, though sometimes I can hear thoughts, too.

Cara's pregnant, but her body wants to reject the embryos. I know – somehow, some inexplicable way – that it won't reject them outright yet, not until they've grown enough to show, but not so grown that they could survive outside her body, even with the best hospital care. I want to tell her to spare herself, and Magne – especially Magne – the sorrow, to abort before the two of them get used to the idea of being parents, but how can I say that to them?

Magne's body is telling me has hasn't been out of the city enough lately, running as a wolf. Cara has kept him busy, not by being demanding, but by being the focus of his lust, maybe even of his love. He has been too caught up in her, and ignoring his werewolf nature. It's making him unwell. But I can't tell him that, either, that his girlfriend is negatively affecting his health.

From strangers, these details would be amusing but meaningless, but I can't handle it from my friends. It feels like I'm spying on them. I need to be alone until I can learn to mute this new ability.

I'm not sure my explanation makes all that much sense, but I think Magne understands, at least a little, so he leaves me, after making sure I have a well-stocked fridge and enough money to pay the rent – thanks to his foresight I already have both. Then he leaves, promising to come back every few days to check on me. I want to hug him as he leaves, to show him physically what I can't put into words, but I don't. I don't want to seem too needy.

Alone in my dark apartment, I spend a lot of time just lying on the couch, staring at the ceiling. Not thinking, just staring. I let the thoughts of the people downstairs drift through my brain, and slowly, I learn how to shut them out. It's not so different from managing my older witch abilities, my thought-probing power and my ability to shut out other witches. Once I get the hang of it, it quickly becomes automatic. So I venture outside at night, walk among people, and I'm okay. I can ignore them or read them as I wish, almost without thinking about it.

And I can distinguish regular humans and *others* easily, just by shifting my attention. To my new senses, *other* and human are surprisingly alike, and true magic strands apart from both like bright flares in smoke. There is more of that magic in the world than I would have thought, and I begin to practice reading the people who carry it. I am careful, because I'm unfamiliar with what beings I might meet, and I quickly realize that if they realize I am noticing them, most of them vanish into the crowd, their bright flames doused and hidden from view. So I learn to hide my own flame, too. And eventually, I can find many of the magic folk even when they are hiding.

Twice a week, Magne checks on me. It's the only way I realize time has passed. After the first week, he tells me Su is due back from Germany soon.

"I don't think I can see her," I say. "Not yet." I am afraid I won't be able to resist using my new abilities on her, to read her, to learn things even she might not know.

Magne shakes his head. "Don't break her heart," he says. What he doesn't say is that his own heart is breaking, and at least part of it is my fault. I try not to read him, but I want to know how he is, need to know he is well, and I don't quite dare ask. I can't ask without admitting I can read him, and I don't want him to mistrust me, even if I deserve it.

But I can tell he's unhappy, that he has not forgotten what I said on the ferry. I want to explain, and I think maybe he wants to ask, but he doesn't. At least I can tell Cara hasn't lost the pregnancy yet, though it would be easier for them both if she did.

"I just need time to figure out what I am now," I say.

"And what are you?" he says, "besides the Evgeny she loves as much as breathing? You haven't said anything about Wonder Island. Except –" He stops before he mentions what I said to Cara.

"I'm your friend," he says, as if he hasn't said it over and over this past week. "And Su loves you. You don't have to do everything alone." He says it as if this time, I'll remember, I'll listen to him and let him help. I want to. I want to curl up in his lap, crawl into Su's arms when she gets home, and let my loved ones take care of me. But I can't.

"I don't know what I am yet," I say, trying to keep irritation out of my voice. I vowed not to let Wonder Island turn me into an asshole, and Magne doesn't deserve it. So I relent, finally, and tell him a little about being able to hear thoughts, to read people, and how I'm learning to block it out because it's too much to bear. I tell him I don't know yet what else I might learn about myself, what I might now be. And there is no one else that can tell me.

"What about your scary old vampire dude?" he says. "Karasu? He seemed to know a thing or two."

I shake my head, and tell him what I learned about Karasu's involvement with Alexei. I guess telling him that much makes him feel better, because he doesn't press for more. He just says, "You know I can't stop Su from trying to see you." He slaps my shoulder and he still doesn't seem as strong as he once did, and I can't tell if it's a change in him, or a change in me. "But I'll let her know you want to be alone."

And maybe that's something else that's changed in me – wanting to be alone. I used to like people around. Su, Magne, and even just random people on the street. Now I want to be by myself.

But the solitude can't last, of course. Magne sends me a text when Su's plane lands – he just says, "Su's landing," with no mention of Alex or Li. I spend the rest of the day pacing, picking at housework even thought my place is already clean and tidy.

She doesn't appear at my door that night, but I can't settle down. Finally, my unnecessary tidying brings me to my camera. The roll of film with the moth picture on it is still loaded, a few frames still unexposed. Purely for something to do, I rewind the film, then take it to my light-tight bathroom and makeshift darkroom to develop it.

It's amazing how easily I slip back into the rhythm of working with film and it distracts me enough that I wish I had more than one roll to develop.

When I'm done, I pace again, but this time it's because I'm impatient for the film to dry so I can make a contact sheet, and not because I'm worrying about Su.

Once the film is dry, hours pass and I hardly notice, I've become so absorbed in printing. I ignore the city shots for now, and focus on the moth frames. I have a couple of useable images, so I choose the one with the best composition and work on compensating as much as I can for the contrasty light of the street lamp. In the end, it's not an image I would choose as an example of the kind of work I would like to do. I will never be an insect photographer. But it's a good picture and captures the mood I was in at the time.

I'm about to print a second copy, when there's a tentative knock at the door and all at once I realize I have worked through the night and the next day and it is night again. And I know it's her immediately. I have to clamp down on my new senses, because it's almost a reflex to reach out and read her.

Before I can completely shut her out, I read worry – concern for me and fear that things have changed between us. And I can feel that she's free of the bonds Alex accidentally put on her, and worried about Alex, and something has happened to Li. And Su, my beautiful, glorious Su, is so much more powerful than when she left. But most of all, I feel love.

I drop the photograph onto the coffee table where I have left all my test prints spread out and I'm at the door almost without thinking. And maybe that's another new ability: even faster than vampire-fast speed.

For a long moment, an eternity it feels like, I hesitate with my hand on the doorknob, as all my fears and uncertainties and insecurities flood back.

She taps again, a little harder, and I make myself turn the knob, pull open the door. And there she is.

She smiles, uncertain. "Hey," she says.

I smile back, and feel all the love I locked up in my heart, safe from the demon, come pouring out, filling me with warmth down to the ends of my toes. "Hey," I say.

And then she is in my arms, and everything is right with the world again.

But of course that it not true. Everything is not right with the world, and never can be again, but for that moment it feels like it is. Like I am complete again, whole, and happy.

"I missed you," I say, into her hair.

"I hear you got into some trouble without me to keep an eye on you," she says, then she kisses my ear and I have to fight not to flinch. That same ear Jinny bit, and Magne, and Luke.

"You talked to Magne," I say, stepping out of her embrace so she can come inside. The air outside smells crisp and fresh. Su smells warm and wild.

"He picked me up at the airport," she says. "He insisted on telling me the whole story before I came to see you." She smiles. "So I didn't so much talk to him as he talked *at* me. But there's a lot he still doesn't understand."

She looks at me closely. "Like why you insist on going through this alone. Are you all right?"

"I think so," I say. "I will be."

"You really freaked Cara out. She wants Magne to move away with her. Away from here."

I bite my lip. "The words just came out."

"Are they true? Will she miscarry?"

I nod. "I can… I can sort of read things a person's body is broadcasting. It… I could tell what's happening in her."

"Jesus, Ev." She sits on a stool at the kitchen island, looks at me like she doesn't know what to say, like I'm fragile and might break if she uses the wrong words. And maybe she's not wrong. "Magne said you had changed."

"I guess I have." I sit across from her, though what I really want is for her to be in my arms. Her body tells me she wants that, too.

"You seem pretty much the same," she says. "But there *is* something different." She cocks her head, as if trying to decide if she can act towards me as she always has, or if she needs to treat me differently. It wounds me that she needs to think about it.

"Su," I say. "My heart." And she really is my heart, she was when I was dealing with the demon, locked up and safe in the core of my being.

"Tell me," she says. "If you can."

"You tell me first," I say. "I don't think you were sipping beer and eating sausages or whatever tourists do in Germany."

"It's a long story," she says.

"So is mine, but you already heard a good part of it from Magne."

She takes my hand, gently, like she's not certain if her touch is welcome. I lace our fingers together and she relaxes.

"I love you," I say.

She smiles and it lights up her face. "I love you," she says. "Whatever you might be now, I love you."

She stands, walks around the kitchen island, and pulls me to my feet so we can press our bodies together. And then she kisses me, softly at first, and then more insistent. And my body wakes for her. My heart speeds up, my skin warms, and my breath quickens. A shift of her pelvis against mine, and I start to get hard.

"I missed you," she whispers into my mouth.

I don't reply, because I'm too busy tasting her tongue. It feels like she has been gone much longer than… How long *has* she been gone? Two weeks? A month? I have completely lost track of the passage of days. But it feels like she has been gone forever and I have to relearn everything about her, the feel of her skin, the sound of her breathing.

And it feels like no time has passed at all.

I hardly notice that we bump off walls and furniture as we make our way out of the kitchen and across the living room. I only want to get her clothes off, to be close to her.

By the time we sprawl across the bed together, we're naked, even socks abandoned somewhere along the way. I stop, pull away from her a little, and just look at her.

Her hair seems longer than when she left, so long that it flows across the pillow and onto the floor. Her eyes are bright with mischief and desire.

I trace a finger across her jaw, down her neck, and along her collarbone, then flatten my hand to caress her ribcage, her stomach, her breasts. She arches towards my touch, gasps when I slide my hand between her thighs to tease her, stimulate her. She retaliates by grasping my erection and stroking.

I ache for her. I want to savor this, to take my time to explore her all over again, to taste her mouth, her skin, between her legs, to smell her, to feel her from inside and out, but I also want to be inside her right now, to fuck her until the ache goes away.

She's pushing against my hand, her breath quickening, and I slide my fingers inside her, push them deeper when she moans into my ear. Then I slide my fingers out, slide them farther back, and push inside her again. Her breathing changes and a frown touches her face, but she doesn't say anything. I can tell, even if I couldn't read her, that she doesn't really like my fingers in her ass. I pull them out and she relaxes.

"Sorry," I whisper.

She shakes her head. "Worth the try," she says. Then she lets go of me, moistens her fingers in her own fluids and slides her hand between my legs. She raises her eyebrows in a question, touches a fingertip to my anus, and I gasp.

A smile teases the corner of her mouth. "Well," she says, and pushes two fingers slowly in.

I try to bite back the moan that bursts from my throat. "Oh God," I try to say, but I'm pretty sure it's unintelligible.

She shifts her position under me so she can have one hand on my hardness and her other in my ass and for a moment, I can't breathe at all.

"Oh fuck," I say. "Don't stop." Then I say, "No, wait, do stop."

"Changed your mind?" she says, and nibbles my nipple, tugging at the piercing gently.

"Fuck no," I say. "But I want to be inside you. If you keep doing that, I'm going to come all over the place."

She moves her hands away slowly, wraps a leg around mine and looks me in the eyes. She looks at me a little funny, because I really don't swear much, though it's not unheard of. So I kiss her, nibble my way down her neck to her left breast, where I flick my tongue across her nipple, then take it into my mouth and suck.

It's her turn to moan, and she pushes against me, more insistent, rubs against the hand I've slipped between her legs.

"Now, Ev," she says.

I fumble in the bedside table for a condom and tear at the package with my teeth. I can't get it open.

Su laughs, takes it from me, and with an ease that might come from her kung fu practice, or maybe from whatever new strength she gained in Germany, she flips me over onto my back.

She straddles my legs, opens the condom, and checks to make sure it's right side out. Then she leans down and takes me in her mouth, slides her tongue over me.

I tangle my hands in her hair, arch towards her, but she pulls back, sits up, that teasing smile on her mouth. Then she puts the condom on me, unrolls it, and climbs on top of me.

She's about to lower herself onto me, when I say, "No." She stops, cocks her head at me. And it's my turn to flip her onto her back, to lean over her.

"You're mine," I say, fierce, in a voice that sounds more possessive than I ever have before.

"You know I am," she says. "And you're mine."

I look down at her, panting, wanting, and I grab her hair, pin her to the pillow. She looks startled but not worried. Her smile grows, shows teeth, and I pin her tighter and pull her legs apart with my other hand.

"Where'd my shy, gentle boy go?" she says, but she doesn't sound concerned. Her body is still yearning for mine, I can feel it. The hot center of her sex is like a beacon to my new senses.

I growl and she growls back.

I push down on her thigh, maneuver my hips into place and I'm about to slide into her when she says, "Ev? That kind of hurts."

I look at her face and there's a tiny drop of moisture in the corner of her eye, not quite big enough to be a tear.

"Your hand," she says.

My left hand has pinned her head to the pillow at an awkward angle, and my right hand holds her thigh, bent and pressed to the bed. I stare. My nails are digging into her skin and at least one has drawn blood.

"Jesus Christ," I say. "I'm so sorry." I relax, let go, bend and twist to kiss her leg where I've wounded her. "I'm so sorry." I lay my head on her stomach and she strokes my hair.

"I didn't want you to stop, vampire boy," she says. "Just ease up a little."

It's true. Her body still calls to me, muted a little maybe, but still strong. I look into her eyes and she smiles. "I can take it rough," she says. "Just not with actual bloodshed."

"I'm sorry."

"You *have* changed," she says. "You're stronger, more forceful. But I'm stronger, too. I can take you."

The teasing again, gentle, loving. She wraps her legs around me and pulls me towards her. My erection rubs against her soft wetness and then nothing else matters but to be inside her, to feel her climax as I take pleasure in her, to know I've made her feel as good as she's made me feel.

I slide against her, back and forth, feel her excitement and need grow, feel myself pushing past the point of control, then I slide into her, feel her heat surround me, feel the pulse of her body as she comes and cries out and feel my own urgency grow and grow, and it does not break.

I look at her face and suddenly see her as the demon imagined her, bruised and bloody, empty-eyed. And then I feel my climax coming and I can't do this and see her like that.

I pull violently away and maybe I cry out, but I don't come.

"Ev?"

My erection shrivels to nothing and want to throw up, to weep, but it seems the demon took that from me. Maybe that was the gentleness Wolfram said I lost.

Her arms are around me and I want to seek comfort in her, but I can't. I curl into myself.

"When I was... fighting the demon, it made me imagine things."

"The memories," she says. "Magne told me."

"Not this," I say. "I didn't tell Magne this. I *couldn't* tell Magne this. But it... it showed me what it wanted me to do to you. To hit you, to violate you."

I feel her cheek against my back, the silken movement of her hair. "You would never do that, Ev. I know that much about you."

"It... just now, the memory of what the demon imagined doing to you, it came back." I uncurl a little, pull away to sit against the wall. I hadn't realized I'd moved the whole width of the room to get away from that vision. "It's there, that memory. It will always be there." I realize, now, that I can read my own body like I can read other people's, and my body is saying it will remember violence – even violence that never actually happened – whenever I try to make love to her. Maybe when I get intimate with any woman, though there are none who could hope to measure up to my Su.

And that, I realize, is the demon's final revenge, what it meant when it said it had already done its worst.

Chapter Twenty-Two

SU, OF COURSE, is sweet and understanding. Or she tries to be understanding. There's no way she could really understand, though, and I wouldn't want her to, because to do that, she'd have to go through what I went through.

She washes up and gets dressed and we sit side by side on the bed. At first, I don't know what to say, so she tells me about Germany, and how Li was a puppet of a powerful witch and Alex stayed there to learn. And to win Li back.

She tells me she learned about her ancestors – the German *hexenfuchs* ones – but she's still sifting through it all, trying to fit it all into place. Some of the stories she found are like fairytales, she says, so much so that they repeat over and over, the same kinds of events happening to different ancestors until she's not really sure what happened to whom or when.

And she tells me true magic is real, that *other* lore could never explain many of the things that happened to her. Could never explain *her*. And she shows me her tail – twice as big and fluffy as before she left.

Then I am able to tell her what I learned about real magic, to fill in the blanks Magne left in my story, because he didn't know them. I tell her everything. Not in detail – I would spare her that, though she's the only one I've ever told about being raped by an ex-boyfriend so I know it's safe to tell her about what the demon did to me, and what it made me do.

"I wish you'd said something sooner," she said. "I'd have come home."

"I didn't want your help," I say, more harshly than I meant to.

She looks stung, but doesn't reply.

"I couldn't distract you from the things *you* needed to do," I say.

She puts a hand on my knee, then withdraws it. "That's not all," she says.

I wonder if she can read me the way I can read her. I wonder what powers her own ordeal awakened in her.

I look at my hands. I can't face her eyes. "I needed to rescue myself for once," I say.

My new senses let me feel her smile, even though I'm trying to block them, to not read her. I look up. Her eyes are shining with tears, but she holds them in.

"Magne was frantic that he couldn't help you," she says, the smile curving her mouth a little more. "I never doubted your strength."

"I know."

Then she glances away, and I see her notice something. Something about my hands, clasped tight together around my knees. I can't see whatever she's looking at.

She touches my left wrist with a finger and then I know.

"You took it off," she says. "Or did it fall off?"

The bracelet she made me of her hair.

I cover my wrist with my other hand. "I took it off," I say. "It – it connected me too strongly to you. And –"

"You needed to rescue yourself." She nods, but her voice is sad. "Where is it?"

I wonder if she wants it back. After all, it is a part of her, and maybe a *hexen* or a sorcerer – a *koldun*? – could use it against her somehow. I don't answer, but I can't help glancing towards the box on my dresser.

She follows my look. "Ah," she says. She knows what that box is, what it contains, like she knows almost everything else about me.

"So that's it, then?"

I want her to be angry. I *deserve* her anger, but she is only sad. For me, as much as for herself.

Don't break her heart, Magne said. I guess I couldn't help it. Not with what the demon did. But when I put her hair in my box of old memories, had I already decided?

"Su –" I say.

"No, it's okay." She shifts on the bed, moves to sit on the edge. "If we can't… If the demon left you those memories… I understand."

"I love you," I say. "That will never change."

"I know." She doesn't look at me. "Magne said you met someone else. Said he even thought for a while that you cheated on me."

"I didn't cheat on you," I say. I came close, but I didn't. "He doesn't have anything to do with this." I wave my hand in the air as if trying to grasp the right words, words that will make sense, that won't hurt her. "I want to be with *you*. My beloved. My heart."

She smiles sadly, but still doesn't look at me. "You want to, but you can't. The demon's memories, its fantasies, won't let you."

"Yes," I whisper. The word hurts to say.

Then she does look at me. Her eyes are clear, no tears, but they burn amber, fox-bright. "When I brought him up, your other… friend…" She pauses, waiting for something.

"Luke," I say.

"When I brought him up, I wasn't accusing you. I only wanted to say that if you can't be with me, then maybe you can find some happiness with him." She looks away, at the door, like she wants to be gone already. Then she meets my eyes again.

"Is he nice? Is he good to you?"

"I don't really know him that well," I say, and realize with surprise that it's true. I really only know that his presence filled me with lust – and how much of that was the demon? – and that he can make me laugh.

She laughs, a short, bitten-off sound. "Well, get to know him," she says, suddenly fierce. "And if he makes you happy, if your demon memories will let you be with him, then do it." She tilts her chin up, silent now. She stands and walks to the door.

Before she walks out, she says, "I love you, but if this is it, don't expect me to wait for you."

"I won't," I say. I think maybe it is *my* heart breaking, not hers. She was always too good for me.

"If he makes you happy, then be with him, love him, fuck him, and be happy."

Then she's gone, so fast the sound of the door closing recaches me before I realize she has really left.

And, stupidly, all I can think about is that I never showed her the moth photograph.

But I can't really be with Luke, can I? He's human and I'm not. I'm even less human that I was when I first kissed him.

I think about going back to work. I will have to, eventually, to be able to live. Because I don't think my new powers will include conjuring up cash from nowhere, and the money Magne collected for me will only last a couple of months.

So I mope around my apartment, cooking food I only nibble at, thinking about maybe taking some more photographs. I get so sick of my own self-pity I wish Magne would barge in and punch me in the face again, just to give me something else to think about. But he's stopped checking on me. Magne was Su's friend first, and guess he's her friend last, too.

I finally make prints from some of the city shots I took before I photographed the moth. They don't have the same energy as the images I shot before Su went to Germany, but they aren't terrible. The moth photo I first shove to the bottom of a drawer, then take out again. I decide to frame it and send it to Su. Maybe we're not together anymore, and maybe we never will be again, but she's still my best friend, or I hope she is, and I took the photo for her in the first place.

Finally good and sick of feeling sorry for myself, I leave the house, wander the streets, and watch people again. I practice reading them and blocking them out, and I practice hiding from those who carry true magic, following them, trying to read them and figure out who and what they are.

One particularly bright spark draws my attention one night, and I follow it. I can't tell what this creature is or even what shape he or she might have. It is as if they have hidden everything about themselves except their magic.

I know they are human-shaped at least some of the time, because I glimpse them from time to time, moving along the street ahead of me. At first, they stick to crowds and it takes me a while to pick out the one who carries the bright magic. Dark jeans and a green hoodie are all I can discern. Hair that might be brown or blond, but it's difficult to tell in this light, and even harder when they leave the busy streets for the alternating shadows and pools of light in the park.

I can't read them at all, save that magic, and that they do feel oddly human. I get no sense of *otherness* and nothing like the people I sensed on Wonder Island as it receded behind the ferry after my ordeal with the demon.

Then the bright spark vanishes as if it never existed and the person I was following seems to dissolve into smoke.

Karasu? I wonder. Or someone like him? But I don't feel the danger, the cloaking fear – not even the fainter version that surrounds him when he masks what he is.

Confused, I lose caution, and keep walking to the last place I sensed them. And there they are – there *he* is – sitting on a bench. The very bench where I shared ice cream with Su, and where I saw the luna moth that night I ran into Jinny Greenteeth.

In the pool of light I can see now that his hair is on the blond side of red – "strawberry blond" Magne called it – and he flashes slightly crooked teeth when he smiles.

"Hey," he says.

I expected that if I ever saw Luke again, he would recoil from me, avoid me. I was sure I must have freaked him out completely the last time I saw him, when Magne barged in on us. But there he is, calm and relaxed. No fear. Not even any anxiety.

Surely he's not the person I was following. But his black jeans and green hoodie say otherwise. I reach out with my new senses and there it is, the bright flare of true magic. His body whispers of the things he would like to do with me, and my heart speeds up.

"Hey," I say, and sit next to him, as if he hasn't just surprised me in more ways than one. I want to take his hand in mine, but I don't quite dare, even though his skin responds to my presence, and tells me he would very much like to hold hands.

"How did you do that?" he says.

"I was just going to ask you the same thing."

He grins, his lips curving in a way that makes me desperately want to kiss them.

"I can hide," he says. "But from you, apparently only for a few seconds." He taps my knee with his index finger, then folds his hands in his lap. "Your turn."

"I don't know," I say. "It's new."

"So it's happened? You're a *koldun*?"

I almost get up and walk away. Does everyone around me know more about me that I do about myself? But I force myself to be calm.

"What do you know of that?" I say.

"Almost nothing."

"What are you?"

"Human," he says. "Only human."

"You have magic. Not *otherness*, but real magic."

"Some of us do," he says, like we're talking about having curly hair or an aptitude for drawing.

"I don't understand."

He shrugs. "It's a long story, but some humans can sense magic, and use it. I'm one of them."

"Like the monk."

"Rasputin? Yeah, he was like me. Also bug-fuck crazy and a sadist, too. I am neither of those, in case you're worried."

I shake my head, "I thought you were just an ordinary guy. I thought… I thought I scared you away."

"I *am* just an ordinary guy. And you kind of did freak me out." He gives me a long, considering look. "I've never seen a vampire up close, all hungry."

"Sorry," I say. "I wasn't myself."

He shrugs again. "No big. But tell me something." He waits, so I nod. "When you kissed me, was that really you, or was that your demon?"

"It's complicated," I say.

"Ah," he says. "The amazing girlfriend."

"What? No. Well yes, but…" I hadn't even been thinking about Su then. Maybe I should have been. "We… we broke up. Which is also a long story, but we… can't be together." I look away, watch the moths – none so large or flashy as a luna – batter themselves against the lamp nearby. "The demon made me act when I shouldn't have."

"I was afraid of that," he says, and my new senses feel him withdraw, even though he doesn't move from his seat next to me on the bench.

Then I look at him, meet his eyes without flinching. "But wanting to kiss you – that was all me." I dare to put my hand on his where it rests in his lap and for a moment I think he's going to pull away.

"Will you tell me about it? The demon and all that? Obviously you've defeated it or whatever, but… Is it still in you?"

I shake my head. "Maybe someday I'll tell you. I don't know. But it's gone. Or not gone, but absorbed. No longer something that can control me, or even put ideas in my head." Except it has permanently tainted my thoughts of Su to the point I can't make love to her. So I have left her. But I don't tell him that.

"So, do you want to go to a movie or something?" he says.

"Are you asking me on a date?" I feel my lips, finally, curve into a smile to answer his. It feels good.

"Yes, I believe I am."

"Okay, then."

"Okay?"

"Yes. But…"

"There are conditions?" He stands up, looks at me in mock ire.

"No conditions," I say. "But it's too late to go to a movie tonight." I feel suddenly daring. I stand up, take his hand, and pull him after me.

"You have a better suggestion?"

"I want to take you home," I say. "And I want to do a lot more than kiss you."

He stops, pulls me so close I can feel him, even though only our hands are touching.

"Your huge werewolf friend isn't going to stop by and chase me away again, is he?"

I shake my head.

"Are *you* going to try to scare me away again, or change your mind and leave me hard and hot and frustrated?"

His breath smells like chocolate and I lean closer to answer him, so close my lips brush his as I speak.

"I'll scare you if you want me to," I say, and he shivers, but not in fear. "But I hope you won't run away, because I want to taste you, and I don't mean as a vampire tasting your blood."

His breathing quickens and he leans closer so our bodies just touch. "You can taste me any way you like," he says. "I like the idea of feeding you."

Now it's my turn to shiver. "Don't tempt me," I say.

"I *want* to tempt you, Alexeyevich," he says. "I want to tempt you so much you can't help yourself. I want you to take me."

"I'm not safe," I say. "I don't know what new powers I have since… Or how I might have changed."

"Since the demon," he says. "I've studied magic, and I know a few others who have. I can help you, if you need it. And I may be only human, but I can defend myself if I need to."

"I hope you won't need to," I say. "But I don't know –"

"Then we'll find out together."

"Luke…"

"I love when you say my name."

I need to stop, to think, to clear my head. But then I remember that Su and I aren't together anymore, and the demon isn't a threat anymore. I don't *need* to stop, or think. For once, I can simply *do* and *be*.

So I kiss him. Just briefly, but I put all my longing into it, all my lust. I bite his lip by accident, but he only smiles.

"There," he says.

"What?"

"That's the man I want."

"The one who bites you by mistake?"

"The one who wants me so much he *can* make a mistake."

"I do want you."

"So take me home."

I'm so worked up I feel like I might explode, but I breathe deep, and calm myself, and we stroll – leisurely, even – back to my apartment.

We're barely in the doorway when he turns to me, puts his arms around my neck, and kisses me. He pushes me back against the door, presses against me, and I can feel his body is just as keyed up as mine.

I pull his shirt off, not gently, and he bites my ear. *That* ear. I growl and he kisses me again. He tastes like chocolate, too, and I push my tongue past his teeth to taste him better. I can't seem to get close enough.

"Bite me," he says. He tilts his head so I can better reach his neck.

"If I bite your neck," I say, trying to get my shirt off without stopping touching him, "I could kill you."

"So bite me somewhere else," he says, then he snorts. "Bite my ass." He turns around and wiggles it at me.

I grab him and pull him close. "There's something much nicer I'd like to do to your ass," I say, and press my hips close to his, grinding against his buttocks.

He leans back against me. "I am all yours, Alexeyevich," he says.

"Evgeny," I say. "My name is Evgeny."

"Evgeny," he says, and it turns to a moan when I slide my hands from his chest, over his belly, and into the front of his jeans. The buttons of his fly pop and I pull him free of his clothes, cup my hand around his testicles, and squeeze.

"Evgeny," he whispers.

"Mmm…" I say, too busy kissing his neck to make real words.

"Do you have any…?"

"In the bedroom," I mumble.

"Mmm," he says as I move one hand out of his pants to feel the shape of his abs, his pecs, to tweak a nipple.

"Oh, wait," he says, "I have one," and fumbles for the jeans that are now around his knees and sliding downwards. He bends, and if I wasn't still mostly dressed, I'd be tempted to take him right then, ready or not.

"Luke," I say.

"Tell me I'm yours," he says, "Evgeny."

"You're mine," I say.

"Say it like you mean it."

"I do mean it."

"Say it."

"Luke, you're mine," I growl. "You're mine now and I'm going to fuck you and you're going to like it." It frightens me a little, the way I speak to him, but it feels good, and his body whispers to my new senses that I've said the right thing.

He wriggles to get his hands free, reach back to unzip my jeans and slide them off of me, so we're standing skin to skin, his back to my chest, his ass to my pelvis.

"Bite me, Evgeny," he says.

"I don't want to hurt you."

"I want you to."

He wants me to bite him? Or to hurt him? Or both? He hands me the condom, leans back against me. "Bite me, and fuck me, and make me yours for real." He twists to look over his shoulder at me, and the desire in his eyes is so raw I almost gasp.

"Luke."

He grins. "I can't tell you how long I've wanted this. To be yours. Maybe I have a vampire fetish."

I want to do it, but I'm afraid some vestige of the demon will make me go too far. But just then I remember Su's words. "Love him, fuck him, and be happy."

So I let him see my vampire face, and he doesn't flinch. He licks his lips.

"There you are," he says softly.

He squeezes his hand and I suddenly remember what he's holding.

"Condom," he whispers, and I lean away from him just enough to roll it onto myself, wishing he didn't have to let go of me to do it.

He steps away from me and I think he's changed his mind. I almost reassemble my face to human, but he's bending over the island, looking back at me, waiting.

"Oh God," I whisper, my words slurred by the shape of my vampire mouth.

"Not God," he says, smiling his sauciest smile. "But maybe I can show you heaven. Or else make you see stars." And without thinking any more, I'm behind him, inside of him, and he's grabbing my ass to pull me closer, move me faster, harder.

I move one hand around to touch him, pleasure him, stroke him, and he pushes urgently against my hand.

"Bite me, my vampire," he says.

This is almost my exact fantasy. "Luke, I might hurt you."

"Just do it," he says, his breath ragged, pleading.

So I do. I bite the muscle of his shoulder and drink from him, just a little. I fasten my teeth in him and he cries out and when he comes I can feel his pleasure along with my own, and I don't know how I stay standing when it's my turn to climax.

But I do, and I stay standing just long enough to get us both into bed where we curl up together, and sleep, satisfied and smiling. Both of us, smiling.

SON of WOLVES

read on for a preview of book five of the *Fictive Kin* series

Chapter One

Tʜᴇ sᴍᴇʟʟ ᴡʜᴇɴ I open the door to Magne's apartment is almost overwhelming.

Bleach and fabric softener and carpet cleaner seem to hover and mingle in the air like a noxious fog and I have to take a step back into the relatively clear air of the hallway to take a breath.

"Magne?" I know he can hear me. He'll have heard the grinding of the industrial elevator as I took the one floor up. And no, I'm not lazy; I could take the stairs but we always use the elevator so those of use who live here know when the others come and go. It's a courtesy and a comfort.

I take a deep breath and plunge into the loft, grab a kitchen stool on my way by, and climb up to reach the lever that cracks open one of the upper windows. The old once-industrial building has huge panes of glass on one wall, but they only have small panels at the top and bottom that angle open a few inches.

I pause to suck in fresh air when I get the bottom window cracked, then move on to the next.

Magne doesn't make an appearance until I've got the last one open and a trickle of fresh air has started to clear out the fumes. He looks like hell.

His eyes are red and watery from the cleaning products, and his hair is lank and flat. Unwashed-looking. I mean, his hair is never really *styled*, per se, but it's shaggy unkemptness – looking like he just rolled out of bed and ran his fingers through it – is dead sexy on him. Right now, he looks the opposite of sexy.

"Hey Su," he says, and tries a smile. It looks forced, and this is a man who grins as carelessly as breathing. And he's the only person I've ever met who looks so comfortable in his body that a casual lean looks actually casual and not like he's posing. Now, he looks like he doesn't know what to do with his limbs.

"You look like crap, Mags," I say. No point in being subtle with him. He can probably smell what I'm thinking.

So yeah, I'm Su, and my best friend is a werewolf. A big, hairy man who can take the shape of something more-or-less wolflike, who looks dumb as a truck, but is actually one of the smartest people I know.

He shrugs and puts down the contraption he's hauled with him out of the depths of his apartment. It's a rental carpet cleaner. I'm pretty sure there are no actual carpets in here.

"No one to look hot for," he says.

"And here I thought you went around looking hot just in case." That provokes something like the grin I'm used to. The dimple in his cheek even makes a brief appearance.

He gestures to the living area, with its low sofas and chairs and way more cushions – in all shaped and sizes – than any normal person could ever possibly want. "Just tidying up a bit." Now that I look, I can see lines where he's used the carpet cleaner to steam clean the furniture. I study his face again. I mean, Magne's tidy – way more organized than I am – but I've never known him to be a clean freak.

"When was the last time *you* tidied up?" I say. "Yourself, I mean." Like I said, no point in being subtle.

He shrugs again. "I can't smell myself."

"I don't know how you can smell anything in here." The bleach has dulled my own nose, and mine's even more sensitive than Magne's, because I'm not exactly human either. The air is beginning to clear a bit, at least, as a breeze finds its way in the windows.

"I can smell *her*," he says. He meets my eyes finally. I don't think the redness is from tears, just from cleaning products. Magne is far too macho to cry, even alone, which is too bad, because honestly, a man who's not afraid to cry is deeply sexy. But werewolf culture is pretty focussed on men being manly, apparently.

Her. His recently departed girlfriend – now ex-girlfriend – Cara, a beautiful, powerful, witch woman who decided our friend group was too weird, scary, and dangerous to stay close to.

Who discovered she was pregnant with Magne's offspring and decided she really needed to go home.

"Come on," I say. I take Magne's hand and pull him towards the door. "You're spending entirely too much time feeling sorry for yourself. You need to run. And this place needs to air out."

"Yeah," he says. "Back atcha."

Because, oh yeah, my beautiful vampire boyfriend, love of my life, is now *my* ex. It's a long story, and there are reasons, and it's not that he fell out of love, but it still sucks in every possible way that we can't be together.

Me and Magne, a perfect matched pair of newly-dumped non-humans. Well, matched except that he looks like a brown-haired Viking, and I look like what resulted when a Viking took the Silk Road to China and decided to leave a baby behind.

I barely pause to let him put shoes on before dragging him outside and down the street towards the park. We live in a light industrial area of small factories, buildings converted to loft apartments, and abandoned storefronts. It's popular with *other* kind, because normal humans don't come here too often. We like it because it's only a few minutes brisk walk to a huge park that borders the river.

Under the trees, we stop at a huge oak – a mother tree if I ever saw one – so Magne can undress and stash his clothes. I step around the tree to give him privacy – not that he cares; he's the least shy person I know and always seems as comfortable naked as clothed. But I move out of sight also because – once I finally got the hang of it – shifting for me is as simple as walking through a door, and I don't even have to undress.

Between one heartbeat and the next, I go from being a mid-height Euro-Asian woman with absurdly long hair to being a rusty-red fox with an absurdly bushy tail.

Yeah, how that came about is a story for another day.

I wait until the creaking of joints and snapping of tendons stops and all I hear is Magne breathing. Werewolves aren't really supernatural; they're made when a symbiotic organism takes over the running of a human body and transforms it. New joints form and old joints move in different ways until a perfectly human-looking person can transform – like those cartoon robots – into a creature you might mistake for a wolf in a dark forest.

In full daylight, what Magne looks like is harder to describe. One of those old-school movie werewolves that seems to be caught halfway between human and canine is probably the closest thing I can think of, but Magne has a wild, terrifying beauty that those movie monsters lack.

"Shall we?" he says, his voice rough and slurred around his massive teeth. It's hard to talk when your mouth has turned into a muzzle, I guess.

I turn and let my legs carry me. I could answer, but even I find it weird to hear my perfectly human-Su voice coming out of my completely fox body.

Magne follows and for a long time we just run. Under and around trees, in and out of dappled sun. The trees here aren't as big as they are farther north, but they're big enough and leafy enough that they keep a lot of the smaller plants from getting much light, so its easy to weave a path around and over the undergrowth. It's been too long since I had a good run, and judging by the way Magne's lungs are working, it's been too long for him, too.

When we reach the river, I find a nice mossy spot to bask in the last of the afternoon sun while Magne wades right out into the water. I'm not sure how were physiology works, but I do know he won't feel the cold much until he's back in human shape, and anyway, it's nearly summer. Once he's back in human form, though, he'll be wanting a hot drink and a warm blanket. Too bad our lofts aren't equipped with fireplaces.

At first he just splashes in the shallows, but then he spies something under the water and goes still, and stalks, and pounces.

In human shape, Magne's pretty nice to look at, even if he is a bit too hairy for my taste. Or so I keep telling myself. In wolf shape he moves like liquid, smoother than the river he's hunting in, and watching him is like listening to the finest poetry.

There was a time when we might have been lovers – the attraction was there on both sides – but then I met Evgeny and fell head over heels despite my best efforts not to. I mean, vampires kept trying to kill me; why would I want to even want to have sex with one, let alone *love* one? And Magne met Cara. And that was that. But watching him emerge from the water with a gleaming silver trout in his mouth, I wonder if we're better as friends or if we should see if we can build something more.

I mean, I do love him. I have for ages, but he was always relegated to the "friend who is not for snogging" part of my brain. And he always acted like an older brother. Now with both of us single again, and him hurting – okay, *both* of us hurting – I just want to make everything better.

Well, not in these shapes we're wearing now. I'm not into bestiality, thanks ever so much. Besides, in our *otherly* shapes, Magne's like ten times my size. Or several times, anyway.

We share the fish he's caught. My fox nature makes me much less squeamish than I might be, and anyway I've always like sashimi. Then we curl up side by side on the moss and watch the sky fade from bright blue to a deeper shade and then to black, and lights appear on the shore of Wonder Island, just visible poking out around the end of a bend in the river.

"I thought this end of Wonder Island was all wild," I say, curling in closer to Magne's body heat.

He lifts his head to look, then relaxes back onto the moss. "It is," he says, sounding sleepy. We should head back soon and see if I can convince him to take a bath and get some sleep. I could probably use both of those things myself.

"I see lights there," I say.

"Maybe someone's camping." I can hear his lips sliding over his teeth as he speaks, trying to keep the words clear.

"That's a lot of light for camping," I say. It looks like a couple of floodlights, maybe, and little points of hand-held flashlights moving here and there. There's no way to tell, but I'd bet something's happening over there. The people who actually live on the island are extremely private, though, so we'll probably never know.

I stir again when I feel Magne shiver. I guess his wolf shape isn't entirely immune to the cold, and since it isn't even – strictly speaking – an actual wolf shape, he doesn't have a full coat of fur like I do. The promise of an early summer has faded with the sunlight and the air has become crisp.

"Yeah," he says, when I stand. "Time to face my empty apartment."

"I'm sorry," I say, as if it's my fault Cara chose to leave. It isn't; I wasn't even in the country. But if I'd been home to deal with Evgeny's … situation … maybe she'd have stayed.

Magne butts his head against mine and then we're racing back through the trees towards the mother oak. I could, if I wanted to, leave him far behind. Werewolves have better night vision than humans, but nothing near as good as a fox's, so he has to run slow enough to let his other senses keep him from running into trees. And whatever variety of fox woman it is that I am is crazy fast anyway, whether that comes from my dad's *hexenfuchs* ancestry or from whatever powers the old fox Asian fox ladies who once saved my life gave me. But that's another story for another time. What it means is that I'm never quite sure what I'm capable of.

But anyway, I'm some kind of magic fox hybrid shifter, and I can be very, very fast. So I could leave Magne far behind, if I wanted to. But he's my friend and I don't want to bruise his manly ego too badly, so I just run fast enough that we arrive back at the tree at the same time. I mean, I may be soft-hearted, but that doesn't mean I have to let him *win*.

I take his hand – once it's hand-shaped again – as we walk home. His fingers are freezing.

"One of these days you're going to get hypothermia," I say.

"I've got a nice bottle of Scotch waiting for me," he replies, and pulls his hand away so he can drape his arm across my shoulders. It's a friendly gesture, not a come-on and I wonder if I want it to be him making a move. Back in our human shapes, I remember how it felt when we were newly neighbours and I desperately wanted to get him naked.

I like sex. A lot. And with Ev gone, maybe I don't really want Magne. Maybe I just want someone to fuck. Except I don't think that's the case. I mean, I don't go out a lot, but I haven't found myself drooling over every hot man or woman I run into when I do go out.

"You know that doesn't actually work, right?" I say. "The booze just makes you *think* you're warm."

He pulls me closer and kisses the top of my head. Only the fact that he smells like he hasn't showered recently and like he just ate a fish raw, guts and all, keeps me from reacting to the kiss like it's more than he meant it to be.

"I'll put it in hot chocolate," he says. "Want some?"

"Only if you take a bath first."

"You know you love my manly scent." He growls into my hair, then tilts his chin towards his armpit. "Okay, maybe I smell a little *too* manly."

Without even saying anything, we decide to leave Magne's place to its airing out, and keep going up to the third floor, where my loft is.

My place is much less homely than Magne's, really. It's mostly open space. Handy for practising kung fu, but not really inviting. But I've got a reasonably comfortable collection of mis-matched couches and easy chairs, a kitchen area to which I recently added an actual stove, and a huge bed with curtains that pull around it for the days when I want to hide in a dark, enclosed space.

The bathroom is the only part of the loft that's got walls and that's where Magne heads as soon as he's got his shoes off. Even before I knew him very well he had a tendency to treat my place as an extension of his own.

I put the kettle on as the shower starts up. I try not to think of him in there, naked. He's in the shower a long time – he must have been even colder than I thought – and when he comes out he's just got a towel wrapped around his waist. Because he couldn't make it easier, could he?

"I should have stopped at my place for clean clothes," he says.

I try very hard not to look at his chest, broad and furry and covered, like the rest of his body, with a tracery of thin white scars. They're the result of the brutal process of being made a werewolf and the only place nearly free of their map-like lines is his face. Only one thin scar bisects his right eyebrow and another follows the line of his left cheekbone.

"I don't mind," I finally say, aiming for a cheeky grin, and then hand him a cup of tea with a healthy dollop of whisky – not as top-shelf as what he usually drinks, but still decent. I go to step around him for my turn in the shower and he stops me by moving between me and the bathroom.

"Are you okay?" he says. "Really?" I rest my forehead on his chest and feel the solidness of him.

"Not really," I say. "But I will be."

"Yeah," he says, and I feel the movement of his lips against my hair. "Me too." He gathers me close in a gentle hug, like he's afraid of breaking me. I hear him sip his tea, feel the bunching of his muscles. Evgeny was my true love, but Magne is my rock, solid and immoveable and always there to anchor me.

"It's funny," he says. "When I started seeing Cara we agreed we didn't want anything serious. It was a fling for both of us. Fun, good sex, a bit of companionship." He sips his tea again, and I turn my head to listen to his heartbeat, slow and strong.

"Then all that shit happened with Ev." Yeah, another story for another time. "And she was there, helping. I don't think I could have got him to Wonder Island without her. And I started to think maybe we could be more than short-term bedpartners." He pauses again, sips his tea, then puts the mug on the counter. His hand, when it puts it on my back, is extra-warm from the heat of the mug.

"And then we found out she was pregnant," he says. His smoked-whisky voice is soft but steady, like he's just stating facts, but I can feel the tension in the way he holds me.

"I'm so sorry, Mags."

"Yeah," he says. "Me, too. I never thought I'd want to be a father. I mean, I figured someday, but not yet." I feel his sigh, deep like it's moving through his whole body.

"I mean, she wasn't even far enough along to show. It was just two little clumps of cells inside her, barely big enough to see. But the *idea*...." He pauses, takes a deep breath. "I suddenly wanted that more than anything. I think I might have wanted those babies more than I wanted Cara."

"Magne..." I start to say, but he pulls away far enough to press a finger to my lips.

"She texted this morning," he says. "To let me know the ... the appointment went well. She's fine and the pregnancy was terminated." His voice breaks a little on the last word and his arms tighten. "She *texted*," he says. "She couldn't even *call* me."

I can't help it. I don't want him to be hurting. So I stretch up to put my arms around his neck, stand on tiptoes, and kiss him.

I feel him hesitate, like he's going to pull away, but then his muscles soften, his body relaxes against mine, and he kisses me back.

And there's the sudden loud buzzing of the building intercom and we pull apart to stare at each other. I can't remember the last time someone buzzed either of us. Anyone who comes here usually calls, or texts, or has a key.

I let go of Magne reluctantly, feeling the absence of his warmth like a cold wind, and go to the wall by the door, press the button.

"Yeah?" I say. My voice comes out shaky.

"Miss Fuchs?" The voice is vaguely familiar, pronouncing my last name like the speaker knows German, and I sense Magne go still behind me. Very still.

"Yes?"

"It's Detective O'Malley. Magne's friend. I … may have some news about your sister."

About the Author

NICO SILVER LIVES like a hermit on the edge of the woods, but haunts used bookstores like a wraith. They fully expected to be found someday as a mummified old corpse crushed under a toppled to-be-read pile, but the rise of e-books has made that somewhat less likely, though the books will always outnumber even the dustbunnies. Nico will read just about anything, including the instructions on the back of medicine bottles, but has a particular fondness for good stories with a hint of magic. They write dark, sexy urban fantasy, and sometimes dream in black and white.

www.ingramcontent.com/pod-product-compliance
Lightning Source LLC
Chambersburg PA
CBHW022128310726
48972CB00007B/2251